Murder
on the
Sea Witch

A Redmond and Haze Mystery
Book 7

By Irina Shapiro

Copyright

© 2021 by Irina Shapiro

All rights reserved. No part of this book may be reproduced in any form, except for quotations in printed reviews, without permission in writing from the author.

All characters are fictional. Any resemblances to actual people (except those who are actual historical figures) are purely coincidental.

Cover created by MiblArt.

Table of Contents

Prologue 5
Chapter 1 8
Chapter 2 11
Chapter 3 17
Chapter 4 28
Chapter 5 32
Chapter 6 41
Chapter 7 47
Chapter 8 53
Chapter 9 67
Chapter 10 72
Chapter 11 80
Chapter 12 90
Chapter 13 93
Chapter 14 105
Chapter 15 115
Chapter 16 119
Chapter 17 128
Chapter 18 131
Chapter 19 146
Chapter 20 153
Chapter 21 163
Chapter 22 172
Chapter 23 184
Chapter 24 197

Chapter 25 204

Chapter 26 213

Chapter 27 233

Chapter 28 238

Chapter 29 247

Epilogue 250

Excerpt from Murder in Half Moon Street 253

Prologue...253

Chapter 1 255

Chapter 2 264

Chapter 3 271

Prologue

The museum had finally closed, the lofty halls echoing with Mason Platt's footsteps as he hurried through the silent rooms toward the rear of the building, where the storerooms were located. Mason was giddy with excitement as he pushed open the door marked 'Private' and trotted into the vast space beyond. It had been empty this morning, but now the area was full of crates, the shipment from the *Sea Witch* having finally arrived a few hours ago, the caravan of wagons delayed by heavy traffic from Southampton. Mason had to admit that he liked the name of the vessel and found it appropriate to the cargo it had carried. A sea witch was a mythical creature, someone found in legends and spooky stories told by sailors, as were some of the artefacts that had been stored in its spacious hold.

Up until a few years ago, mummies and hieroglyphs had been the stuff of legend, but now the museum had its very own Egyptian Hall filled with breathtaking artefacts, the display open to the public, rich and poor alike able to see the glorious finds for the price of an admission ticket. Maybe one day archeologists would find a sea witch, Mason mused as he gazed around the room, his heart thumping with anticipation. A mermaid skeleton would be nearly as exciting as the unique find he was about to behold.

Mason Platt had been a curator at the British Museum for nearly twenty years, but it was only recently that he had finally been promoted to director of the Egyptian section, a position he'd coveted for years. Mason was the in-house expert on anything pertaining to Egypt and one of the few people in London who could be called a true Egyptologist. Although he had never set foot in Egypt, he'd read everything he could get his hands on and always personally catalogued and arranged the displays, complete with a detailed description and background of each item.

He'd been waiting for this hoard for more than a fortnight now, the ship's departure having been delayed by Egyptian authorities, who'd demanded to come on board and personally examine the artefacts that were being taken out of their country. As a historian, Mason could certainly understand their reluctance to part with such important bits of their history, but, on the upside, the treasures would be displayed in one of the greatest museums in the world, something the Egyptians should be grateful for, in his opinion.

But, at last, the *Sea Witch* had docked this morning, and now Mason could spend a few happy hours examining the newly arrived treasures before getting down to the business of cataloguing. Only this morning, he'd thought he'd leave the best for last, but he simply couldn't wait. Blake Upton, the archeologist in charge of the expedition, had written to him about his momentous find. It was an almost perfectly preserved painted wood sarcophagus, complete with a mummy. The sarcophagus had been discovered in the Valley of the Kings in a tomb that Upton and his team had found, a previously unopened chamber filled with grave goods and wall paintings.

Having studied the images painted on the walls and the papyrus found inside the tomb that had been painstakingly translated by the two archeologists on the team, Blake had concluded that the tomb belonged to an important nobleman who'd lived during the New Kingdom, which encompassed the eighteenth, nineteenth, and twentieth dynasties of Egypt. The find was an absolute triumph, and the sarcophagus would be displayed in a glass cabinet in pride of place, the lid stood up vertically to be more clearly seen by the visitors, while the coffin itself would be low enough so that they could gawk at the mummy within.

Mason carefully lifted the lid of the appropriately marked crate, removed the padding used to keep the sarcophagus intact, and drank in the gorgeous colors and workmanship of the coffin. It really was breathtaking, the image of the occupant depicted in golds, reds, and blues, the kohl-rimmed eyes staring as if they could see him, their painted expression condemning Mason for what he planned to do. Mason looked away from the painted face. He didn't think displaying a mummy was quite the same as laying out an Englishman's corpse for everyone to see. That would be inappropriate and disrespectful to the deceased, but this person had died thousands of years ago. He no longer deserved consideration or respect, only interest.

Sniffing experimentally, Mason leaned forward, bringing his face closer to the sarcophagus. There was an odd smell, but he supposed it was to be expected, given its contents. He couldn't wait to see the mummy. Blake might have liked to be present during the opening of the crates, but since the ship had only just docked that morning, he wouldn't be making an appearance until tomorrow afternoon at the earliest. He'd be tired after the voyage and would probably wish to spend a few hours with his wife before setting off.

Mason held his breath as he carefully lifted the lid of the sarcophagus. It was heavier than he had expected, but he was able to lift it high enough to get a good look inside. Mason stared in horror at the contents, gripping the lid so as not to drop it from sheer shock.

There was a corpse within, but it wasn't a dusty old mummy. It was Blake Upton, his face pale, his eyes closed as if he were merely taking a nap, his arms crossed over his chest just like the depiction on the lid.

"Blake?" Mason whispered, praying this was some sort of joke and Blake would open his eyes and sit up, but no such miracle occurred.

Mason Platt couldn't see any signs of violence, but it was painfully clear to him that Blake Upton was very dead.

"Mr. Howe," he said softly to the hovering watchman, as if afraid to disturb the dead man. "Alert Scotland Yard that we have a suspicious death."

Chapter 1

Tuesday, March 31, 1868

Jason Redmond yanked open the door and stepped aboard the London-bound train just as it began to move out of the Brentwood station, the passengers who'd just disembarked becoming blurry shapes as the locomotive picked up speed. Settling by the window, Jason set down his medical bag, then removed his hat and gloves and unbuttoned his coat, glad he had the compartment to himself and could make himself comfortable. It would have been a shame if he'd missed the train, but he'd stopped off to send a wire and hoped Daniel Haze would receive it before the train arrived in Charing Cross station. If not, Jason would simply take himself to Scotland Yard in the hope that Daniel would be there.

The telegram from Daniel had been brief and utterly lacking in information, but it was a plea for help, and Jason was only too happy to lend a hand. It'd been more than three months since they'd worked on a case together, and much had changed in the interim. Daniel had moved to London in January after accepting a position as a detective inspector at Scotland Yard. The offer had been as flattering as it was unexpected, since he hadn't been an inspector with the Brentwood Constabulary for long, but it seemed his reputation as a man who got results had spread as far as Scotland Yard, and he'd be a fool to pass up the opportunity.

Daniel would have been a happy man had Sarah agreed to join him, but she had chosen to remain in Birch Hill with their infant daughter, Charlotte, and her mother. Jason could understand Sarah's reluctance to return to London after the accident that had claimed their son's life but suspected there was more to Daniel and Sarah's separation than just a question of location. Neither had taken Jason into their confidence these past months, so Jason had kept his distance, not wishing to intrude on what was clearly a private matter.

He'd spent most of his time at home, keeping Katherine company as they awaited the birth of their first child. Jason's face split into a happy smile as he thought of Lily. She'd turned one week old yesterday, and already he was so besotted, he could barely believe he was leaving her, even if only for a day. Had Katherine not encouraged him to go, he might have refused Daniel's request for help, but Katherine understood him better than most wives understood their husbands. His desire to live a life of purpose and utilize his surgical skills prevented him from settling down into a life of lord of the manor. He wasn't cut out for idleness, nor did he feel that using his skills to help the police was beneath him. The work also kept him from losing his edge and reminded him of the frailty of human life.

Daniel hadn't described the case in the telegram, and Jason wondered why he hadn't simply trusted the postmortem to the Scotland Yard surgeon. Surely they had a competent man. Either way, Jason was glad Daniel had sent for him. He missed working on a case and hadn't held a scalpel in months, a situation that he hoped to rectify in short order. Before Lily's birth, he and Katherine had talked of moving to London so that Jason could either volunteer his time at a hospital or possibly teach. He liked the idea of shaping young minds and sharing his knowledge and expertise with a future generation of surgeons.

The move would have to wait until Lily was at least a few weeks older, but it was time to start making plans, and this trip to London could be a start. He'd stop into his lawyer's office and check on the status of the Kensington townhouse he'd inherited from his grandfather. The house had been let, since Jason wasn't using it, but perhaps now would be a good time to speak to the current residents about moving on. Katherine had yet to figure out who in the household would be coming up to London and for how long, which could mean either hiring new staff or making room for the staff they already employed at Redmond Hall. And then there was Micah. He'd been boarding at the Westbridge Academy since the start of the academic year, but Micah would be coming home for the summer holidays and wouldn't want to remain in Birch Hill when he could be in London.

Jason missed the boy, but he was doing well in school and making new friends, his fear of being ostracized for being an American Irish Catholic no longer dominating his decisions. Micah was happy, and Jason was happy for him and hoped Micah might take an interest in medicine once he was of an age to decide what he wanted to do with his life.

Greening fields and homey cottages were left behind as the train approached London, the rookeries coming into view, with their air of decay and dejection. Jason looked away, saddened by the poverty that seemed to hover over the slums, the residents either resorting to petty crime to survive or dead-eyed with utter loss of hope. He wasn't naive enough to think he could make a difference, but maybe someday these people would have access to medical care, and some of the surgeons he helped to prepare might be the ones to offer it.

Jason put on his hat and gloves as the train pulled into Charing Cross station, the doors slamming along the length of the train as the passengers began to disembark and head for the exits. He pushed open the door and stepped onto the platform, where young boys yelled themselves hoarse trying to sell the day's papers, and vendors sold hot pies and fragrant oranges to passersby who might wish to fortify themselves before continuing to their destination. He scanned the area for the familiar profile of Daniel Haze, spotting him further down the track, his spectacles fogged up with the steam from the engine, his face anxious. Daniel hadn't seen him yet, so Jason had a moment to observe the tense set of his shoulders and the pallor of a man who'd spent the winter amid the smog and chill of the city. Jason bypassed a matron with several large cases who nearly blocked the entire platform and strode purposefully toward Daniel. He couldn't wait to hear about the case.

Chapter 2

It had rained earlier, but the sky had cleared, and a fresh breeze that caressed Daniel's face felt almost springlike as he recalled that Easter was less than two weeks away. He hated to admit it, but he'd felt a childish sense of relief when Jason's cable had been presented to him as soon as he'd arrived at Scotland Yard this morning, ready to begin the investigation in earnest, whether Jason had agreed to come or not. This was his first high-profile murder case since joining Scotland Yard a few months ago, and he was unsurprisingly nervous. It was one thing to investigate a knifing in Spitalfields or a shooting in Seven Dials, but this victim was a prominent archeologist, whose name had been on everyone's lips when the last Egyptian exhibit opened at the British Museum, Blake Upton's contribution to the display unequalled by any other scholar of Egypt.

It would have been standard procedure to have the body sent to the morgue last night, as soon as Daniel had arrived on the scene and conducted a preliminary investigation, but he'd decided to try his luck and summon Jason, since he didn't quite trust the police surgeon attached to the Yard. Dr. Fenwick was a fine fellow, if one wanted to go for a pint at the local pub or discuss the latest developments in politics, but after working with Jason, Daniel found Dr. Fenwick to be crude in his methods and too quick to pronounce a verdict, often basing his conclusions on the obvious instead of taking the time to look for that which could be hidden.

Dr. Fenwick didn't usually make an appearance before ten o'clock and probably wouldn't begin the postmortem until he'd finished with the one he'd already had scheduled for this morning, so Daniel could afford to wait. He'd left Constable Putney to stand guard over the scene and keep the night watchman company. Between the two of them, they'd keep the evidence and the body secure until Jason either arrived in London or replied in the negative.

Daniel's face split into a grin when he saw Jason striding toward him, his gait brisk, his medical bag in hand. He was here to help, and Daniel felt a surge of gratitude toward his friend, secure in the knowledge that if there was anything untoward to find, Jason would find it and help Daniel solve this puzzling case.

Daniel raised a hand in greeting, and Jason gave him an answering smile.

"Daniel," he said as he clasped Daniel's hand in a firm handshake. "Pleasure to see you. How have you been?"

"Well, thank you," Daniel replied. "And you? How's Lily?"

Jason had sent Daniel a note announcing the birth of his daughter, and Daniel secretly hoped he'd be asked to be the child's godfather, but he didn't dare presume, given his current domestic situation. If he were to be asked, Sarah would have to be asked to be godmother, and Daniel wasn't at all sure either Jason or Katherine would want Sarah to hold such a responsible position, given past events.

Jason's smile grew wider. "She's perfect. It was difficult to leave her, even for a day."

"I'm sorry to tear you away for your family. I know what it's like to have a new baby."

"Katherine is already planning the christening. It will be sometime next month at St. Catherine's. She has asked the squire and Mrs. Talbot to stand up as Lily's godparents. I do hope you understand, Daniel," Jason added apologetically. "The Talbots are Katherine's only family, besides her father, and given their recent loss, she thought it would be the right thing to do."

"Of course, I understand," Daniel hurried to reassure Jason. "Sarah and I are hardly in a position to take on such a weighty role just now."

"Thank you. I was worried you'd feel slighted."

"Not in the least," Daniel said and knew it to be true. It was right and proper that Jason and Katherine should ask a respectable, middle-aged couple, who would honor their obligations to Lily and be a steadying presence in her life.

"I do hope you and Sarah plan to attend," Jason said.

"We wouldn't miss it."

The two men walked out of the station, where several boys were selling newspapers and penny dreadfuls to passengers who'd passed up the opportunity to purchase a copy inside. Daniel was relieved to see no mention of Blake Upton's death in the papers. The press hadn't got wind of the story yet, so that bought him at least a day until public opinion and external pressure to solve the case became a factor. The public was mistrustful of the police and expected them to solve every case within twenty-four hours to prove their mettle. Some cases were straightforward and required a minimum of investigation, but this wasn't one of those cases, and Daniel had to brace himself for the outcry that would follow if he didn't apprehend a suspect soon.

The crowd had thinned, so Daniel had no difficulty finding a cab.

Jason settled into the hansom and set his medical bag on the floor, looking like a man on a mission. "I'm glad you sent for me, Daniel. As much as I love my wife and daughter, I need something to occupy my mind. I haven't worked on a case since you left the Brentwood Constabulary. There's a new police surgeon, a Mr. Norton, who's perfectly capable of dealing with any corpses that come his way."

"So, you find yourself at a loose end?" Daniel asked, thrilled that Jason was eager to help.

"Indeed, I do." Jason laughed. "I'm starting to sound like a real Englishman."

"Don't worry. You've a ways to go yet," Daniel replied, referring to Jason's American accent.

13

Jason's wife privately called him 'Yank,' an apt description, since Jason had been in England less than two years and had previously resided in New York. He'd attended medical school there and had later spent time there recuperating after his imprisonment in a Confederate prison, where he'd almost starved to death along with his ward, Micah Donovan, whom Jason had brought to England with him when he inherited his late grandfather's estate.

"How's Micah?" Daniel asked.

"Fine. Enjoying school. But tell me about the case. I'd like to know what you've been able to learn before I see the deceased."

"Well, Jason, this one is a corker," Daniel said, pushing his spectacles up his nose.

"Do you know the identity of the victim?"

"Yes. His name is Blake Upton, and he's a well-known archeologist. He arrived home from a six-month dig in Egypt just yesterday. His body was discovered yesterday evening by Mr. Mason Platt, a curator at the British Museum. The body was hidden in an ancient sarcophagus, which had been delivered to the museum in the late afternoon. There are no signs of violence that I can see."

"Might it have been an elaborate suicide?" Jason asked.

"I really don't think so. According to Mr. Platt, Mr. Upton was very excited about a burial chamber his team had uncovered during the dig. He was coming back to accolades from the Archeological Society, numerous newspaper write-ups, and an exhibition of the artefacts at the museum. There would be no reason for a man in his position to take his own life, but anything is possible, so the first thing we must do is determine the cause of death."

"Has his family been informed?"

"Not yet. According to Mr. Platt, Mr. Upton is married but has no children. His wife wouldn't have known definitively that the ship was coming in yesterday, so she probably doesn't realize anything is amiss unless a member of the expedition has called on her. I thought it prudent to wait until the cause of death has been ascertained."

"Where can I perform an autopsy?" Jason asked.

"You may use the mortuary at Scotland Yard. I cleared it with my superior as soon as I received your telegram. He's heard of you and is very eager to make your acquaintance."

"Is that where the body is?" Jason asked, already in pathologist mode.

"No. I thought you'd want to see the body in situ before having it moved to the mortuary."

Jason nodded. "Yes, thank you. I would like to examine the sarcophagus as well, once the body has been removed."

"I left a constable guarding the crate, and he'll assist with moving the body to the mortuary. I'm afraid the sarcophagus must remain at the museum. It's a priceless artefact."

"I really see no reason to move it," Jason replied. "I simply wish to look at it and see if there are any traces of blood or tissue."

"I'm sure Mr. Platt can be persuaded to let you do that," Daniel replied. He handed a few coins to the cabbie, who was perched on his elevated seat behind the cab, and the two men walked the short distance to the museum, which had just opened to the public for the day.

The museum was vast, built in the Greek Revival style that made Daniel feel as if a temple had been erected in the heart of London. There was something grandiose in the design, and he supposed it was appropriate to the treasures housed within, but the sheer size of the place intimidated him. Sarah had suggested a few times that they visit the exhibits, but he'd always found an excuse, not really interested in the dusty relics found within. He was more interested in modern inventions and scientific discoveries, like photography and fingerprinting, than bits and pieces of old tombs and statues that had lost their noses and limbs centuries ago.

This morning, Daniel was glad that he didn't have to pass through the echoing exhibit halls to get to his destination. Mr. Platt had given him leave to use a back door that led directly to the storage area for the Egyptian exhibit, so he led Jason around the back of the building and knocked on the door, glad to see Constable Putney was still alert after spending all night with a corpse for company.

"Good morning, Inspector," the constable said. He was a young man of about twenty-one with reddish hair, wide pale blue eyes, and sparse facial hair, a sad attempt at growing a beard.

"Good morning, Constable. This is Lord Redmond, who'll be performing the postmortem. Please ask Mr. Platt to join us and then see about a wagon. We'll need to transport the body to the mortuary as soon as possible."

"Yes, sir."

"All was quiet?" Daniel asked as the much-relieved constable turned to leave.

"Yes, sir."

"Thank you, Constable," Daniel said, but his attention was no longer on the young man.

Chapter 3

Jason pulled off his gloves, removed his coat and hat, and placed his things on a nearby bench before approaching the crate. Nothing had been touched since Daniel had been called to the scene, the lid of the crate closed but not nailed down.

"Good morning," a middle-aged man who could only be Mr. Platt said as he hurried through the door that led into the museum.

"Mr. Platt, this is Lord Redmond," Daniel said.

Mr. Platt looked mildly surprised, but his concern seemed to be for the sarcophagus rather than for Jason's unexpected rank. "Do be careful," he pleaded after greeting Jason absentmindedly. "It really is very delicate."

"Please don't worry, Mr. Platt. I will be most careful," Jason assured him. He studied the crate, then ran a hand along the top. "Tell me, Mr. Platt, do you use your own wagons to pick up the crates from the port?"

"Yes, we do. The museum has a fleet of wagons that we use to transport artefacts and various supplies."

"I'd like to speak to the driver of the wagon," Jason said.

"Of course." Mr. Platt turned toward the guard, who was watching the proceedings, and motioned with his head. "Get Eugene Moore."

The guard left, and Jason turned his attention back to the crate. "Daniel, help me lift the lid."

Mason Platt stood off to the side, nervously wringing his hands. "When do you think you'll be removing the body?" he asked Jason. "It really is rather…" He let the sentence trail off, probably because he was about to say the remains were an inconvenience and prevented him from getting on with the business at hand.

"Within the hour," Jason assured him.

"This sarcophagus is a very rare find. It's so beautiful, so well preserved." Mason Platt sounded as if he were about to cry with frustration. "Once word gets out that it held a corpse, the exhibit will be tainted by scandal."

"It's a coffin, Mr. Platt," Jason pointed out. "It's meant to hold a corpse. I have no doubt your exhibit will be a great success. People will flock to it all the more because it's part of a murder inquiry."

"Do you really think so?" Mr. Platt asked, instantly brightening.

"I have no doubt of it. Now, if you don't mind—"

Jason braced his hands on the sides of the crate and leaned forward as much as the side would allow, his face mere inches from the victim. Blake Upton was around forty, with thick fair hair, sun-bronzed skin, and an athletic build. Had he been taller or huskier, he wouldn't have fit into the narrow coffin designed for someone short and slender. Blake's arms were crossed over his chest, his eyes closed as if he were taking a nap. At first glance, there were no signs of violence, just as Daniel had suggested.

Having studied the body for a few moments, Jason carefully turned the man's head to the right and then to the left. It wasn't easy, since rigor mortis had set in, but he was able to move it far enough to see if there was a wound on the back of the skull.

"Well?" Daniel asked impatiently. He was eager to begin the investigation, but for that, he needed something to go on.

"Give me a moment," Jason replied. He unfolded the man's arms with some difficulty and unbuttoned the jacket, running his hands along the torso, then down his legs, before carefully rolling the body onto its side so he could examine the back.

The door opened, and Constable Putney walked in, followed by two men. One of the men was introduced as Eugene Moore.

Jason turned away from the corpse to greet the man. "Mr. Moore, were you the one to collect this particular crate from the port?" he asked.

"I was, sir."

"And was the crate in good order? Was it sealed?"

"I didn't check, but the lid didn't shift or nothin' when the crate was loaded."

"Did you come to the museum directly from Southampton?" Jason asked.

"Aye, sir. Didn't even stop for a piss, beggin' yer pardon," he added. "Too valuable a cargo to leave unattended."

"Was anyone with you?"

"Not on the bench, but there were two other wagons followin'," Mr. Moore said. "We came straight back 'ere."

"Thank you, Mr. Moore," Jason said. "You may carefully lift the body out of the coffin onto this board," he indicated the lid of the crate, "then cover it with a length of canvas and deliver it to the morgue. Constable Putney will direct you."

"Yes, sir," the men replied in unison.

Jason oversaw the removal of the body, then turned to the coffin. He'd seen a sarcophagus once before when visiting the museum with Micah, but not this close up, and he was mesmerized by its beauty. This was no pine box to bury the dead; this was a work of art that had survived thousands of years. The paint looked as fresh as if the box had been painted just recently, the face of the deceased so skillfully depicted, Jason almost felt as if the kohl-painted eyes were following his every move. The hair, or headpiece, was painted black, and there were numerous images on the lid, possibly telling the story of the man's life. Or perhaps it had been a woman. It was difficult to tell just by looking at the facial features.

Tearing his gaze away from the lid, Jason turned his attention to the interior. There were several strands of fair hair, possibly having fallen out when the body was placed in the coffin, but other than that, Jason couldn't see anything that might resemble bodily fluids or tissue. Not even a broken nail. The inside of the coffin had an unpleasant smell and was a bit dusty, but that was partly due to the contents it had held for centuries and the more recent body that had lain inside. There were no other odors that aroused Jason's suspicions. He briefly wondered what happened to the mummy but decided not to ask since its whereabouts had no bearing on the task at hand.

Mr. Platt hovered at Jason's elbow, clearly terrified Jason would inflict damage on the artefact. Having examined the interior carefully, Jason turned away from the sarcophagus, Mr. Platt's exhalation of relief almost comical.

"Is there anywhere we can talk?" Jason asked.

"Of course. Follow me."

They adjourned to Mr. Platt's office, which was large and comfortable. There was a walnut desk, studded leather chairs, a glass-fronted cabinet stuffed full of well-read books and small knickknacks, and a decanter of something that might have been whisky or brandy on the sideboard. Jason and Daniel took the guest chairs, while Mr. Platt sat behind the desk.

"Mr. Platt, what can you tell me about Mr. Upton?" Jason asked.

"What do you wish to know?"

"How long have you known him? How well? Was he prone to bouts of melancholy? Did he perhaps have a fondness for opium?"

Mr. Platt looked astonished, as did Daniel, but he remained silent, allowing Jason to take the lead. Daniel had spoken to Mr. Platt last night, so this was Jason's turn to ask questions.

"Mr. Upton has had an association with the museum for the past five years. He's been instrumental in expanding our Egyptian exhibit and providing us with background information on the artefacts he's unearthed. The museum does organize its own excavations, but Mr. Upton's efforts were sponsored by Lord Belford, who's a long-time patron of the museum. He donates all the finds to the museum and allows us to display them for as long as we care to. I must tell you that the burial chamber Blake Upton discovered on this dig, the sarcophagus, and the grave goods inside, is the most important discovery since John Turtle Wood uncovered the Temple of Artemis at Ephesus. The temple is fourth century B.C., but according to Blake, this burial chamber dates further back, to the New Kingdom, which we believe to have been at its peak in the seventh century B.C."

Jason nodded, not really interested in a history lesson. The only history he needed was that of Blake Upton. "Was Mr. Upton given to bouts of melancholy?" he asked.

Mr. Platt paused, clearly surprised by the question. "I really wouldn't know. Perhaps he was, and maybe he had a fondness for the opium pipe, but I'm not the right man to ask."

"Did you spend time with him socially or only in your professional capacity?" Jason inquired.

"We saw each other at several museum functions, but we weren't friends, if that's what you're asking."

"Do you have Mr. Upton's home address?"

"I already gave it to the inspector."

"Very good," Jason said, rising to his feet. "Thank you for your help."

"Can we display the sarcophagus now?"

"I don't see why not."

"Oh, thank you," Mr. Platt gushed. "And I hope you find whoever did this terrible thing. Mr. Upton's death is a great loss to archeology."

"What do you think?" Daniel asked as soon as they were outside again. He looked around for a hansom, but there wasn't one in the vicinity, so they started to walk, hoping they'd find one on the way. "Is there any possibility this could have been suicide?"

"I really don't think so, unless someone else was in on it. Even if the man had taken a lethal dose of poison, he'd still need someone to close the lid and then seal the crate. He could hardly have done that himself. Besides, why go to such lengths?"

"Perhaps he wanted to be forever linked to the sarcophagus he'd found," Daniel suggested.

"He'll be forever linked to it anyway, if it's as great a discovery as Mr. Platt said it was. Seventh century B.C.," Jason said, shaking his head in wonder. "I can't even wrap my mind around that. To think that there was a thriving civilization in the sands of Egypt all those years ago, and they were such skilled craftsmen."

"Yes, it really is amazing. I can certainly understand why there's such a fascination with all things Egyptian. I read an article quite recently that suggested the ancient Egyptians and modern-day Englishmen have much in common."

Jason turned to look at Daniel. "What could they possibly have in common?"

"The Egyptians had the utmost respect for death. They planned for it and those who could afford it spent a fortune to bury their dead. Those tombs took decades to build, and they needed a large amount of goods to send their dead well prepared for the afterlife."

"Are people now burying pots and candlesticks with their dead?" Jason said, a smile tugging at the corner of his mouth.

"Not yet, but there's been a mummification right here in England," Daniel said, his eyebrows lifting with the incongruity of that statement.

"What? Really?" Jason asked, turning to gape at him.

"This happened long before you arrived on our shores," Daniel replied, "so you wouldn't have seen it in the papers, but I remember reading about it and discussing it with my father, who'd been absolutely horrified by such an unchristian treatment of the body. The tenth duke of Hamilton had requested that he be mummified according to all the rules and traditions of the process and be buried in an Egyptian sarcophagus that he had purchased for that very purpose in a tomb he'd built in his native Scotland."

"And who mummified him?" Jason asked.

"Thomas Pettigrew. He was a surgeon," Daniel added.

"The eccentricities of one wealthy man don't account for the tastes of an entire nation," Jason said.

"No, but you must admit that our society on the whole is fascinated with death. We have elaborate funerary and mourning traditions. When the average lifespan is no more than forty years, to spend two years in mourning for a loved one is a lot, don't you agree?"

"I agree that a person should mourn for as long as they see fit. No one should impose a timeframe on grief. Not everyone handles loss in the same way, and some people could benefit from distraction whereas others prefer solitude. I do feel sorry for the poor woman whose life we're about to change forever," Jason said, referring to Blake Upton's widow.

"As do I. Losing a spouse is nearly as bad as losing a child," Daniel said softly.

"Yes." Now that Jason had a child of his own, he could understand only too well what Daniel was referring to. The thought of anything happening to Lily was so acutely painful, he couldn't bear to contemplate it for even a moment.

"Jason, we have some time before the body gets to Scotland Yard. What say you to a spot of lunch? I don't want you to get lightheaded while you're working," Daniel added solicitously.

Normally, Jason didn't eat before performing an autopsy, but lately, if he didn't eat every few hours, he grew lightheaded and shaky. As a doctor, he knew these were symptoms of hypoglycemia, and he suspected he was at risk for diabetes mellitus, a condition that might have been brought on by his lengthy incarceration at Andersonville Prison. Some men were able to recover with no long-term ill effects, but Jason hadn't been so lucky. Almost a year of near starvation had taken its toll, and now his body was letting him know that it would never be the same. Jason had curbed his sugar intake and tried to eat protein with every meal, since he found it kept the bouts of hypoglycemia at bay.

"A steak and ale pie or a sausage roll will do," Jason replied. "I can't eat a full meal before performing an autopsy, but I would very much like to take you out to supper this evening, if you're free."

"I would like that very much," Daniel replied.

"Excellent. Would you like one?" Jason asked as they approached a street vendor who had about a dozen steaming pies laid out on a tray slung around his neck with a leather strap. They must have just come out of the oven, and they smelled divine.

"Why not?" Daniel said. "I can never say no to a hot pie."

By the time Jason had purchased the pies, Daniel had secured a hansom, and they ate their impromptu meal on the way to Scotland Yard.

Jason had been curious to visit the Yard, and he enjoyed a brief tour and a warm welcome from the policemen Daniel introduced him to.

"Let me introduce you to Superintendent Ransome," Daniel said. "He's head of Detective Branch. He's eager to meet you. He's something of an admirer." Daniel knocked on a glass-fronted door and was bid to enter.

"Sir, may I present Lord Redmond, lately of the Essex Police," Daniel said, beaming with pride.

John Ransome got to his feet and held out his hand. "It's an honor to meet you, sir. I've heard a lot about you."

"Thank you," Jason said, glad the superintendent didn't resent his presence. At first glance, John Ransome was nothing like Superintendent Coleridge, who had been Daniel's and, by extension, Jason's superior at the Brentwood Constabulary. For one, John Ransome was much younger, possibly in his late thirties. He wasn't very tall, but he had a lean, wiry frame and intense dark eyes beneath finely shaped eyebrows. His hair was very black, and his handlebar moustache was waxed into neat points. He smiled, but his gaze was watchful, appraising.

"I appreciate you helping us out," John Ransome said as he resumed his seat and gestured for the two men to settle themselves in the guest chairs. "We have our own police surgeons, of course, but this is going to be a highly publicized case, and your expertise certainly won't hurt. And, of course, you will be compensated for your time," the superintendent added.

"I'm not doing this for the money," Jason replied.

"Nevertheless," Ransome replied, dismissing the issue of money. "Have you come to any conclusions after examining the body?"

"I would prefer to wait until after the postmortem to share my findings," Jason said.

John Ransome smiled widely, as if Jason had just passed some unspoken test. "Good man," he said. "A good detective never rushes to conclusions. Please, share your findings with me once you have them."

"Of course, sir," Jason promised. "Now, if everything is in readiness, I would like to begin."

"Dr. Fenwick's next client has been moved to the City Mortuary, so the premises are at your disposal for as long as you need them. Inspector Haze will take you down."

The mortuary at Scotland Yard was like every mortuary Jason had ever worked in— sterile, cold, and utterly without character. He could have been anywhere in the world, including the hospital where he'd worked in New York before the war.

The body of Blake Upton was laid out on the granite slab, still fully dressed, as Jason had given express instructions not to touch anything. Jason dropped his walking stick in a metal stand by the door, removed his overcoat, hat, and jacket, and hung them up on a coat rack, then reached for the leather apron hanging behind the door. From his medical bag, he extracted the linen cap he wore when working to keep the hair out of his eyes.

Checking that he had everything he needed to begin, Jason approached the corpse and began to slowly undress him, not an easy task given that his limbs were as stiff as wooden planks. Jason sniffed the clothes before folding them and putting them aside, just in case there was any telltale odor of poison, but he would have smelled it back at the museum had there been anything to detect. Once the corpse was naked, Jason performed a thorough examination, checking everything from the scalp beneath his thick hair to the toenails before picking up a scalpel. He wouldn't have minded a bit of company, but Daniel was squeamish and never attended postmortems, preferring to wait outside and hear the results afterwards.

More than three hours later, Jason washed his hands with carbolic soap, removed the cap and the bloodstained apron, and donned his jacket before draping his coat over his arm and retrieving his hat, gloves, and walking stick. He was ready to share his conclusions with Daniel and John Ransome.

Chapter 4

Jason found Daniel in the office he shared with another inspector, working on a report. Daniel looked up and smiled. "You finished faster than I had anticipated," he said. "I'm eager to hear the results, but let's talk in Ransome's office. He wants to hear all the details."

They walked the short distance to John Ransome's office and were admitted instantly, even though the superintendent had been speaking to someone else. The man was dismissed, and Daniel and Jason settled into the guest chairs they'd occupied before.

"So, what say you, your lordship?" Ransome asked, his eyes twinkling with amusement. Many people found it puzzling that a member of the nobility would want to spend his time cutting up corpses and assisting the police, and no doubt John Ransome was one of them. Police surgeons were generally men who couldn't get work in a hospital or private clinic, having either crossed someone in a position of power or disgraced themselves in the operating theater. Pathology was not a popular field of surgery and not overly appealing to those who didn't care to find the key to the mystery that was death. Jason would have preferred to work on living patients as well, but he found pathology fascinating, the surgeon drawing up a map of the exact road the deceased had taken to his or her final destination. It was particularly gratifying in the case of violent death, since Jason's findings could be the key to catching the killer.

Jason met John Ransome's amused gaze. "This is rather a unique case," he said.

"What's the cause of death?" Ransome asked impatiently. "Let me guess. Poison, right?"

Jason shook his head. "There are no traces of poison in the body. There is also no bruising, no entry wound, no defensive wounds, and no evidence of a lethal bite that might have been the cause of death. The deceased had particles of sand and residue of hashish beneath his fingernails, but no tissue or blood. Likewise, I found no physical ailment that would account for sudden death. Mr. Upton was in excellent health and would have had decades left had he not been murdered."

"Then what killed him?" John Ransome asked, clearly disappointed. He'd probably been hoping for something sensational, something that would make the papers and then make him look like a hero once the case was neatly solved. Jason could see the man was a political animal whose ambition didn't end with the superintendent placement. John Ransome aimed to be the commissioner of police, if Jason's hunch was correct.

"Excerebration," Jason said, watching the man's face with some satisfaction. He was sure John Ransome didn't recognize the word, so he spelled it out for him. "The victim's brain has been removed. Partially," he added.

"What?" John Ransome and Daniel asked in unison, leaning forward in their eagerness to hear more.

"It would appear that a long, thin instrument was used to puncture the ethmoid bone. Once there was an opening, the instrument was then used to extract the brain through the nostril. Parts of the brain were still intact, since whoever did this probably doesn't have much experience in performing such a procedure."

John Ransome paled. "Are you certain?" he rasped.

"I would be happy to show you," Jason replied.

"I'll take your word for it," Ransome said, raising his hand in a gesture of acquiescence.

"Were any other organs removed?" Daniel asked.

"No, just the brain. I did get a whiff of chloroform when I cut into the lungs. I believe Blake Upton was unconscious at the time of death."

"Not suicide, then," Ransome said with a sardonic smile. "Well, well. Now I've heard it all, I think. How long has he been dead? Is there any possibility he was murdered at the museum?"

"No. Mr. Upton's been dead for over twenty-four hours. He was dead upon arrival in Southampton."

"So, he was murdered aboard the ship," John Ransome said.

"He was. Most likely shortly before the ship docked."

"Would death have been quick?" Daniel asked.

"Yes, but not instantaneous," Jason replied.

"That's most unexpected," John Ransome said, nodding as if deep in thought. He turned to Daniel. "Had Mr. Upton been murdered at the museum, I'd turn this over to Division F, since the British Museum falls within their jurisdiction, but since Mr. Upton was killed aboard a ship, we'll keep this one." It wasn't hard to see that he was pleased as punch. "Inspector Haze, you're in charge of the case. Whatever resources you require are at your disposal. I hope to see a result sooner rather than later," he reminded Daniel, as if he weren't already under pressure.

"Yes, sir," Daniel said, rising to his feet.

"Goodnight, gentlemen," John Ransome said. "And thank you again, Lord Redmond. It is truly my pleasure to be working with you, since I assume you will be assisting Inspector Haze in apprehending the killer." His eyes twinkled.

"I will help Inspector Haze in any way I can," Jason said.

"I wager he'll be holding a press conference first thing tomorrow," Daniel grumbled as soon as they left the Yard. "This is a high-profile case that will show the powers-that-be what sort of depravity we're dealing with and highlight the importance of a well-trained police force. Your average clodhopper can't be expected to handle a case of this delicacy, and Ransome hopes to attract men of intelligence and ingenuity to the police service."

"Like us?" Jason asked innocently, making Daniel laugh.

"If you've no objection, I'd like to speak to Blake Upton's widow before we finish for the night," Daniel said.

"I can wait," Jason replied. "I think Mrs. Upton must be informed of her husband's death with all due haste."

Chapter 5

The Uptons lived in a Georgian terraced house in Grenville Place, an address in keeping with Mr. Upton's station, Daniel speculated as he and Jason approached the front door. The Uptons were clearly well off but not extremely wealthy or titled. A young maidservant opened the door and invited Daniel and Jason to wait in the foyer while she informed the mistress of their visit. At least she didn't leave them to wait on the doorstep, since it had grown colder, and Jason thought it might rain.

The maid returned a few minutes later, took their things, and directed them toward the drawing room from which she had just emerged. Mrs. Upton rose to greet them, her face tense with anxiety.

"You are from the police?" she asked, even though she already knew the answer. "Is this about Freddie?" She looked around as if suddenly remembering her manners. "Please, do sit down."

She sank onto a butter-yellow settee, but her back remained rigid, her shoulders tense. Daniel and Jason sat across from her, neither one relaxing into the settee but sitting as upright as the new widow. Serena Upton appeared to be in her early thirties. She had fair hair, the front cut short to curl charmingly around her heart-shaped face, wide brown eyes, and a pert nose. Her stylish gown was of pale blue silk, and she wore a necklace that could only have come from Egypt, depicting a colorful scarab on a gold disk. Her hand subconsciously went to the necklace as she looked from one man to the other.

"Sorry, but who's Freddie?" Daniel asked carefully.

"My brother. He's always getting into trouble and was arrested only a fortnight ago for public drunkenness. It was all very embarrassing. My father gave him a stern warning, but knowing Freddie, it fell on deaf ears." Mrs. Upton went quiet, as though suddenly realizing that this visit had nothing to do with her brother. "Why are you here?" she asked softly.

"Mrs. Upton, I'm Inspector Haze, and this is my colleague, Jason Redmond," Daniel began, even though he'd already given the names to the maidservant. "I'm very sorry to tell you that your husband's body was discovered inside an Egyptian sarcophagus by Mr. Mason Platt. I apologize for not coming to see you sooner, but we wanted to determine the cause of death before bringing you the tragic news."

Mrs. Upton's eyes filled with tears, and she bit her lip to keep it from trembling. She lowered her head and clasped her fingers around the scarab necklace, as if it might give her strength.

"I'm sorry," Daniel said again.

She nodded, still clutching the necklace.

Neither man said anything until Mrs. Upton looked up a few moments later, having composed herself. "So, the ship docked today?" she asked.

"Yesterday," Daniel replied. "Did you know your husband was on his way home?"

"Yes. He'd written to me saying he'd be sailing back on the *Sea Witch*. I thought it an awful name. It sounds evil," she added, looking to them for understanding. "It was a bad omen. I just knew it. I wish he'd taken the necklace." She seemed to be speaking almost to herself, her pale fingers now caressing the scarab at her throat.

"The necklace you're wearing?" Jason asked.

She nodded. "He gave it to me after his first Egyptian excavation. He was so excited. He found it hidden inside an earthenware jug. It was crusted with dirt and he thought it was a piece of rubbish, but then, once he'd cleaned it, he realized he'd found something precious. The scarab is a symbol of immortality and rebirth, you know. Blake said it would keep me safe while he was away."

"Was your husband a superstitious man?" Jason asked.

It was actually a silly question. The English were a superstitious lot, and all their beliefs had to do with impending death. Jason had had a crash course in ill omens from Mrs. Dodson when he and Micah first arrived and neither fainted from terror when a firefly—an incontrovertible harbinger of death— flew into the house. Mrs. Dodson found Micah examining the insect as it sat on his finger, a smile of delight on his face. She swatted Micah's hand with a tea towel and killed the poor bug, throwing it on the fire and muttering a prayer under her breath. Then the lecture came. If one saw an owl in daytime—death. If a bird flew into a closed window—death. If someone smelled roses when there were none nearby—death. If a sparrow landed on a piano—death. If one met a funeral procession head on—death. And on and on it went. The list was endless and utterly devoid of any logic, but Jason tried to humor Mrs. Dodson and the rest of the household staff or they would leave him without a second thought for fear that he would cause their untimely demise.

Mrs. Upton cocked her head to the side, considering the question. "Yes, I suppose he was, but not in a general sort of way. He didn't believe that if you don't cover your mouth when yawning, your soul will escape, or that if you open an umbrella indoors, there will be a murder. He thought all these notions superstitious claptrap, but he did fear the wrath of the dead," she said, lowering her voice as if the dead could hear her. "He laughed off ancient curses, but I know that he always asked for forgiveness when disturbing someone's resting place. He believed their spirit was still present."

"He didn't think they moved on to the afterlife?" Daniel asked, clearly curious.

"He did, but thought some part of them remained, to guard their tombs."

"Mrs. Upton, when was the last time you heard from your husband?" Jason asked.

"I had a letter several weeks ago, but it was posted at the beginning of March. It takes a long time for a letter to reach one when sent from such a distant place."

"Did you ever go on excavations with your husband?" Daniel asked.

"God, no," Serena Upton exclaimed. "What would I do in a place like that? It's so…" Her brows knitted delicately as she searched for the right word. "Heathen," she said at last. "And Blake always went for such a very long time and stayed in awful native-run hotels. He took pleasure in roughing it, as he called it."

"Mrs. Upton, do you know the other members of your husband's team?" Daniel asked, his notepad at the ready.

She nodded. "Yes. Most of them. We all had dinner together the night before they sailed."

"Can you please list them for me?" Daniel asked gently.

"Of course. There is Jock Thomas. He is also an archeologist. Adam Longhorn, who holds the purse strings."

"Sorry?" Daniel asked.

"Funds can go very quickly if one is not careful, Inspector. Blake trusted Adam to keep track of every penny and negotiate various fees."

"What sort of fees?" Jason asked. "I can't begin to imagine how one organizes a dig."

"Well, the party has to have accommodation, food, various supplies, sufficient funds to bribe various officials and grease palms to expedite the work. And, of course, there are workers to be paid, the price of the voyage, which is quite lengthy, the cost of sending cables and such. Oh, and of course there's the photographic equipment."

"Thank you. Please continue," Daniel invited.

"There is Peter Moffat, the photographer. Also, Dr. Richard Scarborough."

"Your husband brought his own physician along?" Jason asked, surprised.

"Oh, yes. You wouldn't believe the number of injuries and odd ailments that can befall Englishmen in a foreign land." Mrs. Upton looked momentarily panicked, her anxious gaze flickering between the two men. "Inspector, what did Blake die of?"

"I'm afraid he was murdered, Mrs. Upton," Daniel said softly. It was obvious he felt sorry for the woman. She was past the first flush of youth but still managed to appear fragile and childlike.

"Murdered?" Serena Upton cried. "Who by? Oh, but I don't understand." She was wringing her hands, her eyes shimmering with tears. "I assumed he'd been ill."

Jason felt a pang of sympathy at her obvious confusion. She must have thought Blake Upton's body had been placed in the sarcophagus as a sign of respect by the members of his team. It had never occurred to her that the death was unnatural.

"Mrs. Upton, it would have been over very quickly. He didn't suffer," Jason assured her.

"But how did he die?" she moaned, her tearful gaze begging Jason for an explanation.

He might have tried to downplay the real cause of death if not for the fact that the papers would be full of the case tomorrow, complete with photographs of the corpse ensconced in his brightly painted coffin. Daniel had mentioned that it was standard procedure for the Yard to send a photographer to every crime scene, so the photographs had been taken last night when Daniel had first arrived on the scene. The images would be released to the press by Superintendent Ransome.

"I'm afraid his brain was removed," Jason said very softly. "He wouldn't have suffered," he reiterated. "I believe he was unconscious at the time."

Mrs. Upton began to shake, her hand clutching the necklace again as if it could protect her from the horror of what she was hearing.

"Mrs. Upton, I'm a doctor. Shall I give you a mild sedative?" Jason asked, watching the woman with concern.

She shook her head, then pulled a lacy handkerchief out of her sleeve and dabbed at her eyes. "I always knew Blake would come to a bad end," she whimpered. "It's bad luck to disturb the resting places of the dead. He knew that, and still he went."

"That's what an archeologist does, by definition," Daniel said, "so I don't suppose he could have avoided it."

"But the Egyptians cursed those who would disturb their dead," Mrs. Upton cried. "Blake said the workers were always warning him."

"Did he believe in curses?" Jason asked.

"He believed in evil," Serena muttered. Her hand went to her breast, and her breathing had grown shallow.

Jason thought of fetching the smelling salts from his bag should Serena Upton faint, but she was holding on. "Mrs. Upton, would you like to lie down?"

She shook her head vehemently. "No, thank you. I'm fine now. I will answer your questions so that you can apprehend whoever hurt Blake. Please, go on, Inspector," she urged.

"Was there anyone else in your husband's party who would have traveled back with him on the *Sea Witch*?" Daniel asked.

"Yes. Michael Dillane."

"And who is he?"

"He is employed by Lord Belford, who sponsored the dig."

"So, Mr. Dillane was there to see that Lord Belford's money was well spent?" Jason asked.

"Yes. And he reported directly to his lordship. If he felt the funds were being inappropriately spent, the funding would stop."

"Mrs. Upton, did your husband have any disagreements with any members of his party? Did anyone threaten him or take issue with his leadership?" Daniel asked.

"I honestly wouldn't know. Blake never mentioned anything like that in his letters. In fact, he didn't go into detail. He often told me of the finds and even drew pictures of the items in order to help me visualize them, but he never spoke about money or about the working relationships between the various individuals. He didn't wish to upset me."

"How did he sound in his last letter?" Jason asked.

"He was ecstatic. He had found a buried tomb that had been sealed for thousands of years and was bringing home a sarcophagus that was perfectly preserved. He couldn't wait to show it off. He thought he was going to be the toast of London and would be honored at the BAA," Mrs. Upton said, her pride in her husband obvious.

"And what is the BAA?" Daniel asked.

"It's the British Archeological Association. He was a longstanding member."

"Mrs. Upton, do you have anyone who can come and stay with you?" Jason asked. She'd been on her own for the past six months, but she'd thought her husband was coming home. Now she was a widow, her husband murdered, possibly by someone he trusted. She'd need support.

Serena Upton nodded. "I'll go stay with my father. And Freddie," she added softly.

"Thank you, Mrs. Upton. If you think of anything else, please send for me at Scotland Yard."

Mrs. Upton looked up, her expression anxious once again. "When will Blake's body be released?" she asked. "I'd like to start planning the funeral."

"It will be a few more days, but you can certainly go ahead with the planning," Daniel assured her.

"I'm sure Lord Belford will wish to contribute," she said under her breath. "It must be a grand affair, with black-plumed horses and a patent hearse. And mutes. Lots of mutes."

She was still muttering when Daniel and Jason said their goodbyes and were shown out by the spooked maid.

"Poor woman," Daniel said as soon as they stepped out into the street. "She seems mentally fragile."

"Yes, she does," Jason said, but his mind was still on the interview.

"What are you thinking?" Daniel asked.

"I wonder if you should have asked for her husband's letters," Jason said. "She might not have spotted anything alarming, but you might."

"That is a very good point. I'll be right back."

Daniel returned to the house and exited a few moments later, shaking his head.

"She wouldn't hand them over. Said they're private and there's nothing in them that would help us catch Blake's killer."

"Perhaps she'll change her mind once she's had time to think it over," Jason said. "Daniel, what are mutes?"

Daniel chuckled. "Paid mourners. They follow the hearse, looking bereft."

"Of course. Why did I even bother to ask?" Jason said, a tad sarcastically.

"Do they not have mutes in America?"

"Not as far as I know. Shall we have that supper now?"

"I know just the place," Daniel said as he peered down the street in the hope of spotting a cab. "Jason, my landlady has a spare room if you'd like to stay the night. And I would very much value your assistance on this investigation."

Jason considered the suggestion but dismissed it immediately. Katherine would be frightened if he didn't return home, and he didn't want to give her a moment's worry.

"Tonight, I must return home, but perhaps I'll take you up on the offer of the room tomorrow. I'll bring a change of clothes and stay for a day or two. I actually have some personal business to see to while I'm here. So, where are we going?"

"I thought we could dine at Lake's. It's reasonably priced and has decent fare."

"How about Verey's?" Jason asked. "I heard good things about it from Mr. Sullivan."

Jason could tell by the look on Daniel's face that the place was pricey and he felt awkward about allowing Jason to pay.

"Daniel, it's been ages since I've been to a fine restaurant and I'd really like to go, if you don't mind."

Daniel smiled. "All right."

Jason hailed a cab and directed the driver to take them to Verey's in Regent Street.

Chapter 6

Daniel normally stopped for supper at a chophouse a few doors down from his rented rooms, so Verey's came as a surprise. The dining room was spacious, and the tables were sufficiently far apart for the conversations to remain private. The walls were hung with pale green silk and decorated with gilt mirrors and wall sconces, and the tables were all decked out in snow-white tablecloths, the silverware and crystal a cut above any establishment Daniel could afford to frequent. A white-gloved waiter took their order, poured the wine, and retreated as quietly as he had come.

"This is certainly more upscale than anything they have in Brentwood," Daniel observed, taking a sip of his claret and nodding in appreciation.

"Yes, it is. I should bring Katie here once she's fully recovered. She deserves a night out." Jason leaned back in his chair and smiled at Daniel. "Do you miss the Brentwood Constabulary?"

"Yes and no. I liked working with Superintendent Coleridge. I saw him as a mentor. Superintendent Ransome is a very different kettle of fish," Daniel said.

"What sort of fish is he?" Jason asked, obviously liking the quaint expression.

"The kind that swallows you whole," Daniel joked. "He's not given to mentoring or sharing the spotlight. But I'm happy in my work, and there's room for advancement. If I prove myself, I can keep moving up the ranks of the police force."

"And living in London?" Jason asked carefully. Daniel was meant to visit his family in Birch Hill on his days off, but he was making the trip less and less frequently, a fact that Jason was no doubt aware of.

"I have no plans to return to Essex, if that's what you're asking."

The waiter reappeared and placed the first course before them, oysters for Jason and a consommé for Daniel. They'd both ordered venison with roasted potatoes and vegetables for their second course, and Neapolitan cake for dessert. Mrs. Dodson was a fine cook and offered a varied menu at Redmond Hall, but for Daniel, this was a real treat. He didn't have the means to splurge on such a fine meal.

"How does Sarah feel about you remaining in London?" Jason asked once the waiter had gone.

"To be honest, we haven't discussed it." Daniel looked away, hoping Jason wouldn't pursue the matter. He had no wish to talk about Sarah, even though he desperately needed to unburden himself.

Jason nodded. "Daniel, if you ever need to talk or would like to ask for medical advice, I'm here," Jason said.

"I know, and I appreciate that," Daniel said. "But I'm not ready."

"I understand," Jason said. He always knew when it was prudent to change the subject and did so now. "So, what's your plan, Inspector?"

"I think we should start by questioning the crew of the *Sea Witch*," Daniel said. "I don't know how soon the vessel will be leaving, and I don't want to miss my chance to question everyone on board."

"Is the crew English, do you think?" Jason asked.

"I don't know. I suppose we'll find out tomorrow. Given that Blake Upton was murdered aboard the ship, it's imperative that we learn as much as we can and see if we can find the murder scene."

42

"It would have taken a minimum of a half hour to perform the procedure and hide the body, so it would have to be a place that would guarantee privacy."

"Agreed. What did you make of the wife?" Daniel asked.

"Six months is a long time to be apart," Jason said. "I'd like to think that were I to go off for such a long period of time, Katie would come with me."

"That's what I was thinking," Daniel said. "And since they have no children, there's nothing to prevent Serena Upton from joining her husband except her fear of the unknown."

"Or perhaps her fear of her husband," Jason pointed out.

"How do you mean? You think he'd hurt her?" Daniel asked, surprised by Jason's observation. He'd sensed no fear in Mrs. Upton.

"Sorry, wrong turn of phrase," Jason amended. "What I meant was that perhaps she realizes her husband wouldn't give her the attention or the support she'd need in a place like Egypt, and she would find herself largely ignored while he concentrated on his efforts and spent most of his time with his men."

"Ah, I see," Daniel said. "Yes, that would certainly make it unpleasant for her, more so since she seems to have no interest in visiting the place."

"Or maybe has no interest in her husband, or vice versa," Jason pointed out.

The waiter returned with the venison and placed the plates before them with great flourish. "Enjoy, gentlemen," he said, and withdrew.

Oh, I will, Daniel thought as he inhaled the heavenly aroma. He picked up his knife and fork, ready to sample the food.

Jason took a bite, nodded in approval, then swallowed and continued, "Given the advancement of rigor mortis and the consistency of the food in the victim's stomach, I believe he was killed soon after a meal. It may have been lunch, but given the contents and the amount, I suspect it was dinner."

"You think he was murdered after dinner the night before the ship docked?" Daniel asked. He found that talk of the victim's stomach contents did nothing to put him off his own food.

"I think that's likely."

"But that would mean that no one would have seen him at all yesterday. How would the rest of his team account for that?"

"That's what we need to find out. I must admit, this is rather good," Jason said, spearing another bitesize piece of venison. "Mrs. Dodson is a fine cook, but sometimes I miss dining out."

"Will you be bringing the Dodsons to London? You are still coming to London, aren't you?" Daniel asked.

"That's the plan," Jason replied. "We just need to figure out who'll be joining me."

Daniel smiled at his friend. "Lady Redmond is not Mrs. Upton. She won't let you out of her sight for more than a few days."

"That's what I'm hoping," Jason replied. "But I wouldn't like to force her hand. Katie enjoys London, but she's never lived in a big city. She's used to open spaces and country walks."

"I'm sure she can divide her time between London and Birch Hill," Daniel said.

"She could, but that would mean maintaining two separate staffs," Jason pointed out.

"Ah, the problems of the rich," Daniel joked, and drained the last of his wine. He would gladly trade his own problems with Jason's.

The rest of the meal passed in pleasant conversation, and all too soon it was time to go. Jason had a train to catch, and Daniel would return to his lonely lodgings.

"I will meet you tomorrow at Charing Cross," Daniel said. "And then we'll head over to Southampton to interview the crew."

"I'll be there."

"Get home safe," Daniel said, and watched as Jason hailed a cab and got in.

A thin drizzle had begun to fall, and the gas lamps emitted a hazy glow that did little to dispel the darkness. Daniel barely noticed. He should have been thinking about the case, but his mind was on Sarah and the trial their marriage had become. How he wished he could go home, climb into bed, and hold Sarah close as he told her about his day and shared his thoughts about the case. She would have been shocked but also deeply interested and perhaps even helpful. But the days of loving and sharing were long gone.

When Sarah had found herself pregnant with Charlotte, Daniel had believed that they'd finally turned a corner. He understood that Sarah would never get over Felix's death, and he didn't expect her to forget or stop loving him, but he'd thought the worst of her grief was over and they might have a fresh start. She'd been so happy when Charlotte was born. It was as if she herself had been reborn. Daniel had allowed himself to relax, and to hope. But what took place at Ardith Hall last December had changed everything, and he had no idea how to move forward. He could hardly pretend not to know what Sarah had done, nor could he hope to convince her that she wasn't to blame for the death of the man whose carriage had run down their son.

Sarah put on a smile when he came home, and they carried on like nothing was wrong, but the truth was that Sarah was broken, and Daniel had no idea how to fix her. The darkness inside her seemed to be growing, her guilt and grief impenetrable. He'd considered suggesting a consultation with a specialist in London but was afraid of the outcome. Daniel was no doctor, but he had an inkling of the diagnosis that would be passed down. Hysteria. And there were only two solutions for that affliction—surgically removing Sarah's womb or confining her to an asylum, where she would be subjected to various treatments until she either learned to conform or she'd crack, the fragile thread of her sanity finally snapping. And then she'd never be able to come home or be a wife to Daniel or a mother to Charlotte.

No, they would continue as before, he decided, as heavy raindrops plopped onto the brim of his bowler and ran down the back of his neck and into the collar of his shirt. Maybe in time, the pain would dull and the wounds would begin to heal, but the scars would always be there. He knew that now. But there was reason to hope. The past few times he'd returned to Birch Hill, Sarah had seemed calmer, more at peace. Perhaps all she needed was time to finally come to terms not only with Felix's death but with what she'd tried to do. Still, he couldn't just leave her to cope on her own. Daniel pulled up his collar and quickened his step. He wouldn't consult a specialist, but he would talk to Jason and see if he might help them both.

Chapter 7

It was past ten o'clock by the time Jason finally got home. He'd been pleasantly surprised to find Joe Marin waiting for him at the station. The poor man had been there for over two hours, meeting every London train in the hope that Jason was on it.

"I'm sorry you had to wait, Joe. I was going to take a cab from the station," Jason said as he climbed into the brougham.

"It's no trouble, sir. I knew you'd arrive sooner or later." Joe didn't seem put out, so Jason let the matter drop.

Joe shut the door, and Jason relaxed into the luxurious interior, eager to get home. Lily would be asleep, but he hoped Katie would still be up and he could tell her about his day.

"Good evening, sir," Dodson intoned when he opened the door and took Jason's things. "Would you care for some supper?"

"Thank you, I've eaten. Please feel free to retire," Jason added, knowing Dodson required reassurance that he was no longer needed.

"Goodnight, sir." Dodson gave a stiff bow and walked away. He'd come back in a few minutes to lock up for the night.

Katherine was in bed, her spectacles perched on her nose, a book in her hand, but her eyes were closed, and she was breathing evenly. Jason carefully removed the book and tried to take off the glasses without waking her, but her eyes fluttered open, a sweet smile spreading across her face.

"Jason, I was waiting for you," she murmured.

"Go back to sleep," Jason said as he turned off the lamp. "We'll talk tomorrow."

"I'm awake now. Tell me about the case. I want to hear all the details."

"It's gruesome," Jason warned.

"Isn't it always?"

"Yes," Jason conceded. He pulled off his clothes and climbed into bed, wrapping his arm around Katherine when she rested her head on his shoulder.

"Well, go on," she prompted, so Jason filled her in on the particulars and watched her eyes widen as she looked up at him. "Goodness me. How awful."

"Yes, it is, and completely unnecessary," Jason said, not bothering to hide his disgust.

"What do you mean?"

"Being a surgeon, I could easily cut out someone's liver or heart if I wanted to be dramatic, but if my objective was to kill someone, I'd choose a simpler and cleaner method."

"Do tell," Katherine teased. "How *would* you kill someone?"

Jason chuckled. "You know what I mean. Why show off? I'd probably use poison or stick a knife between my enemy's ribs. I certainly wouldn't bother with the drama of removing their brain."

"Good to know. I'd hate to be married to a man who's utterly depraved. I'm glad you would either knife or poison your victim. Much more civilized, I say," Katherine joked.

"Katie," Jason said, smiling despite himself.

"So, what exactly are you saying, that this murder was staged?"

"Yes, I think it was. Whoever killed Blake Upton could have simply knocked him over the head and stashed him in a crate or tossed him overboard. Why the theatrics?"

"Well, possibly because they wanted to blame it on the curse of the mummy," Katherine replied, lowering her voice to sound menacing like said mummy and making Jason laugh.

"Exactly. They wanted to make the killing about the artefact."

"Professional jealousy, do you think?" Katherine asked.

"Possibly."

"How difficult would it be to perform this procedure?"

"I'm really not sure, but it wouldn't take too long for the victim to die, so the perpetrator would have plenty of time to work on him as long as he wasn't disturbed."

"And do you have a list of suspects?"

"In broad terms, everyone aboard the *Sea Witch*. More specifically, the members of Upton's team."

"I take it you'll be returning to London tomorrow to assist Daniel?" Katherine asked innocently.

"Do you mind? Daniel has invited me to spend a few days. His landlady has a spare room."

"No. Why would I mind? You're happiest when your mind is occupied by some puzzle. And speaking of keeping your mind occupied, did you have time to stop at the lawyer's office?"

"I'm afraid not, but I will try to do it this week, since I'll be in London. Have you reached a decision about who'd be coming to London?" Jason asked carefully, not wanting to pressure her.

"All of us," Katherine replied, looking at him as if the answer were obvious. "I wouldn't dream of leaving the children in Essex, and the staff is eager to join us in London."

"All of them?" Jason asked. He was frankly surprised that the Dodsons would be willing to make the move, even if it might be temporary.

Katherine smiled. "I think they're excited at the prospect. Even Kitty said she'd come."

"And Henley?" Jason asked, wishing his troublesome valet would seek other employment. The man's fondness for strong drink really was a liability, but Jason couldn't bring himself to dismiss the man, partly because he believed Henley's alcoholism was a disease and partly because he was the Dodsons' nephew.

"Yes, Henley would like to come. And so would Fanny. And, of course, we'd need a bedroom for Micah for when he comes home from school."

"Of course," Jason said. "I look forward to seeing him at Easter. He is coming home, isn't he?"

"Yes, he is. He'd been invited to stay with a friend, but I think he misses us too much to pass up this opportunity to come home. And, of course, he wants to see Liam."

"Good. I miss him too," Jason said. "Katie, have you seen much of Sarah?"

"No, not really. I called on her twice in the past few weeks and was told by Tilda that she's not receiving. Why do you ask?"

"Just something Daniel said. Or, more accurately, what he didn't say. I think he wants my opinion but feels uncomfortable to ask for it outright."

"Opinion on what?"

"Whether he should seek medical intervention for Sarah," Jason replied.

"And do you think he should?" Katherine asked carefully.

"I think Sarah is riddled with guilt, both over Felix's accident and her attempt on the life of the man who's responsible for his death. Subjecting her to inhumane treatment will not rid her of her guilt. If anything, it might turn her already fragile mind. What Sarah needs is to talk about her feelings until she finds a way to come to terms with reality."

"Is there such a thing as a talking cure?" Katherine asked.

"Not yet, but I think in time there will be a branch of medicine that deals with the psychological effects of certain traumatic events."

"Somehow I doubt that. When has talking ever helped anyone?" Katherine looked troubled. "Do you think Daniel is considering locking Sarah up in an asylum?"

"No, of course not. He only wants to help her. And himself. I think going off to London was not the most prudent decision he could have made, but everyone deals with difficulties in their own way."

"I think perhaps Sarah is trying to find her own way back to a state of grace," Katherine said.

"What makes you say that?" Jason asked.

"She seems less agitated when we see her at church. She's downright serene."

"Is that what you'd call it?"

"What would you call it?" Katherine asked.

"I'd call it vacant. She is present physically, but her mind is miles away. I'm not sure she even acknowledged our presence last Sunday."

"She has a small child, and she worries about Daniel. Don't judge her so harshly, Jason."

"It's not Sarah I'm guilty of judging," Jason replied. "I can't help thinking that Daniel's timing couldn't have been worse. Perhaps he could have deferred his new job for a few months and taken the time to see to his wife."

"So you wouldn't just leave if you thought I was mad?" Katherine asked, only half-joking.

"Katie, I would never leave you out there in the wilderness and try to save myself. You are a part of me, the mother of my child. I would do everything in my power to bring you back from the dark place you found yourself in."

"You are a rare man, Jason Redmond, and I love you," she said simply as she snuggled closer to him. "Goodnight."

"Goodnight," Jason replied. "I love you too."

But Katherine was already asleep.

Chapter 8

Wednesday, April 1

The day dawned cloudy and cold, a dense fog blanketing the streets and swallowing all sound. Despite the early hour, carriages had their lamps lit, and shimmering orbs of light hovered above the streetlamps that had yet to be extinguished. Having fortified himself with a hearty breakfast provided by his landlady, Daniel set off to meet Jason, who was just walking out of the station, newspaper in hand, as Daniel's hansom pulled up. Jason climbed in and they proceeded to Waterloo, where they would board a train to Southampton.

Daniel held out his hand, and Jason handed him the paper. The headline screamed:

THE CURSE OF THE MUMMY

There was a photograph of the sarcophagus, which was thankfully closed. At least the editors had had the decency not to print the image of the victim. That had to be Ransome's doing. Not because he had any respect for the deceased but because he didn't care to be censured by either the commissioner or the public. To depict the dead man without the express permission of his family would have been a gross miscalculation.

"I don't know why we're bothering to go to Southampton," Jason said conversationally as Daniel set the paper aside.

"Why wouldn't we?" Daniel asked, confused. "We still need to question the crew."

"We have our culprit. It was the mummy," Jason said, tapping the headline with his finger.

Daniel laughed. "Yes, that would be convenient. Incidentally, I wonder what happened to the mummy that was meant to be inside that coffin. I reckon the poor chap was thrown overboard—not the afterlife he'd envisioned."

"It is fascinating, isn't it?" Jason asked, looking dreamy. "Such a different culture and way of looking at things. I would love to see Egypt for myself. What about you?"

"I have to agree with Mrs. Upton," Daniel said. "Too heathen for my liking. I hear there are vendors selling mummies in the street. Can you envision bringing that home and propping it up in the foyer to greet the visitors? Ghoulish is what it is."

"It's certainly disrespectful to the dead. They were living, breathing people once. Their final resting places should not be disturbed. It's no wonder the Egyptians keep pushing this idea of a mummy's curse. Their history is being desecrated by the West."

"Absolutely," Daniel agreed. "Take the statues, the tablets, the photographs, but leave the dead be."

"So maybe it *was* the mummy that did it," Jason said, lifting his eyebrows suggestively. "It says that the mummy sucked out Blake Upton's brain through the nostrils."

"How did the mummy even come into this?" Daniel asked, annoyed with the balderdash the newspapers were printing.

"Sensational headlines sell papers," Jason said.

"I'd say this murder is sensational enough without making up nonsense," Daniel said, his tone gruffer than he'd intended. It wasn't Jason's fault the newspapers were making light of the man's death. It was John Ransome's, who should have kept the case out of the papers, but this was too good an opportunity to miss for someone as ambitious as the superintendent. Apprehending the killer would generate favorable publicity for the Yard, and Ransome would have his killer, even if the wrong man got collared for the crime. Ransome was not known for his scruples.

"I have been thinking about the logistics of the murder," Jason said once they were seated in an otherwise empty compartment of the Southampton-bound train. "The interior of the sarcophagus was clean, so the actual murder took place elsewhere. Where was Blake Upton killed, and how did the killer get him into the coffin? Upton wasn't a slight man. He wasn't very tall, but he was muscular. I expect he toiled alongside the workers, digging and lifting buckets of sand. There were callouses on his hands," Jason added.

"How do you think it might have happened?" Daniel asked, sure Jason had a theory.

"Say Blake Upton was asleep in his cabin when the killer came inside, drugged him, and forced the instrument up his nose, puncturing the bone and violating his brain. First of all, there would have been blood and gore, which the steward would have discovered as soon as he entered the cabin. I assume there was a steward, or a sailor who was tasked with cleaning the cabin. Second, the killer would then have had to drag Blake Upton's body down to the hold, where he would have to lift it high enough to get it into the crate containing the sarcophagus."

"How much blood and gore are we talking about?" Daniel asked.

Jason considered the question for a moment. "Probably not a lot," he conceded. "There would have been a nosebleed, of course, and then the brain matter, but to an untrained eye, it might have easily been mistaken for porridge."

Daniel made a moue of distaste as he unwittingly imagined globs of brain littering the floor of the cabin. "Do you think he was killed by more than one person?" he asked. "That would have made it easier to dispose of the body."

"It's certainly possible. Or Blake Upton went down to the hold of his own free will. Either there was something he wanted to see, or perhaps he intended to meet someone. His killer, most likely. It would be much easier to kill him down there, extract his brain, and then get him into the crate. It would still take some effort to lift him, but at least the killer wouldn't have to drag him all the way from his cabin down into the cargo hold, where anyone would hear the noise and might come out of their cabin to investigate."

"We need to search the cabins and the hold," Daniel said.

"Let's hope the ship hasn't been cleaned yet," Jason said. "If the floors have been swabbed, we won't find a thing."

"Maybe not, but surely someone would have seen the blood and the brain matter. Would they not have reported it to the captain?" Daniel asked.

"If they had, the captain did not alert the authorities upon coming into port."

"Perhaps he didn't realize it was significant," Daniel pointed out. "If there wasn't a lot of blood, and brain matter could be mistaken for oatmeal, whoever cleaned the cabin may have assumed someone cut themselves and then dropped a bowl of porridge," Daniel theorized. "Or maybe the killer cleaned up himself."

"I would," Jason said. "If Blake Upton was murdered in the cargo hold at night, the killer would have plenty of time to see to the details, since there'd be no one around. I can't imagine there's much danger of being caught red-handed. And if the killer was calm and collected, as he would have to be to carry out the procedure, he'd make sure there was nothing to tie him to the murder. This crime was well planned, not a spur-of-the-moment act that took the killer as much by surprise as the victim."

"You know, I honestly hope you never decide to go on a killing spree. You'd never be caught," Daniel quipped.

"Funny, Katie said something along those lines only last night," Jason replied, grinning. "Just because I can put myself in the mind of a killer doesn't mean I am one."

"I never said you were. It's just fascinating to me how you think of every detail."

"As a surgeon, I have to think several steps ahead or I might lose precious time during the operation while I consider my next move or have to react to an unexpected development. Strategic thinking comes naturally to me." Jason smiled at Daniel, easily reading between the lines of Daniel's insecurity. "I've been practicing medicine for nearly a decade. You've been a detective for just over a year, Daniel. Don't be so hard on yourself. We all learn on the job, and you've come a long way from settling disputes over stolen livestock."

Daniel felt a warm glow at Jason's encouragement. Jason understood and didn't judge his lack of experience or fear of failure. Few men weren't nervous when trying to impress a new superior.

"We'll get to the bottom of this," Jason promised just as the train arrived in Southampton. They disembarked and walked toward the port, which was a beehive of activity as vessels were loaded and unloaded and passengers queued for departure before a liner that was due to leave that afternoon.

The sky had darkened since they'd left London, the sullen gray reflected in the water that lapped gently at the quay where the *Sea Witch* was moored. She loomed out of the mist as they approached her, the hull towering above their heads like a leviathan rising out of the water, its gunports firmly shut. The Union Jack hung limply off the main mast, since there wasn't a breeze coming off the water, the air heavy with moisture and the odors of seaweed and damp wood. The vessel was an East Indiaman, an armed merchant ship most often used for long-distance voyages to China and India, and in this case, Egypt. The ramp was conveniently down, so Jason and Daniel were able to get aboard without much difficulty.

"Hey, what d'ye want 'ere?" a passing sailor demanded rudely.

Daniel held up his warrant card. "Take us to the captain."

The sailor looked surprised but led the way to the captain's cabin. He knocked on the door, and once the captain bid him to enter, pushed it open, blocking the entrance with his stocky body.

"The police are 'ere, sir." He stepped aside to allow Daniel and Jason enter the cabin, which was spacious and well appointed, a haven of comfort and privacy in the midst of a normally crowded vessel.

Daniel showed his warrant card again and introduced himself and Jason. "Your name, sir?" he asked.

"Captain Jeffrey Sanders," the captain said, motioning for the visitors to take a seat. He was around fifty and stout, with woolly brown whiskers liberally streaked with gray and curling hair that encircled his balding pate like a crown of laurels. His pale blue eyes regarded the two men with obvious wariness.

"What can I do for you, gentlemen?" he asked.

"Mr. Blake Upton's body was found concealed in one of the Egyptian artefacts that arrived aboard your ship. We need to ask you a few questions," Daniel explained.

Captain Sanders looked genuinely shocked. "Mr. Upton is dead?"

"He is."

"How did he die?"

"He was murdered, sir," Daniel replied. "His brain was partially removed."

The captain's mouth opened in astonishment as he absorbed Daniel's words. "Anything I can do to help, Inspector. Anything at all. Mr. Upton was a good man."

Daniel flipped open his notepad, ready to take notes. "When was the last time you saw Mr. Upton?"

"We all had dinner the night before we arrived in Southampton."

"Who was present?"

"Myself, Mr. Crowther the quartermaster, Mr. Upton, Mr. Thomas, Mr. Longhorn, Mr. Moffat, Dr. Scarborough, Mr. Dillane, and the two ladies."

"What ladies?" Daniel asked.

"Mrs. Foster and Miss Gibb."

"Were they part of the archeological team?"

"No. The ladies had been traveling on their own and were returning home. They met the archeological crew when they boarded in Alexandria."

"Were there any other passengers aboard?" Daniel asked.

"No. The *Sea Witch* is a cargo vessel, but we do have several cabins that we use for paying passengers. They go quickly," he added. "There are always Britons bound for home."

"Did you sail directly from Alexandria to Southampton?" Jason asked.

"Yes. Alexandria was our last port of call before sailing to Southampton."

"Where did you stop before Alexandria?"

"Izmir and Antalya. The Ottoman Empire," Captain Sanders added for their benefit.

"And how long did the voyage take?" Jason asked.

"Nearly three weeks. I'm really looking forward to the opening of the Suez Canal, I don't mind telling you," Captain Sanders said. "It will greatly reduce sailing time between Egypt and England. Possibly even by a week or two. We'll be able to make twice as many trips per year as we make now."

"That's a long time to be aboard a ship. Were there any tensions among the members of the archeological team?" Daniel asked.

"Not that I know of."

"What was the mood like at that final dinner?" Jason asked.

"Jolly. Everyone was excited to get home."

"And the ladies? How did they fit in with the other passengers? Was there a possibility of a shipboard romance?"

"If there was, I wasn't aware of it. I don't spend much time with the passengers."

"Can you tell us about the women?" Jason asked.

Captain Sanders shrugged. "Mrs. Foster is thirty-five or thereabouts. She's rather stern. Miss Gibb is younger. Twenty, maybe. She's a lovely creature," the captain added with a warm smile.

"Not stern, then?" Jason asked.

"She's a bit flighty, actually. At least that was my impression."

"Is she a paid companion?" Daniel asked.

"Miss Gibb is Mrs. Foster's niece. I'm not privy to their financial arrangements."

Daniel noted all this down, then turned his mind to more pertinent questions. "Did anyone see Mr. Upton the morning the ship docked?"

"I can't speak for the rest of the crew, but I didn't," Captain Sanders replied.

"Was that odd? Would you have seen him had he been alive?" Daniel asked.

"Not necessarily. I took breakfast in my cabin and then went up on the bridge, where I remained for several hours. I assumed Mr. Upton had disembarked without saying goodbye."

"Did any member of the crew report finding anything that would appear abnormal?" Jason asked.

"They did not."

"I would like to speak to the crew, Captain," Daniel said.

"I'm afraid that's not possible, Inspector. We're not due to sail for a fortnight, so most of the crew has gone home to visit with their families. In fact, had you come a few hours later, you would have missed me as well. I'm homeward bound."

"And where is home, Captain Sanders?" Jason asked.

"Bristol. I will return in ten days' time, when the cargo for our next voyage will be ready for loading." Captain Sanders looked thoughtful. "I don't know if you want my opinion on the matter, Inspector, but I don't think the crew will be much help. Had anyone seen anything overtly suspicious, they would have reported it immediately. And none of my crew would have any reason to kill Mr. Upton. They only met the man when he came aboard in Alexandria and had no personal dealings with him. Except for Mr. Crowther, members of the crew are not permitted to mix with the passengers. I would turn my attention to his companions."

"Thank you, Captain Sanders. I appreciate your input," Daniel said. "All the same, I would like a list of crew members and their addresses, if you have them. And also the addresses for the passengers. I assume you have that information."

The captain nodded and opened a desk drawer, taking out a ledger. He flipped it open to the appropriate page and turned the ledger toward Daniel. "This is the list. You may copy it. These brackets indicate which passengers shared a cabin."

Daniel copied the names and returned the notebook to his pocket. "And now we'd like to take a look at the cabins and search the cargo hold," he announced.

Captain Sanders looked surprised, then shook his head sadly. "I'm afraid you won't find anything. The cabins have been thoroughly cleaned, and the hold was swabbed as soon as it was empty of cargo. You're welcome to look, though. Hammond!" Captain Sanders bellowed.

The sailor they'd met before appeared as if by magic.

"Show these gentlemen all the cabins, and take them down into the cargo hold," Captain Sanders said.

"Aye, Captain."

"Good luck to you," Captain Sanders said in parting. "I hope you find whoever did this."

"Good day, sir," Daniel said.

Hammond took them to every cabin and waited patiently as they examined every inch of the narrow spaces fitted only with berths that were screwed to the walls, a small table, and tallboys built into the foot end of the berths, where the passengers could keep their clothes and other personal items. All the drawers were empty, and there was nothing to be found beneath the berths or on the floor, which had been scrubbed clean.

"Imagine spending weeks cooped up in a space this small," Daniel remarked as they entered the last cabin, which had been Blake Upton's. He was the only member of the team to have a cabin to himself."

"It would be difficult," Jason agreed. "I would require a lot of reading material to pass the time."

Having found nothing, they stepped out into the narrow corridor.

"I think you're correct in assuming that Blake Upton met his killer in the hold," Daniel said, taking in the proximity of the cabins. "Any altercation would be clearly heard by the other passengers, even if they were fast asleep."

"Yes, and it would take a good deal of strength and stealth to move the body from the cabin to the hold. I think we can rule that out."

"Let's take a look at the hold," Daniel said. "Lead the way, Mr. Hammond."

Mr. Hammond lit two lanterns and handed one to each man before leading them into the bowels of the ship. "There's no light down there," he explained.

The hold was divided into two levels. The top level was fitted with rows of wooden bunks for the crew. The chances of Blake Upton being murdered there were slim at best, since dozens of men would have witnessed the crime, but Jason and Daniel performed a cursory search of the quarters. There were no telltale stains or evidence of recent violence, but the whole area stank of stale sweat, tobacco, and spilled grog.

They then descended to the vast and empty cargo hold. The smell that greeted them wasn't very pleasant but was not as overpowering as the one they'd just left behind, since no one lived down below. It smelled of a combination of various shipments that had been transported over time, from tea and spices to lumber and salted fish. Here, the floor had been swept clean but not swabbed, which was more promising. Jason and Daniel split up and began at the far ends, examining every inch of the scarred wooden floor as they searched for evidence of murder, while Mr. Hammond stood by, watching them, his impatience obvious.

"Over here," Daniel called as he stopped close to the wall near the center of the space.

Jason instantly joined him. There were several small, dark stains on the floor that might have been blood, and then a few inches to the left, two pale beige blobs that had dried onto the wooden planks.

Bending down, Jason used his finger to first touch the dark stain, which left a dry red smudge, and then the beige bits. He nodded. "I believe this is where Blake Upton was killed. The blood would be from his nose, and those particles are the brain matter."

Daniel shuddered. It really was too disturbing to contemplate.

Jason pivoted on his heel very slowly, looking for more blood and gore, but there didn't appear to be any, nor were there any signs of a struggle. "Had the killer not cleaned up, there would be more evidence," Jason said at last. "A good portion of the brain was removed, and there would have been more blood. Mr. Hammond," he said, "is there normally fabric to be found down here?"

"Aye," the sailor replied. "There's canvas as used to replace torn sails. Sheets of it."

Jason nodded. "The killer might have spread a sheet of canvas beneath the body, excerebrated the victim, then, once the body was in the sarcophagus, rolled up the canvas and disposed of it, thus destroying the evidence." He turned to the sailor again. "And where were the crates from the excavation located?"

"Just 'bout there," Mr. Hammond said, pointing to the spot where Daniel stood. "Rest of the 'old was already full of cargo from the Ottomans," he added with some distaste.

"And how are the crates lifted out of the cargo hold?" Daniel asked. He couldn't imagine that they'd carry the crates up the stairs, into the upper level of the hold, through the passenger quarters, and onto the deck.

Mr. Hammond pointed to a large square trapdoor in the ceiling, now firmly shut. "The crates are tied with ropes and lifted out of the 'old using a pulley system, then lowered onto the dock."

"Are any wheeled carts used to move the crates into position?" Jason asked. The crates stowed in other areas of the hold would need to be maneuvered to the spot just beneath the trapdoor in order to be lifted out.

"Why, yes, sir. We 'ave some 'ere." He pulled a two-wheeled hand cart from behind a narrow cupboard.

Jason nodded. "Thank you."

"What are you thinking?" Daniel asked as he studied the handcart.

"The body might have been moved using the handcart. Likewise, if the handcart with the body was positioned against the side of the crate with the body facing the killer, all the killer would have to do is lift the bottom and then allow the body to slide into the sarcophagus. One person would be perfectly capable of doing it."

"Was there any evidence of the body being manhandled?" Daniel asked.

"No, but if it happened postmortem, there'd be no noticeable bruises. Besides, the crate used for the sarcophagus was long and shallow, so the body wouldn't have far to fall," Jason explained.

"The crate was sealed," Daniel said. "Are there any tools down here?"

Mr. Hammond nodded. "We keep an 'ammer and nails, just in case something ought to be secured."

"I doubt the killer would risk hammering the crate shut," Daniel said, "but it would take only one or two nails to keep the lid in place. If something soft was placed over the nails to muffle the sound, no one would be the wiser."

"Yes," Jason said. "And the stairs to the upper deck don't pass through the quarters of the crew, so no one would have seen anyone going down into the hold or coming back up again, even if they were still awake."

Daniel nodded in agreement. "We now know where Blake Upton was murdered and how. All we have to do is figure out who's clever enough to have planned this and why they wanted to kill Upton in the first place."

"Are ye done 'ere, then?" Mr. Hammond asked, looking from Daniel to Jason.

"Yes. Thank you, Mr. Hammond," Daniel said, and they made their way up to the deck.

"The quartermaster lives right here in Southampton," Daniel said once they were walking down the quay. "I think we should pay him a visit."

"Absolutely," Jason replied. "Since we can't question the crew, he's the next best thing."

Chapter 9

Mr. Crowther lived in a narrow stone house in Redbridge and opened the door to them himself. He was a tall man, gaunt and serious looking, with neatly pomaded dark hair, sparsely lashed brown eyes, and a trim beard. He was in his shirtsleeves, but his trousers, waistcoat, and cravat were unrelieved black, so he looked somber and unwelcoming.

"Yes?" he demanded.

"Mr. Crowther, I'm Inspector Haze of Scotland Yard, and this is Lord Redmond, my colleague. We'd like to ask you some questions regarding the murder of Mr. Upton."

Mr. Crowther stared at Daniel, uncomprehending. "Mr. Upton's been murdered?"

"Yes, aboard the *Sea Witch*," Daniel replied.

"But that's not possible," Crowther said, staring at Daniel as if he were mad.

"Mr. Crowther, may we come in?"

"Of course. I do apologize," he said. "I'm just a bit shocked is all."

"That's understandable. Have you not seen the papers?" Daniel asked.

"No. I only just arrived at home on Tuesday and haven't gone out."

"Do you live here alone?" Jason asked as Mr. Crowther led them into a small but welcoming parlor.

"No. I reside with my wife and daughter. They went for a walk," he explained as they all sat down. "Please, tell me what happened."

Daniel related the details of the crime, all the while watching the man's face for any signs of awareness but seeing none. Mr. Crowther appeared genuinely shocked.

"You believe Mr. Upton was murdered in the hold, stuffed into the very sarcophagus he'd discovered, and delivered to the museum?"

"In a nutshell, yes," Daniel replied.

"I see."

"Mr. Crowther, let's begin with the crew. Did any members of the crew have disagreements or voice complaints about the archeological team?"

"No. The sailors went about their duties. They were respectful and polite, but they had no personal dealings with the members of the team. They're not permitted to mix with paying passengers."

"Did anyone report seeing or hearing anything out of the ordinary?" Daniel asked.

"Yes," Mr. Crowther said, his brows knitting in displeasure. "I should have taken more notice, but at the time, I had no reason to be alarmed."

"What happened?" Jason asked.

"Mr. Mulligan, the steward assigned to Mr. Upton, informed me that he brought Mr. Upton his breakfast on the morning of our arrival but did not find Mr. Upton in his cabin, as he normally would. His bunk didn't look slept in."

"What of his things?" Daniel asked.

"His trunk was offloaded with the rest of the passenger luggage. I suppose it was sent on to his home address if he didn't claim it at the dock."

"Mr. Crowther, how easy would it be for someone to go down into the cargo hold unnoticed?"

"Easy enough. Most of the sailors retire after supper, with only a few reporting for the night shift. They have a bit of time to themselves, but then it's lights out at nine. Had Mr. Upton gone down to the hold after ten-thirty, when he was last seen alive, then no one would have noticed."

"How closely are the crates stacked?" Jason asked.

"We try to utilize the space efficiently, but we do leave enough room between the rows of crates to pass, should we need to get to a particular area of the hold."

"Then if the killer were to spread a sheet of canvas between the crates, he'd have enough room to perform the procedure, but would also be blocked from view should anyone come down?"

"Exactly so, except that the light from their lantern would be seen. It's pitch dark in the hold at all times. They would need to bring their own light."

"But each passenger had an oil lamp in their cabin, correct?" Jason asked.

"Yes."

"Were the passengers allowed up on deck at night?" Daniel asked.

"Only if they needed to visit the head. Otherwise, they were asked to keep to their cabins after supper. Some did come up for a bit of air after the meal but stayed for only a few minutes. Generally, by ten o'clock, the ship was a ghost town."

"Did the ladies use the head as well?" Jason asked.

"No. That would be rather difficult while wearing crinolines," Mr. Crowther said. "The ladies were provided with a chamber pot, which was taken out by their steward."

"So, if someone was seen moving about the ship at night, any passing sailors would assume they'd gone to the necessary?" Daniel clarified.

"That's correct."

"Is there anything else you can tell us, Mr. Crowther?" Daniel asked as he closed his notebook with a slap of disappointment.

"Sorry, no. I don't spend much time with the passengers. We dined together several times, but everyone was amiable and full of good humor, and no incendiary topics were discussed, since the ladies were present."

"What did you make of the ladies?" Jason asked.

"They were pleasant enough. I suppose it's nice that they can afford to pursue their interests. Not many unmarried women have such freedoms."

"Thank you, Mr. Crowther," Daniel said as he pushed to his feet. "Please write to me care of Scotland Yard if you happen to remember anything else."

"I will most certainly do that. Good day to you, gentlemen."

Mr. Crowther saw Daniel and Jason out, and they headed back toward the train station.

Having just missed the train when they arrived, they took the opportunity to have lunch at a nearby chophouse, which was clean, pleasant in appearance, and offered a nice variety of dishes to choose from. They ordered the fried fish and pints of ale.

"I don't think we should focus on the crew," Jason observed. "If they only met Mr. Upton in Alexandria and, as their names indicate, they're all English, I don't think scooping out his brain would be their chosen method of murder, even if some altercation had taken place between the victim and a crew member.

A knife between the ribs, a blow to the head, a push overboard, but not brain removal. I think we should concentrate on the members of Upton's team."

Daniel nodded. "I agree, but we should still speak with the women. They might have seen or heard something."

"Of course, but I think we should begin the interviews with Dr. Scarborough. As a physician, he'd have the knowledge required to puncture the bone and draw out the brain quickly and efficiently."

"Are you suggesting that you could perform that procedure without having tried it before?" Daniel asked.

"If I had prior knowledge, gleaned from texts or verbal accounts, then yes, I would be able to do it."

"Hmm," was all Daniel could say to that.

Chapter 10

Once back in London, they proceeded to the Bloomsbury residence of Dr. Richard Scarborough. It was in Gower Street, and the three-story terraced house bespoke wealth and comfort. If the good doctor could afford to go off on an expedition for six months, he didn't need to see to his London patients, which meant he was either independently wealthy or extremely well paid for his services.

A maidservant showed them into the drawing room, where Dr. Scarborough was seated before the fire, smoking a cheroot, a newspaper in his lap. He set aside the paper and came forward to greet them, his face tense and his gaze anxious.

"Please, come in," he said. "Make yourselves comfortable. Would you care for some refreshment? I'll ring for tea," he offered before they had a chance to reply.

Dr. Scarborough appeared to be in his forties, a man of middling height and build, with the unusual combination of red hair and very black eyes in an unnaturally pale face, especially in one who'd just returned from a hot, sunny climate. He looked from Daniel to Jason as they settled on a peacock-blue settee across from their host.

"It's shocking. Absolutely shocking," Dr. Scarborough said when neither Daniel nor Jason spoke. "A dreadful loss to archeology and to those of us who knew Blake."

"Were you and Mr. Upton friends?" Daniel asked, slipping open his notebook.

"Oh, yes. We've known each other since our days at Oxford. That's why Blake asked me to join the excavation. He trusted me to look after his men."

"Dr. Scarborough," Jason said, his gaze pinning the doctor, "Blake Upton was excerebrated."

"What?" Dr. Scarborough cried. "I saw that bit about the mummy sucking out Blake's brain, but I thought it was just sensational guff made up by some unscrupulous journalist."

"It isn't."

"How do you know?" Dr. Scarborough demanded.

"I performed the postmortem," Jason replied calmly.

"Are you the police surgeon? I thought—" He turned to Daniel, searching for a plausible explanation.

"Lord Redmond is a trained surgeon, Dr. Scarborough. He's worked with the police on a number of cases."

With Dr. Scarborough, there was no sense in leaving out Jason's rank. If anything, it might impress him and get him to open up. Having gone to Eton, Richard Scarborough had been surrounded by titled men all his life.

The doctor shook his head in disbelief. "I can't begin to imagine who'd do such a thing."

"So, it wasn't you?" Daniel asked, goading him.

The man's head snapped up, eyes opening wide. "Me? Why would you think it was me?"

"Because you were the only medical man on board, unless there was a ship's doctor," Daniel replied.

"There wasn't, but just because I'm a doctor doesn't mean I'm the only one capable of performing the procedure."

"Who else would know how to excerebrate a man?" Jason asked, clearly interested.

"All of us," Dr. Scarborough replied.

"All of you?" Daniel demanded. He hadn't expected that answer.

"Inspector, this wasn't our first trip to Egypt. Everyone in our group had been part of two previous expeditions. Blake was an excellent archaeologist and a dedicated historian. He didn't just dig in the sand, he studied the culture, customs, and beliefs of the ancient Egyptians. And not just from books. He'd invited various experts to come talk to us. One such expert was Dr. Ibrahim, a local specialist. He spoke extensively about the process of mummification and described the process, in detail, I might add. Everyone asked questions and even took notes."

"And how does Dr. Ibrahim feel about Westerners coming to Egypt and stealing its history?" Jason asked.

Dr. Scarborough glared at him. "The Egyptians don't care about their culture. They'd sell their own mothers if they could make a profit. Why, there are countless merchants who spread their wares right on the sidewalk and sell everything from jewelry they'd found in the sands to actual mummies. The mummies stand lined up against the walls, sold for a pittance to anyone who has a mind to have an unwrapping party."

"An unwrapping party?" Jason asked, while Daniel jotted down the term.

"Oh, yes. It's all the rage, my lord, or haven't you ever been invited to one?" Dr. Scarborough asked sarcastically. "Engraved invitations go out, the guests enjoy a wonderful dinner and then adjourn to another room, where the mummy is laid out on the table. The lights are turned down low to create an atmosphere of mystery, and then all the guests take turns unwrapping the bandages until the remains are exposed, what's left of a human being nothing more than a few minutes' entertainment for bored, wealthy people. And then there's the mummy wheat," he added angrily.

"Sorry, what?" Jason asked.

"Mummy wheat. The participants search the wrappings for seeds of grain, then plant them in their own gardens. They believe that the wheat or corn that comes up is thousands of years old and a direct link to the person the seeds were found upon."

"Is such a thing even possible?" Daniel asked.

"Of course not," Dr. Scarborough scoffed. "The host will often slip a few seeds between the wrappings before the party in order to make things more interesting. It's a parlor trick, nothing more. As a doctor, I think the whole things is an outrage, especially the desecration of the mummy."

"Then why do you take part in these expeditions if you morally oppose the desecration of someone's final resting place?" Daniel asked.

"I'm not an archaeologist, Inspector Haze. I'm a doctor. I'm there to look after the men, and believe me, they need looking after, and no Egyptian doctor, if such a thing even exists," he added with disdain, "can be relied upon or trusted to treat an Englishman."

"What do you treat them for?" Jason asked.

"Everything," Dr. Scarborough replied. "We've had bouts of malaria, dysentery, bites that could turn septic, food poisoning, and even melancholy."

"Melancholy?" Daniel echoed.

"Of course. It's not easy being away from home for such a long time. We all miss civilization and our loved ones."

"Are all the members of the team married?" Daniel asked.

"Everyone except Peter Moffat. He's the photographer. Oh, and Michael Dillane."

"And what's his role?" Daniel asked, eager to compare it with Mrs. Upton's description.

"He's a spy."

75

"For the British government?" Daniel asked.

"No, for Lord Belford, who funds these expeditions. He's there to ensure that we don't get too comfortable or waste time mooning about."

"I see," Daniel said. "Were there any tensions on the dig?"

"There are always tensions," Dr. Scarborough replied. "When people live and work in such close proximity, they will get on each other's nerves. That doesn't mean they'll scrape each other's brains out."

"When was the last time you saw Blake Upton?" Daniel asked.

"At dinner, the night before we docked. That would have been Monday night."

"Were there any disagreements or resentment between members of the team?" Jason asked.

"No. Everyone was in high spirits. We couldn't wait to get home. In fact, everyone got rather foxed."

Jason glanced at Daniel for an explanation.

"Was Blake Upton drunk as well?" Daniel asked, simultaneously answering Jason's query.

"He was."

"I found traces of hashish beneath his fingernails. Did he smoke on a regular basis?" Jason asked.

"We all did. I find it to be rather medicinal under certain circumstances."

"Do you now?" Daniel asked, failing to disguise his disapproval. "How does it make one feel, doctor?"

"Happy," Dr. Scarborough replied. "It relaxes the body and the mind and has no lasting effects, unlike opium, for instance, which is highly addictive."

"Was Mr. Upton fond of the pipe?" Daniel asked.

"No. He never partook, at least not as far as I know."

"Did anyone else?" Jason asked.

"No. Opium doesn't mix well with working ten-hour days in the heat of the desert."

"Dr. Scarborough, it is my belief that Mr. Upton was killed during the night. Did no one find it odd when he was nowhere to be seen on the morning of your arrival in Southampton?" Daniel asked, watching the man closely.

"It was odd. I remember Michael Dillane asking after him, and then Jock Thomas kept asking if anyone had seen Blake."

"Did no one look for him?"

"I knocked on his cabin door around ten, but there was no answer, so I went away. I had no reason to suspect he was ill, or dead, so I went back to my own quarters to pack the remainder of my belongings."

"Why did you not think something was wrong?" Jason asked.

"Blake rose precisely at six every morning while we were in Cairo and didn't retire until midnight, but he saw no reason to keep to the schedule aboard the ship. It was a time to rest and reflect. I simply assumed he was sleeping off the drink."

"Did no one wonder where he was when disembarking?" Jason asked.

"Honestly, no. Blake always supervised the offloading of the cargo, fearful that the workers might drop something of great value. We simply assumed he was down in the cargo hold, and frankly, we were all too eager to get home."

"What about Mr. Thomas? Did he not participate in the offloading of the cargo?" Daniel asked.

"He did. He was down on the docks. I saw him as I walked down the ramp."

"Would he not have questioned Blake Upton's absence?" Jason asked.

Dr. Scarborough shrugged. "You'd have to ask him that."

"Doctor, did Mr. Upton have any enemies that you can think of among the group?" Daniel asked. He was getting desperate. He'd interviewed three people and learned next to nothing of value.

"No. As I said, except for basic human impatience and bouts of irritability, which we're all afflicted with, no one really went head to head."

"And what of the ladies aboard the ship?" Jason asked.

"The ladies kept mostly to themselves. They were returning home after traveling in the Middle East."

"Did they mix with the members of your group?" Jason asked.

"Given the close quarters, they had no choice but to mix with us, but everything was above board, if that's what you're asking. Besides, Mrs. Foster kept rather a sharp eye on her niece."

"Is she not of age?" Jason asked.

"Yes, but an unmarried young lady can hardly be left to her own devices, can she?" Dr. Scarborough said. "Especially among more than two dozen men."

"Did members of the crew ever act inappropriately toward her?" Daniel asked.

"Captain Sanders would never allow it. He runs a tight ship," Dr. Scarborough said, clearly pleased with his choice of phrase. "But men will be men. I saw them ogling her and smiling at her when no one was about. She's a lovely young woman."

"And Mrs. Foster? Did anyone smile at her?" Jason asked, trying to hide his own smile.

"Not nearly as much. She's something of a dragon, although she's an attractive woman in her own right. I believe she lost her husband not too long ago. I think she still misses him."

"Thank you, Doctor," Daniel said, and closed his notebook.

"Do you think he was being truthful?" he asked once he and Jason were outside once more.

"I really couldn't say. I would have to meet the other members of the team before passing judgment. Who shall we call on next?"

Daniel consulted his watch. "Perhaps we should split up. I will call on Mrs. Foster and Miss Gibb, and you call on Mrs. Upton. I would like to know if her husband's trunk was delivered to the house and if there's anything in it that might help us. Perhaps he kept a journal."

"Yes, that sounds like a sound plan. Shall I meet you back at your lodgings?"

"Yes. And I told Mrs. Pimm—that's the landlady—to expect us for dinner. It's included in the price of the lodgings," Daniel added. "She's a fine cook."

"Excellent. I look forward to hearing what you discover," Jason said, and tipped his hat to Daniel before heading off.

Chapter 11

Having said goodbye to Jason, Daniel decided to walk to Cavendish Square, where Mrs. Foster and Miss Gibb resided. He needed time to consider, and he did his best thinking while walking. The sky had cleared, and weak late-afternoon sunshine washed the streets, the temperature now mild enough to make Daniel uncomfortable in his wool overcoat. He unbuttoned the two top buttons and continued to walk, his mind on the case.

Jason was correct. Unless Blake Upton had had a run-in with a member of the crew, which was unlikely, given the manner of his death, then Daniel was down to seven suspects: the five team members and the two ladies. Mrs. Foster and Miss Gibb would likely know nothing about the mummification process, but they might have seen or heard something that could help Daniel catch the killer. Women were observant creatures, and having been confined aboard a ship for the past few weeks, they would have formed strong opinions about the members of the team.

When Daniel knocked on the door, a middle-aged maidservant directed him to the top floor, where it seemed Mrs. Foster was renting rooms. A young girl with flaming red hair and pale blue eyes answered the door that led to the apartment and left him to wait outside while she consulted with her mistress.

"Mrs. Foster will see ye now," the girl said imperiously, and opened the door to allow Daniel to come in. The rooms Mrs. Foster rented were spacious and well appointed, with several paintings on the walls and souvenirs from previous travels scattered about the parlor. From the parlor, Daniel could see a small dining room dominated by a highly polished dark-wood table and four chairs, and two other doors that presumably led to the bedrooms.

Mrs. Foster was seated on a sea-green settee and did not rise to greet him. She was in her late thirties and slender, with a narrow nose, slanted brown eyes, and ash-blond hair worn in a simple chignon at the back of her neck. There were no curls or embellishments of any kind, nor did she wear any jewelry, except for a plain silver band on the fourth finger of her right hand. Mrs. Foster wore a navy-blue skirt and a white blouse, the collar resembling a man's shirt, with a striped navy and pale gray tie. Had she been wearing trousers, she would have looked like a man in his shirtsleeves. A gold-rimmed pince-nez hung on a velvet ribbon around her neck, and she lifted it to her eyes to study Daniel as if he were part of some museum display.

"Good afternoon, Inspector," Mrs. Foster said. Her voice was throaty and unexpectedly pleasing to the ear. "Do sit down. Staring up at you is going to give me a crick in the neck."

"Do you know why I'm here?" Daniel asked as he sat in a wingchair that matched the settee.

"I can only assume it's to do with the death of Mr. Upton."

"The murder of Mr. Upton," he corrected her.

She inclined her head in acknowledgement. She must have seen the newspaper. That was the only way she would be aware of Mr. Upton's passing.

"How can I help you, Inspector?" Mrs. Foster asked. Daniel was surprised to note that she appeared to be amused by him.

"You shared a confined space with the archeological team for weeks. I was wondering if you might be able to shed some light on the interactions between the members of the team."

"Susanna and I didn't spend much time with the archeologists, but I will gladly answer whatever questions you put to me," Mrs. Foster said.

"When did you first meet the members of the team?" Daniel asked, pencil poised to take notes.

"We met when we came aboard in Alexandria. All the men were up on deck, so the introductions were made right away."

"What can you tell me about them?" Daniel asked.

Mrs. Foster shrugged delicately. "Mr. Upton was a charming man. Handsome, intelligent, and ambitious. I'm very sorry to hear he's been a victim of a crime. I must write a letter of condolence to his wife," she added under her breath.

"And the others?"

"Well, let me see. Jock Thomas is rather bullish, and competitive," she added, almost as an afterthought. "Adam Longhorn is pleasant and unassuming. Sue and I thought he was good company. Peter Moffat is quiet, but very handsome," she said, a ghost of a smile hovering about her lips. "He reminded me of Michelangelo's David. Male perfection captured in marble."

"Please, go on," Daniel invited, somewhat embarrassed. He had never seen the statue, either in person or in a book, but he was fairly sure the subject was nude.

"I didn't much care for Dr. Scarborough. Boorish, full of himself, and not up on the latest advances in medicine, if you ask me."

"Do you know something of medical matters?" Daniel asked.

"I make it my business to read the medical journals to keep abreast of the latest discoveries. He suggested Susanna take laudanum for seasickness. Imagine that! Nothing like bracing sea air to make one feel better. It took her a day or two, but she got her sea legs in the end. The man is a fool," Mrs. Foster said with feeling.

"And Michael Dillane?"

"Mr. Dillane is the odd man out in that group. Everyone treated him like a pariah. He didn't seem to mind overmuch, though. He's fairly self-contained and spent much of his time reading in his favorite spot on the deck."

"Did you happen to overhear any arguments or threats made against Mr. Upton?" Dare he hope someone had threatened Blake Upton?

"I overheard several," she considered her choice of words, "spirited conversations between Mr. Upton and Mr. Thomas."

"What about?"

"Their discoveries. Mr. Thomas didn't agree with Mr. Upton's conclusions regarding the sarcophagus they found, or more accurately, its occupant."

"What was Jock Thomas contending?" Daniel asked.

Mrs. Foster shrugged. "I really don't know. You'd have to ask him. I didn't hear enough of the conversation to draw any conclusions."

"Anything else?" Daniel asked.

Mrs. Foster began to shake her head but stopped, as if recalling something. "Yes, there was a disagreement. It was early on in the voyage, so I forgot all about it."

"Between whom?"

"Between Blake Upton and Adam Longhorn."

"They argued out in the open?" Daniel asked, thinking it probably wasn't anything too important if anyone could overhear.

"No, the argument took place in Blake Upton's cabin, which was just across from ours. I just happened to be passing by and overheard snatches of the conversation. Their voices were raised, you understand."

"What did they argue about?"

"As I said, I only overheard a few phrases, so I might have taken them out of context, but it sounded like Mr. Upton was accusing Mr. Longhorn of misappropriating funds. It was rather heated."

"Misappropriating funds?" Daniel asked. "Did you hear Mr. Longhorn's response?"

"Well, of course he denied it. He would, wouldn't he?" Mrs. Foster said, raising her eyebrows at Daniel's obvious naivete. *Who would admit to skimming funds?* her expression seemed to say.

"Did you notice any ill will between the two men for the rest of the voyage?" Daniel asked.

"As I previously stated, Inspector, we didn't spend that much time with the other passengers, so I can't really answer that. They were cordial enough when we dined together."

"When was the last time you saw Mr. Upton?"

"At dinner, the night before we docked."

"And how was the mood at the table?" Daniel asked.

"Very amiable. Mr. Upton was extremely excited at the prospect of the new exhibition and couldn't wait to show off his finds to the curators of the museum and Lord Belford."

"Did Mr. Dillane indicate whether his employer was pleased with the results of the excavation?"

"He did, as a matter of fact. He said Lord Belford was very pleased and would most likely sponsor another dig."

"Did you notice Mr. Upton's absence on the morning of your arrival in Southampton?" Daniel asked.

"No, I didn't. Sue and I finished packing and then we went up on deck. We did see Mr. Thomas down on the wharf, hailing the wagons that were to take the crates to London. He became agitated after a time, but I really wasn't paying much attention. I was eager to begin the journey home. After three weeks spent sleeping on a narrow wooden bunk and washing in parts, I was eager for my own bed and the luxury of a hot bath."

"Do you rent these room?" Daniel asked, even though the answer seemed obvious.

"No. I own this house," Mrs. Foster said, taking him by surprise. "I let the two lower floors. Sue and I don't need the space, and the money supplements my income and funds my love of travel."

"And Miss Gibb?" Daniel asked. "What is her role?"

"Sue is my friend and companion. She is my late husband's niece. She lost her parents at a young age."

"How long have you been widowed, if I might ask?"

"Nearly eight years. Alan was a dear man. We were great friends."

"Can I speak to Miss Gibb?" Daniel asked, having run out of questions for Mrs. Foster.

"Of course." Mrs. Foster sounded agreeable enough, but a note of reserve crept into her tone, as if she felt the need to protect her companion. "Inspector, Sue doesn't know how Mr. Upton died. She's not one to pick up a newspaper. I told her the news, of course, but only in the broadest terms. Please, don't tell her. She'll be terribly alarmed."

Daniel nodded. He supposed the method of the murder could be avoided if Susanna Gibb answered all his other questions willingly.

Mrs. Foster got to her feet and went to knock on one of the bedroom doors. "Sue, dear, Inspector Haze from Scotland Yard is here and would like to speak with you."

A young woman stepped out, and Mrs. Foster entered the other bedroom and shut the door, presumably to give them privacy. Susanna Gibb was slight and short of stature, but she had a graceful way of moving that reminded Daniel of a dancer. Her hair was very dark, almost black, and dressed in the latest style, with soft curls framing her face. Her pale-green eyes were wide and fringed with dark lashes, and her emerald-green gown looked expensive and was of the latest style.

"Good afternoon, Miss Gibb," Daniel said. "I hope you don't mind if I ask you a few questions."

"Not at all," Susanna Gibb said as she took the seat Mrs. Foster had vacated.

"I assume you heard about Mr. Upton's death," Daniel said.

"Yes. It's tragic." Her eyes filled with tears, and she momentarily looked away, needing a moment to compose herself. "He was a nice man."

"Did you spend much time with him?"

"Oh, no. Amelia and I kept mostly to ourselves. But, of course, it's difficult to keep your distance in such close quarters," she added.

"Can you tell me something about the members of the archeological team?" Daniel asked.

Miss Gibb looked thoughtful. "I honestly didn't pay them much mind. They were always arguing, it seemed. Mostly about their discoveries and the history behind the artefacts. To be honest, I find history quite boring."

"What did you do all day while on board?"

"I read, took walks on deck, and drew in my sketchbook," she admitted with a sheepish smile. "It annoyed Amelia when I was concentrating on my book or the drawings because she likes to talk and feels ignored when I'm not paying attention to her."

Daniel could very easily see how Amelia Foster would be irritated by her companion not making herself available. "Where were you before arriving in Alexandria?"

"Damascus," Susanna Gibb said.

"What did you think of it?" Daniel asked, simply out of curiosity.

"It's beautiful, I suppose, but it's Amelia who's fond of the Middle East. She says it's the crossroads of the world. I would have much rather gone to Paris or Vienna. She did say we could go to Italy next year, so I'm looking forward to that."

"How long were you in Damascus?" Daniel asked.

"Close to a month. And before that, we were in Constantinople," she replied.

"Did you like it better than Damascus?" Daniel had no idea why he was asking these questions. They had no relevance to the case, but there was something about Susanna Gibb that made him want to keep talking to her.

"To be honest with you, Inspector, if you've seen one mosque, you've seen them all, but please don't tell Amelia I said that. She can describe the distinguishing features of every building we visited and expound on them for hours, so don't get her started."

"And you?"

"I'm a simple creature. I like to shop and visit exhibits, and just go for walks and look at people. I love people-watching," she said, smiling charmingly. "People are so interesting, especially when they don't realize they're being observed."

"And what did you observe of the archeological team?" Daniel asked.

Susanna Gibb looked him straight in the eye. "I think they strongly disliked each other."

"Was it something they said that led you to believe that?"

"It was what they didn't say," Susanna replied. "What you read between the lines often speaks the loudest, don't you think?"

"Yes, I do. Do you think everyone disliked Blake Upton?" Daniel asked, hoping she'd drop a clue.

She shrugged delicately. "They had a sort of love/hate relationship with him, I suppose. They admired him and were grateful to him for taking them out of their daily routine, but they also resented him. He was a bit of an autocrat, I think."

"And the others? What were they like?"

"Have you asked Amelia? I've no doubt she would be happy to dissect each man until there was no part of him left unexamined."

"She did offer me her views, but I would like to hear yours," Daniel said, smiling at her despite himself. She was enchanting.

"Jock Thomas is single-mindedly focused on his career, probably to the detriment of his family. Dr. Scarborough is as dry as toast. Adam Longhorn is a dear, I thought. He's the sort of man who always puts others before himself. And Michael Dillane is a lot more sensitive than he lets on. Life has not been easy for him."

"And Peter Moffat?" Daniel tilted his head, waiting for Susanna to respond.

A slow smile spread across her face. "Peter is very nice."

"Did you spend any time with him?"

"Not alone, no. Amelia would never permit that," Susanna replied sadly.

"Will you see him again, now that you're back in England?"

"Not unless he pays us a call."

"Do you think he will?" Daniel asked.

"No," Susanna replied with surprising finality.

"Thank you, Miss Gibb. I appreciate you taking the time to speak to me."

"You're welcome, Inspector. Good luck with your investigation."

Daniel donned his coat and hat and stepped out into the spring twilight. The rest of the interviews would have to wait until tomorrow. He was tired and hungry and looked forward to discussing the case with Jason, much as they had done when they'd met in Jason's drawing room at Redmond Hall, enjoying a drink by the fire. Only back then, he'd had Sarah to return home to. Now, he'd go to his lonely bed.

Chapter 12

Having finished with their modest meal, Jason and Daniel adjourned to Mrs. Pimm's tiny parlor. She had retired early to give them a bit of privacy, and Daniel greatly appreciated her tact. Mrs. Pimm didn't offer brandy or whisky to her lodgers, but Jason had had the forethought to pick up a bottle on the way back and poured them each a drink before settling by the fire.

"How did you find Mrs. Upton?" Daniel asked.

"Sad. Lost. She did promise to look through her husband's trunk tomorrow or the day after to see if there's anything that might be of use. I also asked her for the letters again, but she refused to part with them, even for a day or two."

"For a grieving widow, she certainly doesn't seem too eager to help us solve this case," Daniel pointed out.

"I think she's just in shock," Jason replied. "She's just lost her husband, and she has no children to focus on. It's not easy being left alone."

"She does have a father and a brother to look after her," Daniel said.

"Yes, but that's hardly the same as a husband."

Daniel nodded in agreement and took a sip of his rather fine brandy.

"How did your interview with Mrs. Foster and Miss Gibb go?" Jason asked.

"Well enough. They are an odd pair."

"How so?"

"Mrs. Foster is rather sharp around the edges. She is opinionated, decisive, and sure of her place in the world," Daniel said.

"And Miss Gibb?"

"Exactly the opposite. She's young, beautiful, and a little detached."

"Detached?"

"She doesn't seem to care one way or the other what they do. She indicated that it was Mrs. Foster's desire to travel and that she would have been just as happy to remain at home, or perhaps visit Paris. She has no interest in history and appears to be entirely at Mrs. Foster's disposal."

"You mean it's Mrs. Foster who pays the bills and Miss Gibb can't afford to upset her," Jason observed.

"They have a set of rooms on the top floor of a rather fine house. I assumed they were lodgers, but it appears Mrs. Foster owns the building. She is widowed, and her husband seems to have left her well provided for. She lets out the two bottom floors to supplement her income."

"Traveling can be a costly business," Jason said. "Were you able to learn anything of interest?"

"Only that there were tensions between the men, mostly pertaining to their finds and the history behind the artefacts."

"Katherine and I think that professional jealousy is a possible motive," Jason said.

Daniel nodded. "I agree. But let's reserve judgment until we speak to all the members of the expedition. Mrs. Foster also mentioned in passing that she'd overheard an argument between Blake Upton and Adam Longhorn where the former accused the latter of sticking his hand into the till, so to speak. Money is always a motive for murder."

"Yes, it certainly is," Jason said. "But if that were the case, surely Michael Dillane would know something about it."

"I thought so too," Daniel said.

"What's our plan for tomorrow?"

"I think we should start with Peter Moffat, since his lodgings are the closest, then work our way through the remaining members of the team."

"Sounds logical," Jason said. He'd finished his drink and set the glass down.

"Would you like another?" Daniel asked.

Jason smiled. "Why not?"

Chapter 13

Thursday, April 2

When Jason and Daniel left the house the following day after a hearty breakfast provided by Mrs. Pimm, they immediately came across a boy selling newspapers. The headline, as well as the boy, screamed:

WILL THE MUMMY STRIKE AGAIN?

Daniel looked at the newspaper with distaste. Why couldn't the papers print only factual information instead of relying on these silly gimmicks to boost sales? Seeing a second boy hawking the *Illustrated Police News*, he very nearly changed his mind. The front page showed a sketch of a terrified woman standing on a wooden platform, a noose around her neck, the headline announcing the public hanging of Frances Kidder outside Maidstone Prison that morning.

"It's disgraceful," Jason said, following Daniel's gaze. "What sort of person do you have to be to attend an execution for entertainment?"

Daniel shrugged. "People have attended public hangings for centuries. It's a time-honored British tradition," he added bitterly.

"What does she stand accused of?"

"Drowning her stepdaughter. I don't really know the details. Not one of my cases," Daniel replied.

"Somehow, the prospect of a vengeful mummy doesn't seem as objectionable today, given that other headline," Jason said as they walked toward Peter Moffat's lodgings.

A quarter of an hour later, Daniel pulled out his notepad and checked the address. "This is it right here," he said, pointing to a set of windows above a chemist's shop. He knocked on the door, which was opened by a woman in her sixties.

She smiled pleasantly. "How can I help you, gentlemen?"

"Is Mr. Moffat in?" Daniel asked, holding up his warrant card.

"Oh, dear," the woman said. "I hope he's not in any trouble. He only just got back from Egypt, you know."

"Yes, we are aware of that. Mrs…?" Daniel stretched out the question, waiting for her to supply the answer.

"Mrs. Moffat. Peter is my son," she supplied. "Do come in and make yourselves comfortable. I'll tell Peter you're here. He's in the darkroom," she added, once they'd ascended the stairs to the living quarters. "Can I offer you some tea?"

"No, thank you," Daniel said after Jason shook his head.

"All right then," Mrs. Moffat said, and left them in the parlor.

The room was small and not overly bright, since there was only one window and it was west facing, so the sun was on the other side. The space was clean and cozy, but everything was worn, from the rug on the floor to the tapestried cushions on the chairs. There were arrangements of dried flowers and several stuffed birds perched on a branch inside a glass case. On the mantle were several porcelain figurines, two courtly couples painted in garish colors. There were also several framed photographs, presumably taken by the photographer.

At last, Peter Moffat walked through the door. "I'm sorry to have kept you waiting. I was in the darkroom and couldn't open the door until the development process was complete," he explained. He held a cardboard box beneath his arm and set it on the low table.

Peter Moffat had to be one of the most attractive men Daniel had ever seen. Whereas all men were born of a woman, the photographer appeared to have been sculpted by an artist's hand. His fair hair gleamed, and his dark blue eyes were large and thickly lashed. His straight nose, high cheekbones, and full lips put Daniel in mind of the Roman busts he'd seen at the museum. And his physique was that of a fencer, his movements fluid and economical. No wonder Mrs. Foster had compared him to Michelangelo's David. She was right to be impressed.

"It's awful what happened to Blake," Peter said, taking a seat. "I'm in absolute shock."

"Can you tell us about Blake Upton?" Daniel invited.

"Yes. He was a good man. Very passionate about archeology."

"When was the last time you saw him?" Daniel asked.

"It was around ten o'clock on Monday, March thirtieth," Peter said.

"Not at dinner?" Daniel asked, glad to hear someone had seen the victim after the meal.

"I wasn't feeling well," Peter said, "so I went up on deck to get some air. The cabins are close and stuffy, and I bunked with Michael Dillane, so there wasn't much privacy. When I came up on deck, it was quiet and dark. The crew had already retired, and there was just the first mate on the bridge and another sailor whose name I didn't know. Blake was standing by the rail."

"Was he alone?" Jason asked.

"No. He was speaking to someone, but I couldn't make out who it was."

"If you could make out Blake Upton, why couldn't you identify his companion?" Jason asked.

"Blake wasn't wearing a hat, so his face was clearly visible. I called out to him, and he returned my greeting. But in doing so, he turned to face me and blocked the other person with his shoulders. All I saw was that his companion was wearing a black coat and hat, pulled low over the eyes."

"Was this person tall, short, thin, stout?" Daniel demanded.

"He was thinner and shorter than Blake. That's all I can reasonably tell you. Given that I had just left Michael in our cabin, that would leave only Jock Thomas, Adam Longhorn, and Richard Scarborough to choose from. It definitely wasn't Dr. Scarborough. He's stouter than Blake was, and just as tall. I don't think it was Jock either. He has a rather booming voice. I would have heard it. It might have been Adam, but I didn't get the impression it was him."

"Did Mr. Upton seem agitated at all?" Jason asked.

"No. He seemed relaxed. Happy, even," Peter Moffat said. "He was eager to get home."

"Mr. Moffat, we know there were tensions between members of the team. Can you elaborate on that?" Daniel asked.

"Oh, God, where do I even begin?" Peter Moffat said. "Well, I suppose the biggest rift was between Blake and Jock. You see, it was Jock Thomas who discovered the tomb. Blake had marked off several locations and had the workers dig there, but all they found was sand. Jock insisted that they dig further to the east, in the area he'd marked, and that's where they found the entrance to the burial chamber."

"Was Jock Thomas angry with Blake Upton?" Daniel asked.

"He wasn't openly angry, but he was resentful. As the leader of the dig, Blake would take all the credit. He always did. Jock's name might be mentioned in passing, but even the information plate at the museum would most likely say that the discovery was made by Blake Upton."

"Was Jock Thomas resentful enough to kill?" Jason asked.

"I wouldn't have said so," Peter Moffat said. "But they did butt heads. That was the nature of their relationship."

"But this wasn't the first dig they'd gone on together?"

"No, this was the third."

"Were you at the previous two?" Daniel asked.

"I was. I'm not overly interested in Egyptian history, but the job was well paid, and I could use the money," he admitted.

"Who else argued with Mr. Upton?"

"He and Adam Longhorn went at it hammer and tongs."

"Over what?" Daniel inquired.

"Expenses. Blake was willing to stay at dodgy guesthouses and skimp on clean sheets and hot water, but he liked his food and drink, and he hired more workers than was strictly necessary in order to dig in several locations at once."

"And the workers were all local men?" Jason asked.

"Yes, and most of them come in packs. You hire one man and he'll bring his sons, his brothers, his uncles, and even his wife to cook for the men. The profit they make off a dig can probably last them for several years if they are careful."

"So, Adam Longhorn wanted Blake Upton to cut back on expenses?" Daniel clarified.

"Yes. He wanted him to dismiss half the workers and concentrate on two locations instead of four. He also thought we should be made to share rooms at the guesthouse."

"Did everyone have their own room?" Jason asked.

"Thankfully, yes. It's not easy to share a room with someone you hardly know for months on end," Peter said.

"Luckily, no one would ask me to share, since I need a darkroom to develop the images."

"You were able to work in your room?" Jason inquired, clearly surprised.

"Yes, at night. During the day it was too bright, even with the shutters closed, so I had to wait until it was completely dark."

"How could you see what you were doing?"

"I would light an oil lamp and place it behind a thin red curtain I had fashioned. It gave off a muted red light that allowed me to see without exposing the negative. I brought some photos to show you," Peter Moffat said. "I developed these yesterday."

He reached for the box and took off the lid. Inside was a stack of photographs. He took them out carefully and passed them to Daniel, who looked at each photograph in turn and handed it to Jason. There were about ten in total. A group photo of the Englishmen. A photo of the workers, who looked tired and grim as they stared into the camera, their dark faces a stark contrast to the white of their turbans and kaftans. The rest of the photos were of the artefacts. There was a beautiful statue of a black cat decorated with gold and precious gems. There were two photographs of the sarcophagus, one with the lid closed and one with the lid open, the mummy inside clearly visible, its bandaged remains dried up and gruesome. There were also several images of clay pots found with the coffin and several pieces of jewelry. The designs were intricate and exotic, not something one would imagine being crafted thousands of years ago and with crude tools. Even in the black-and-white photos, it was possible to tell that the stones were colorful and vibrant.

Daniel finished with the stack and returned to the first photograph, the group shot. All the men were dressed in light-colored suits, their faces shaded by wide-brimmed hats. They were smiling and looking into the camera, the very picture of camaraderie and purpose.

"What about Mr. Dillane?" Daniel asked. "Which one is he?"

"Bottom right."

"What was his relationship with Mr. Upton like?"

"Excellent. Blake treated Michael Dillane like his long-lost brother because he wanted Michael to send a good report to his employer. Lord Belford is mad for anything Egyptian and wants his name associated with the most exciting finds, so he's willing to pay good money to fund these expeditions. If he's not happy with one archaeologist, he'll simply find another. As I'm sure he will now. If I might venture to guess, I think Jock Thomas will be leading the next excavation."

"And Dr. Scarborough? What do you think of him?" Jason asked.

"He's a pompous arse whose answer to every ailment is either a dose of laudanum or a purging of the bowels. Believe me, when in Cairo, one doesn't need any more purging than happens naturally," Peter Moffat said. "The spices alone are enough to send a man to hell."

"You did not have an English cook?" Daniel asked.

"No. To bring out a cook would be an unnecessary expense. We ate breakfast and dinner at the guesthouse. The owner's wife did her best to accommodate our tastes. During the day, we ate whatever the workers ate. That was usually the problem. Their food is vastly different from anything our English bellies are accustomed to."

"And what of the two ladies onboard?" Daniel asked.

"They were rather bored, I'm afraid. The *Sea Witch* is not a luxury liner; it's a cargo vessel, so there was nothing to do. No entertainments of any kind, and we couldn't spend too much time on deck, since we'd be in the way of the crew going about their work, so we had to take turns. We all spent much time in our cabins. Miss Gibb found an out-of-the-way spot where she liked to sketch."

"Is she any good?" Jason asked.

Peter Moffat smiled guiltily. "No. She has no artistic talent whatsoever, but it gave her something to do. I think she used her desire to sketch as a way to get away from Mrs. Foster, who can be quite overbearing."

"I see you don't have any photographs of the ladies," Daniel observed.

"I would have liked to take a photo of them, but Mrs. Foster didn't like the idea."

"What about Miss Gibb?" Jason asked.

"She wanted to but deferred to her aunt," Peter Moffat replied.

Daniel handed back the stack of photographs. "Thank you, Mr. Moffat. Might I borrow this photograph?" Daniel held up the group photo.

"You can have it. I can just print another copy."

"May I see that?" Jason asked. Daniel passed the photograph to him, and Jason stared at it intently.

"Something wrong?" Peter Moffat asked.

"Yes. There were six men in your group, but there are seven people in the photograph," Jason observed. "Who's the seventh man?"

Peter's face fell. "The seventh man is Henry."

"Who's Henry?" Daniel demanded.

"Henry Ames was Mr. Upton's assistant. He was fresh out of university and wanted to learn the ropes from someone as renowned as Blake Upton, so Mr. Upton took him along, as a favor to Henry's parents, who are Blake Upton's godparents. Henry catalogued all the dig locations, finds, and any information he could find pertaining to each object. He also helped Mr. Upton date the artefacts and the like."

"Where can we find this Mr. Ames? He wasn't on the list of passengers Captain Sanders provided us with," Daniel said. "Did he share a cabin with Dr. Scarborough? Seems the good doctor was the only one to have a cabin to himself, besides Blake Upton."

"Henry died," Peter said quietly. "And Mr. Upton blamed Dr. Scarborough."

"Why? What was the cause of death?" Jason asked, watching Peter Moffat intently.

Peter sighed heavily. "It was about a month after we arrived in Cairo that Henry started complaining of abdominal pain. He consulted Dr. Scarborough, who gave him castor oil. The pain seemed to go away but returned in a few days. Dr. Scarborough prescribed more castor oil. He said Henry needed to purge his bowels. A week later, Henry had another bout. More severe this time, so Dr. Scarborough gave him laudanum for the pain. This went on for about three weeks. The pain would recede, then come back stronger in a few days. One day, Henry cried out while we were eating our midday meal. He was clutching at his stomach, doubled over with pain. His forehead was covered in sweat, but he was cold and shivering. By that time Dr. Scarborough had guessed what was ailing him, but it was too late. Henry died of a burst appendix that very day."

Jason looked horrified. "How could he not have known? There are ways to diagnose an inflamed appendix."

"I don't know, but Mr. Upton was devastated. He felt responsible for Henry's death, since he'd been the one to bring him along. He said Dr. Scarborough was an ignorant buffoon for missing something so serious and he should have acted sooner. He could have saved Henry's life. Mr. Upton threatened to report Dr. Scarborough to the Royal College of Physicians, or whatever body is responsible for the integrity of medical men. He said he'd see Dr. Scarborough lose his license and never practice medicine again."

"Was there a postmortem?" Jason asked.

Peter nodded. "Mr. Upton insisted that there be one. He took Henry's body to an Egyptian surgeon in Cairo, who performed the postmortem. Mr. Upton made sure Dr. Scarborough was there to watch."

"Did the two men resume cordial relations after Mr. Ames's death?" Daniel asked.

"They were civil, but there was tension between them. Mr. Upton suggested Dr. Scarborough return home, but the doctor insisted on staying. I think he hoped to change Mr. Upton's mind and convince him that it was a natural mistake any doctor might have made under the circumstances."

"A natural mistake?" Jason echoed.

Peter shrugged. "I don't know anything about medicine, so I can't comment. I only know that Dr. Scarborough was very upset and sorry about Henry's death. He was only twenty-two," Peter Moffat added quietly. "And we had to bury him in Cairo, in a graveyard attached to an Orthodox Church, since that was the only Christian church in the vicinity. His parents were shattered by the news. I sent them a photograph I'd taken of Henry, so they'd at least have something recent to remember him by."

"That was very kind of you," Jason said.

"It was the least I could do. Henry was my friend. He was the nicest, most likable member of the team. He didn't deserve to die the way he did."

"No, he didn't," Jason agreed.

"Thank you," Daniel said again, and stood to leave.

Jason followed.

"That poor young man. Could they not have sent his body home?" Daniel asked once they were outside.

"It would have taken a minimum of a month to find a ship and then to sail back to England. I'm afraid the body would begin to leak, especially since the weather is so warm in that part of the world."

"It's tragic not to be able to bury your son," Daniel said. At least he could visit Felix's grave whenever he wished.

"Many men die far from home," Jason said, a faraway expression on his face. Daniel let the matter drop, knowing Jason was recalling his own tragic experiences.

"He did seem sincere," Daniel said. "And his account corroborates professional jealousy as a possible motive for Jock Thomas to murder Mr. Upton. The disposal of the body would tie in with that as well. Blake Upton wanted the fame of discovering the sarcophagus, and now, ironically, he'll be eternally associated with it."

"Yes, but Dr. Scarborough would have known how to remove Blake Upton's brain as well, and he most likely had a supply of chloroform in his medical arsenal. And if what Peter Moffat says is true, then he certainly had a motive. He might have lost not only his license to practice medicine but his good name and source of income, and from what we've seen of Dr. Scarborough's home, he enjoys a very comfortable existence."

"Could it not have been an honest mistake that led to Henry Ames's death?" Daniel asked. "Surely there's no way to tell for certain without performing an operation."

"I would have to speak to Dr. Scarborough and look at his case notes. It's difficult to form an opinion without examining the patient myself."

"In your opinion, is Dr. Scarborough capable of murder?" Daniel asked as they continued down the street.

"I think anyone who feels threatened is capable of murder," Jason replied. "But I don't see what Dr. Scarborough would have to gain by waiting until the last minute. If he had planned to kill Blake Upton, he could have chosen a less obvious way to do it. As a doctor, he could have made Upton's death appear to be the result of natural causes. Why go to the trouble of removing his brain and hiding him inside the sarcophagus, where he was sure to be found?"

"Perhaps he wanted to teach him a lesson. Blake Upton was going to ruin his professional reputation, so he decided to kill Upton in a way that would reflect badly on his own professional standing."

"I'm not sure that it does. It's just ghoulish," Jason remarked. "However, the method of the murder does point the finger at Jock Thomas, if we are to believe that professional jealousy is the motive."

"Yes, it certainly does. I would dearly like to know who Blake Upton was speaking to up on deck."

"The person Peter Moffat saw him with may have been the last person to see him alive and could have been arranging to meet Blake Upton down in the hold. Even if whoever it was happened to be shorter and slighter, with the aid of the chloroform, they would have been able to take down Upton easily enough."

"I think it's time we spoke to Mr. Thomas," Daniel said. "And we will need to reinterview Dr. Scarborough."

Chapter 14

Jock Thomas lived in a modest house in Millbank, an area of London favored by tradesmen and merchants. He clearly had to earn his living, unlike Blake Upton and Richard Scarborough, who seemed to be very well off, probably due to inheriting family money. Jock Thomas opened the door himself, his tall frame filling the doorway, his head nearly touching the lintel.

Daniel held up his warrant card. "Mr. Thomas, I'm Inspector Haze of Scotland Yard, and this is my colleague, Lord Redmond. We'd like to speak to you regarding the murder of Mr. Blake Upton."

Jock Thomas stepped aside. "Come in."

They trooped into the narrow entryway that seemed to bisect the house from front to back. There were several doors on either side. Jock Thomas invited them into the parlor, which faced the street, the windows hung with heavy mustard-yellow drapes drawn aside to reveal the lace curtains beneath. The room was modestly decorated and had a lived-in quality particular to houses where the occupants spent much of their time in just a few rooms, not having the space to spread out. Daniel and Jason accepted the offered seats.

"Who is it, Jock?" called a voice, followed by a woman of about thirty with frothy brown hair and dark eyes who peeked into the parlor and seemed astonished to find two strangers. She carried a small boy on her hip and had obviously been feeding him since his face was smeared with food. A girl of maybe seven appeared behind her mother, her dark eyes filled with curiosity about the strangers. She smiled shyly and retreated.

"It's the police, my dear," Jock replied, giving his wife a reassuring smile. "Nothing to worry about. They just want to ask me a few questions about Blake."

The woman inclined her head in understanding but showed no signs of nervousness or panic at being visited by the police. "I'll just be in the kitchen, if you need me." She looked to her husband as if silently asking if she should offer their visitors refreshment.

"We're fine," Jock assured her. "See to the children."

The woman returned to the kitchen, and Jock Thomas shut the door behind her, then folded himself into a well-worn armchair, looking from Daniel to Jason with an air of expectation.

The photograph Peter Moffat had showed them didn't do the man justice. He wasn't classically handsome, but with his jet-black hair, black eyes, and neatly waxed moustache, he had a certain presence and a suppressed energy that seemed to flow outward, as if he were restless. Something about his demeanor reminded Daniel of Superintendent Ransome.

"Am I to be arrested, Inspector?" Jock Thomas asked with barely suppressed belligerence.

"Why do you think we're here to arrest you, Mr. Thomas?" Daniel asked, taken aback.

"I'm the only member of the group who had an obvious motive to kill Blake Upton, or at least that's what any self-respecting prosecutor would suggest."

"And what motive is that?" Jason asked.

Jock looked momentarily confused, as if wondering if he'd just handed the police a reason to suspect him, but then regained his composure and continued. "Blake offered me an incredible opportunity when he invited me to join his dig, but he also made sure I never got any credit. I was the one to find that tomb, you know. Based on my research, I believed there to be a tomb in that very area. Blake argued with me and insisted we dig in several other spots first. We found nothing," Jock said, baring his teeth in triumph. "Only then did he agree to dig where I had suggested. And then we disagreed bitterly about the time period of the burial. Blake believed the man had lived during the twenty-first dynasty, but I was able to date him back to the New Kingdom," Jock explained proudly.

"And how were you able to accomplish that?" Daniel asked.

"I was able to translate the papyrus found inside the tomb and cross-reference the text with the images painted on the walls and the statues found with the grave goods. There are subtle differences in the artistic styles from the two periods, but I won't bore you with the details."

"Did Mr. Upton acknowledge his mistake?" Jason asked.

"He did, after a time, but he didn't deal well with eating humble pie," Jock Thomas said smugly. It was almost as if he wanted to convince them he had a motive for killing Blake Upton, Daniel thought as he noted Jock Thomas's comments in his notebook.

"Were all your differences of an academic nature?" Daniel asked.

"For the most part, but there were other issues as well," Jock replied.

"What sort of issues?"

"I had been the one to persuade the inspector from the Department of Antiquities to allow us to take the sarcophagus out of the country. Blake simply assumed we could remove whatever we found, but this was quite a coup, and the Egyptian officials initially forbade the removal of the artefacts from the tomb."

"How did you persuade them?" Jason asked.

"Well, for one, I didn't treat the inspector like a gibbering monkey who couldn't possibly appreciate the honor we were bestowing on his country by pillaging its history. I explained to him that there was great interest in the West in all things Egyptian, and the sarcophagus and its occupant, as well as the grave goods, would be treated with the utmost respect and tell a story mere words couldn't convey. I invited him to visit London and see the exhibit for himself, all expenses paid by Lord Belford, and he eventually agreed to sign off on the customs form that would finally permit us to leave the country with our discoveries. Blake was thrilled but also resentful that I was the one to talk the inspector round."

"Then you admit you two were at loggerheads quite often," Daniel stated, amazed by the man's willingness to share so much of his relationship with the victim. Few suspects would be as honest.

"Blake was stubborn as a mule, but he was also charming and amusing when he chose to be. He was the one to secure funding and keep Lord Belford happy. His lordship would never have bet on the likes of me. At least not before this momentous find."

"And now you hope to pick up where Blake Upton left off?" Jason asked.

"I do, yes. I have proved that I have the knowledge and expertise to obtain results, not only academically but tactically as well."

"Mr. Thomas, are you admitting to the murder of Blake Upton?" Daniel asked, shutting his notebook.

"I'm doing no such thing, Inspector. I'm simply pointing out why everyone and their mother will assume I'm the murderer."

"And are you?"

"No," Jock Thomas said emphatically.

"Convince me," Daniel said.

Jock shrugged and rolled his eyes in exasperation. "Why would I resort to removing the man's brain on board a ship back to

England? There are easier ways to kill someone, especially during an excavation."

"Such as?" Jason chimed in.

"Such as leaving a scorpion in their bed. Or dislodging a centuries-old piece of masonry and making sure it lands on the victim's head. Shall I go on?"

"What about the curse of the mummy?" Jason asked, a ghost of a smile touching his lips. "Could the mummy have killed him?"

Jock looked even more impatient. "Do you honestly believe all that tripe?"

"No, but there are those who are superstitious and take such prophecies seriously," Jason replied. "Did Blake Upton fear the repercussions of disturbing someone's final resting place, and could the killer have been alluding to his fear by killing him in such a unique way?"

"I don't believe in dark magic or curses that live on for thousands of years, my lord, but as a Christian, I do feel a certain sense of wrongdoing when disturbing a grave. So did Blake. But that didn't stop him from pursuing his goals."

"Did he take the curses seriously?" Jason asked.

"What does it matter?" Jock exploded. "Are you suggesting the mummy came to life and took its revenge on the person who desecrated its grave? That's ludicrous."

"I'm just trying to get into the mind of the killer," Jason replied patiently. "I'm curious what would prompt someone to go to such lengths to kill a man when, as you pointed out, they could have just tipped a piece of masonry on his head or left a scorpion in his bed."

"Blake was interested in the curses, but in a purely academic way. He liked to talk to the workers and hear the stories.

They always blather on about curses and the revenge of the worthies whose graves have been disturbed, but that doesn't stop them from showing up for work. They are dirt poor, and they need the money we so liberally spread about. The curses are just legends, a way to keep unscrupulous people from robbing the tombs. And yes, that's what we do," Jock said angrily. "That's what archeology is—disturbing the dead. But it's also a way to learn about the past and show the masses how ingenious and advanced the people who came before us were. The people of today think they know it all and everyone who came before them was a barbarian, but the ancient Egyptians were brilliant. Have you ever seen the Great Pyramids? They're magnificent, and utterly indestructible. They will still be there long after we are gone. How could primitive people with no formal education, no machinery, and nothing but the most rudimentary tools build such monuments?" Jock exclaimed.

"Using thousands of slaves," Daniel said.

"It's not as simple as that, Inspector. No doubt they used slave labor to haul the stones from the quarries and lay them in place, although I have no idea how they did it, since some of those blocks must weigh tons, but someone was the architect of those structures. Someone designed them and the chambers within. These were people who understood not only mathematics and physics but also astrology. And the artisans of the time were highly skilled. The sculptures and drawings are so detailed and lifelike, it's as if they were created by the finest artists of our time. The temples in Karnak and Luxor are simply breathtaking, the statues perfectly proportioned and intricately carved. It boggles the mind that such craftsmanship existed thousands of year ago and in such a primitive place."

"Be that as it may, Mr. Thomas," Daniel said, "that still doesn't prove you didn't murder Blake Upton."

"No, I don't suppose it does," Jock Thomas agreed. "But I told you the truth of our relationship. We butted heads, we argued, we got angry, and then we had a meal and a drink and put our differences aside until the following day. Besides, as far as I can tell, you don't have a shred of physical evidence against me," he challenged. "Have you found the murder weapon? Fingerprints? Witnesses who'd seen me go down into the cargo hold with Blake? I hadn't set foot in the cargo hold since the day we boarded the ship, when I went down to make sure the crates were securely stowed."

"Mr. Upton's brain was removed in a copycat act of mummification. Who else would know how to perform such a procedure?" Daniel demanded, barely keeping his anger in check. Jock Thomas was absolutely correct. They had nothing against him save his professional resentment against Blake Upton, and although that might be a motive, it certainly wasn't proof.

"Anyone who listened to Dr. Ibrahim's lecture," Jock Thomas retorted. "We were all there. He went on at length about how the dead were prepared for the afterlife. He even showed us the instruments the ancient Egyptians used. All it would take to extract the brain is a bamboo stick. That same stick could be used to puncture the bone, with the help of a mallet or a stone to drive the stick through the barrier. Anyone could have done it. Anyone," he repeated defiantly.

"Even someone like Michael Dillane?" Daniel asked.

"Even someone like Michael Dillane."

"But what would be his motive? Or that of Peter Moffat? What would they have to gain by killing Blake Upton?" Daniel demanded.

"You'd have to ask them that," Jock Thomas replied. He looked angry and defensive. "Just because someone doesn't have an obvious motive doesn't mean they're not the culprit."

"Mr. Thomas, did Mr. Upton ever speak to you about Adam Longhorn?" Daniel asked, changing tack.

"What about him?"

"Did Blake Upton believe Mr. Longhorn was stealing money?"

Jock looked genuinely surprised. "No. He never said anything to me. Who told you that?"

"That doesn't really matter," Daniel replied. "And where did the press get the idea that there was a curse? Did you tell them that?"

Jock Thomas grinned. "A reporter from *The Times* ambushed me outside my front door. I might have mentioned the mummy to deflect his questions."

"Or perhaps you were trying to deflect responsibility from yourself," Daniel suggested.

"By blaming a mummy? Hardly."

"Then you must know that one of your party killed Blake Upton," Daniel said.

"Yes. That would stand to reason, wouldn't it?"

"Mr. Upton was angry with Dr. Scarborough's mishandling of Henry Ames's illness," Daniel said, watching the man intently.

Jock Thomas made a dismissive gesture with his hand. "People are often angry with doctors for failing to save those they care about, but that's only because they need someone to blame. Blake felt guilty for taking Henry along. He was an amiable young man, but he was a bit frail, not suited to life on a dig. He was always complaining of this or that. He was violently ill on the voyage out. Puked his guts out. Then he developed some sort of rash once we arrived and thought he'd been bitten by a poisonous snake. Richard did his best to treat him and keep him calm, but every week there was a new ailment. I suppose he should have taken Henry's complaints more seriously, but many of us had health problems once we arrived. The change in climate and food does a number on your innards. It takes a few weeks to fully adjust."

"Then you don't believe there was anything more Dr. Scarborough could have done?" Jason asked.

"Look, I'm not a medical man, so I really couldn't say, but I do think Blake's anger was directed more at himself than at Richard. Henry's parents are Blake's godparents, so there is a family connection there. Henry wasn't a stranger. Blake had known the boy since birth."

"Mr. Thomas, you seem to be making a case against yourself despite your best efforts," Daniel pointed out.

"I'm not going to point the finger at someone else to deflect attention from myself," Jock Thomas said. "Arrest me if you must, but you'll find no evidence to prove my guilt. I didn't kill Blake, so I have nothing to fear."

"You had much to gain by Mr. Upton's death," Daniel said.

"We've gone on three digs together, and I have never done anything to harm him physically or to tarnish his reputation."

"Ah, but this time you discovered a burial chamber filled with valuable artefacts," Daniel countered. "This time, there was more at stake. And by mentioning the curse, you very effectively raised the public's interest in your find."

"Inspector, no amount of public interest would benefit me if I found myself at the end of a rope. Blake could be bloody-minded and selfish, but he was my mentor and friend, and I wouldn't have harmed him for the world. By the by, what time was Blake killed?" Jock Thomas asked conversationally.

"He was last seen alive around ten and was probably dead by the time the crew woke in the morning," Jason supplied.

A slow grin spread across Jock Thomas's face. "Then I have an alibi," he said.

"And what is your alibi?" Daniel asked.

"I shared a cabin with Adam Longhorn, who is an insomniac. He usually stays up all night reading. It's very annoying, since the light bothers me," Jock said. "But, in this instance, it's a godsend. Adam will confirm that I never left the cabin between those hours, and I would have had to leave for at least an hour to carry out the procedure and hide the corpse," Jock pointed out. He looked irritatingly smug.

"And Mr. Longhorn? Are you sure he didn't leave the cabin while you were asleep?" Jason asked.

"I am. I'm not a heavy sleeper. Never have been. I had to learn to sleep on my side to ignore the light of his lantern, but I could hardly ignore the opening and closing of the cabin door. It tended to stick, so one had to put one's shoulder to it to get it open."

"And what time did you retire?" Daniel asked.

"Immediately after dinner, so it would have been before ten. Adam returned to the cabin with me."

Daniel nodded and pushed to his feet. "Don't leave town, Mr. Thomas," he said as he jammed his bowler on his head.

"I wouldn't dream of it," Jock Thomas replied, his sarcasm as obvious as it was galling.

Chapter 15

After leaving Jock Thomas, Daniel and Jason took themselves off to a coffeehouse a few streets away. Having ordered coffee, cake for Daniel, and cheese pie for Jason, they returned to the case.

"There's no physical evidence against Jock Thomas," Jason said after he stirred in milk and a half-teaspoon of sugar and took his first sip. The coffee was bitter and strong, just the way he liked it.

Daniel leaned back in his chair, looking unusually tired for so early in the day. "Jock Thomas had means, motive, and opportunity, and he might be a flight risk. Ransome will have my head on a spike if I let a murderer get away. Perhaps I should have arrested him."

"If you had, tomorrow's newspapers would be full of the arrest. The man's reputation would be unjustly ruined," Jason pointed out.

"Do you really think he's innocent, Jason?" Daniel asked, clearly annoyed by Jason's defense of the man.

"As Mr. Thomas pointed out, there are easier ways to kill a man. And why wait until they were back in England? I've never been to Egypt, but somehow, I think it would easier for an Englishman to get away with killing an Englishman on foreign soil. I can't imagine that Egypt has an extensive police force."

"Perhaps they had a falling out aboard the ship," Daniel suggested.

"But why go through that ridiculous charade? Why not just poison the man or push him overboard? If Jock Thomas had helped himself to the chloroform, he could have just as easily taken anything else from Dr. Scarborough's stock of medicines. Blake Upton had a cabin to himself. Jock Thomas could have held a pillow over his face, and no one would have been the wiser."

"What are you suggesting, Jason?" Daniel asked warily.

"I'm suggesting that we're on the wrong track," Jason replied patiently.

"And what's the right track, in your opinion?"

"I don't know yet. We need to interview the remaining suspects and then rethink everything we know. If you make a hasty arrest, you'll look a fool."

"I'm already a fool," Daniel said softly. "My wife attempted to kill a man and then carried on as if nothing had happened, and I didn't see it. I didn't suspect her for a moment, even though she had been right there at the scene of the crime. Not much of a detective, am I? Or a husband, for that matter. I'm afraid for her, Jason. She's not herself. She's consumed with grief, guilt, and all manner of feelings I can't understand. Where do we go from here? How do we live together with this always between us?"

"Daniel, what Sarah did was wrong, but ultimately, she wasn't responsible for the man's death."

"But she could have been. She meant to kill him. How do I live with that? How do I pretend everything is all right?"

"You don't. I think you and Sarah need to talk about this. And then you need to talk about it again and again, until you both come to terms with everything that's happened. Daniel, I'm not justifying what Sarah did, but had I come face to face with the person responsible for my child's death, I can't promise you I wouldn't try to exact revenge. It's human nature. Blood for blood. A life for a life. The government does it every single day. They hang people for murder. Sarah simply decided to bypass due process."

"That still doesn't make what she did forgivable," Daniel argued.

"No, it doesn't, but it makes it understandable. And if you can understand what she did and why, then you can start to forgive her." Jason looked at Daniel closely. "Daniel, do you still love her?"

Daniel looked away for a moment, staring at a carriage that had stopped on the opposite side of the street, an attractive woman in a plumed bonnet getting out and disappearing into a doorway.

"I don't know," he said at last. "I love the person she used to be. I'm not sure I can love the person she's become. But I can't do anything to hurt her. She's suffered enough, and I wouldn't cheat Charlotte out of having a mother. Sarah adores her."

"Perhaps if you had another child," Jason said softly.

Daniel stared at him. "Are you mad? We barely look each other in the face. You think we can…" He let the sentence trail off, but his meaning was clear.

"Maybe you need to," Jason said. "You are man and wife, and marital relations are the glue that holds a marriage together."

"Our glue has dried up, Jason, and no amount of stirring the pot will bring it back."

"I'm sorry," Jason said. "I truly am. I wish I could do something to help."

"You are helping. You're the only person I can talk to about this, the only one who understands how I feel."

"I'm here if you want to talk more. Anytime."

"I know, and I appreciate that. You are the only friend I have in the world," Daniel said, smiling sadly, then turned his attention to his cake, shoveling it in like a man who hadn't eaten in days.

Jason sighed and took a bite of his pie. He desperately wished he could help, but this wasn't a medical matter. Daniel and Sarah had to find their own way forward, if there was a way. Just now, Jason wasn't sure.

"Where to next?" Jason asked once the silence became too heavy.

"Adam Longhorn, then Michael Dillane. It's not too far to the Longhorn residence. Are you all right with walking?" Daniel asked.

"Of course," Jason replied with forced enthusiasm. "It's a fine day." And maybe Daniel would be more himself once they arrived at their destination.

Chapter 16

They found Adam Longhorn at his home in Holborn. He had been enjoying luncheon with his wife and daughter but came to join Daniel and Jason in the drawing room as soon as the maidservant summoned him. The house was modest but tastefully decorated. Daniel noted that the furniture looked newish, and the carpet and curtains showed no signs of wear. The Longhorns appeared to be comfortably off, if not wealthy enough to settle in a more desirable neighborhood.

Adam Longhorn was around forty, with thinning brown hair that was silvered at the temples, warm brown eyes, and a pleasant smile.

"Good afternoon, gentlemen," he said. "Can I offer you some refreshment?"

"No, thank you, Mr. Longhorn," Daniel said, eager to get down to business. "I assume you know why we're here?"

"Yes, of course. This is about Blake's death. It's tragic. Truly tragic," Adam Longhorn said, his dark eyes reflecting his pain.

"Mr. Longhorn, can you describe your relationship with the deceased?" Daniel invited.

"We were friends, and colleagues. We'd known each other for years. In fact, I had been Blake's banker before he asked me to join him on his first expedition five years ago. My wife was vehemently opposed to me leaving my position at the bank and running off to Egypt, but I simply couldn't pass up such an opportunity."

"Why was that?" Daniel asked.

"I have spent the best years of my life sitting behind a desk, staring at columns of figures. There were times when I felt as if my very life was draining out of me. And suddenly, I had the chance to shed my black suits, walk in the sun, and be a part of something amazing. I can't tell you what it's like when someone yells, 'Over here!' and everyone comes running, their excitement palpable. Many times, it's nothing but a broken pot or a hunk of a broken statue, but sometimes, it's a once-in-a-lifetime find, like the burial chamber we found, and the sarcophagus within. Knowing that we were the first people to see that face after thousands of years is a feeling I can't even begin to describe. It's euphoric," he added, his eyes glowing with the memory of it. "And we owe it all to Blake."

"Yet someone killed him," Daniel pointed out.

"Yes. I can't imagine who would do such a thing," Adam Longhorn said, his eyes dimming with grief once again. He had a very expressive face for a man, Daniel thought, watching him closely. Someone like Adam Longhorn would never be able to lie effectively.

"You were overheard arguing with Blake Upton about money," Daniel said.

Adam Longhorn smiled sadly. "We argued about money daily. Blake was often stubborn and unreasonable."

"In what way was he unreasonable?" Jason asked.

"There are necessary and unnecessary expenses, Lord Redmond," Adam Longhorn replied. "Blake couldn't always distinguish between the two."

"So, what would be an unnecessary expense?" Jason asked, his curiosity piqued.

"Wine," Adam Longhorn said.

"Wine?" Daniel echoed in surprise.

"Yes. You must understand that the majority of the locals are followers of Islam. The Quran forbids the imbibing of alcohol. In a country where people don't drink, securing an endless supply of wine is costly. The hotel owners and merchants import wine from Italy and Greece expressly for the consumption of Western visitors, and they charge whatever they wish, since the foreigners are willing to pay the price. Blake demanded that there be wine with every dinner, bottles of it. He also had a fondness for Scotch and beer and wasn't willing to go without. I could hardly order spirits for him without providing for the other men. It was one of the biggest expenses after paying the workers and securing lodgings."

"Did you record these expenses accurately?" Daniel asked.

"Of course. Why wouldn't I?"

"Did Blake Upton ever ask you to fiddle with the books to bury these unnecessary indulgences?"

"No, never," Adam Longhorn replied, his surprise at such a suggestion obvious. "Blake felt he was entitled to enjoy a couple of glasses of good wine after a day spent digging in the heat of the desert. He felt no need to hide anything."

"When was the last time you saw Blake Upton alive?" Daniel asked.

"Around ten thirty on our last evening aboard. We met in the corridor just outside my cabin."

"What were you doing in the corridor?"

"I was going to the head," Adam Longhorn said, clearly embarrassed to admit to the need to empty his bowels.

"And Mr. Upton?"

"He had been up on deck and was returning to his cabin. We wished each other goodnight and went our separate ways."

"Was he alone?" Daniel asked.

"Yes, he was."

"Mr. Longhorn, did you see anyone else, either before you met Blake Upton or just after? Someone wearing a black coat and hat."

"No, I'm afraid not."

"Do you know of anyone who might own such items?" Daniel asked.

Adam Longhorn stared at Daniel as if he'd just been asked a trick question. "We wore mostly light-colored fabrics while in Egypt, but everyone had their wool coats and felt hats with them, and we had unpacked them as soon as the weather grew colder. It could have been anyone, Inspector."

Daniel nodded, acknowledging the truth of that. "Did you see any of the passengers once you came up on deck?"

"No, but I didn't really look. There might have been someone there, in the shadows. It's not a crime to go up for some fresh air or enjoy the nighttime sky."

"No, it isn't," Daniel agreed. "But the person Blake Upton was seen with shortly before you encountered him in the corridor might have been his killer," Daniel said acidly.

Adam Longhorn appeared stricken by the suggestion but didn't say anything.

"How did Blake Upton seem when you met him?" Jason asked.

"Fine. Good," Adam Longhorn replied hastily. "He smiled when he saw me and seemed happy and relaxed. He was eager to get home, see his wife, and begin the process of arranging the new exhibit."

"Had you observed any arguments or tensions between the members of the team?" Daniel asked.

"Of course there were tensions. We spent nearly six months together and then another several weeks on board with nothing to do to pass the time. We're only human, Inspector."

"And what about the resentment Blake Upton felt toward Dr. Scarborough over the death of Henry Ames?"

Adam Longhorn seemed surprised by the question but was quick to respond. "Henry's death was unfortunate, but I think Blake's accusations were uncalled for. He called Richard terrible names and threatened to have his license suspended. People die, Inspector. It happens every day. There's no guarantee that had Henry been in England and seen another physician the outcome would have been any different."

"But Blake Upton armed himself with evidence that would have proved his case had he wished to take it before the medical board once back in London," Jason said. "By having an independent surgeon perform the postmortem, he had irrefutable proof that Dr. Scarborough made a tragic mistake."

"To be fair, my lord, few English medical men would take the findings of an Egyptian surgeon as gospel. They would most likely side with Dr. Scarborough because he's one of their own. As you know, medicine is not an exact science. Sometimes things turn for the worse and there's nothing a doctor can do but stand aside and allow nature to take its course."

"I'm not sure this was one such case," Jason argued.

"I really wouldn't know," Adam Longhorn said. "I expect you'll have a clearer picture once you speak to Dr. Scarborough, but I don't believe Blake would have stayed the course. He was angry and upset, and he felt terrible guilt because of his connection to the family and the fact that Henry's body couldn't be sent back for burial, but once he had time to consider, he understood that Dr. Scarborough had done all he could with the tools available to him. Blake was not a vengeful man by nature and wouldn't have hurt someone without a damn good reason."

"You don't believe Richard Scarborough could have murdered Blake Upton to save his reputation and source of income?" Daniel asked.

"I have a hard time imagining Richard as a murderer," Adam Longhorn replied.

"What about the two ladies who were aboard the ship?" Jason asked.

"What about them?" Adam Longhorn asked, his brow furrowing with confusion.

"Did you interact with them?" Jason pressed.

"Not very much. They kept to themselves. We did have dinner together occasionally, but not every night. Sometimes they took a tray in their room."

"Were relations with the ladies cordial?" Daniel asked.

"Yes, of course. They were perfectly pleasant," Adam Longhorn replied.

"Can you elaborate on that?"

Adam Longhorn made a show of thinking. "Mrs. Foster is the older of the two and rather prim. She did display an interest in history and enjoyed talking to Blake and Jock about the dig and history in general. She and her niece had recently visited Constantinople and Damascus, which Blake was curious about since he'd never been. He was considering mounting an expedition to Syria. He thought it might be a nice change from Egypt. He was going to propose the idea to Lord Belford and had consulted with me about the approximate financial scope of such an undertaking."

"Do you think Lord Belford would be open to an excavation in Syria?" Daniel asked.

"I really couldn't say," Adam Longhorn replied. "But I would have gladly joined the expedition were I to be asked."

"And what about Miss Gibb?" Jason asked.

"Miss Gibb doesn't give a fig for history. I assume she's at her aunt's mercy when it comes to financial matters and does what she's told. She's a charming young lady," he added.

"Miss Gibb is very attractive. Might there have been a blossoming romance between her and one of the men?" Daniel asked. "Come to think of it, Mrs. Foster is attractive as well, and you just said she spent time with Blake Upton and Jock Thomas."

Adam Longhorn's eyebrows knitted in concentration. "I—I really don't think so," he replied hesitantly. "I certainly didn't see anything that might be described as a courtship. It was all very cordial and proper. Besides, both Blake and Jock are married."

"Peter Moffat and Michael Dillane aren't," Daniel reminded him.

"No, they're not, but, as I said, it was all above board. I didn't see anything untoward, but I'm probably not the right man to ask. I tend to have my nose in a book when I'm at my leisure."

"Mr. Longhorn, did you share a cabin with someone?" Daniel asked, even though he already knew the answer.

"Yes, I shared with Jock Thomas."

"Did Mr. Thomas leave the cabin at any time after you retired for the night on Monday?"

Adam Longhorn shook his head. "No, he went to bed around ten and didn't wake until seven the following morning."

"How can you be so sure?" Jason asked.

"I don't sleep well. It takes me hours to drop off and then I wake up if there's even the slightest noise. Oftentimes, I end up reading half the night."

"And you're absolutely sure that Jock Thomas couldn't have quietly left the cabin while you were asleep?" Daniel asked.

"I'm positive, Inspector, because the door was warped. It didn't open smoothly. Jock would not have been able to leave without waking me."

"I see," Daniel said, disappointed that Jock Thomas's alibi checked out. "And what about you, Mr. Longhorn? Could you have left the cabin without Mr. Thomas realizing it?"

"No. Jock is a light sleeper. He always complained about my reading light. He'd be up in a flash if I pushed open the door and then tried to close it behind me." Adam Longhorn seemed to suddenly realize what Daniel had just asked, his gaze reflecting his panic. "Are you suggesting I killed Blake?"

"Did you?" Daniel asked.

"Why would I kill him?"

"You were in charge of the money," Daniel said. "If you happened to be diverting funds into your own pocket and Blake Upton realized it, you'd have a motive for murder."

Adam Longhorn instantly looked relieved. "Except I wasn't. You can examine the ledgers, if you wish. I have already submitted them, as well as all the receipts, to Lord Belford, but I have no doubt he'd be happy to show them to you."

"You appear to have redecorated recently," Daniel observed. "The carpet is new, and the furniture looks hardly used."

"So?"

"That's hundreds of pounds out of pocket," Daniel remarked.

"My wife's uncle recently passed. He left her one thousand pounds in his will. Quite a windfall. We had no idea Uncle Everett was so well off. Alice and I decided to save the bulk of the inheritance for our daughter, Eleanor, but we treated ourselves to several new items. This is the room where we spend the most time, and we wanted it to be welcoming. I will be happy to furnish you with the name and address of the lawyer who handled Everett Frye's estate."

Adam Longhorn got to his feet and left the room, returning a few minutes later with a card, which he handed to Daniel. He looked at ease, like a man who had nothing to hide.

"Mr. Longhorn, if you had to choose one person out of your group who you think is capable of murder, who would that be?" Daniel asked.

"I'm sorry, but I would rather not answer that question. You're asking me to point the finger at someone, and I won't do that. I have no reason to suspect anyone."

"Thank you, Mr. Longhorn," Daniel said, feeling somewhat defeated.

"He seemed perfectly genuine," Jason said once they stepped out into the street.

"He did, didn't he?" Daniel grumbled. He pulled out his pocket watch. "The lawyer's office is only a few streets away. Let's stop in and verify the story about the unexpected legacy from the benevolent uncle before speaking to Michael Dillane."

"Lead the way," Jason said.

Chapter 17

The ancient clerk at Mr. Edgerton Esquire's office refused to admit them until Daniel produced his warrant card and threatened to arrest the man for obstruction. Five minutes later, they were seated in Mr. Edgerton's office, which looked and smelled like it hadn't been dusted or aired out in a long time, possibly ever. The man himself could have used a good airing out as well, given his rheumy gaze and dandruff-dusted shoulders. Daniel almost expected him to whip out a hearing horn, but thankfully that didn't seem necessary. Daniel briefly explained the context of their visit, then made his request.

"Mr. Edgerton, we need to verify that Mrs. Longhorn did indeed receive a legacy from her uncle," he said.

"She did, but I suppose you require more than just my word," Mr. Edgerton rasped. He stood and walked on shaky legs over to a row of wooden cabinets. He was well past retirement age and seemed strangely out of touch with the world, as if he'd been hidden away in his office for decades without setting foot outside. It took him a maddeningly long time to locate the will, which he then consulted, squinting at the document through a less-than-clean pence-nez. Returning to his desk, he laid the document before Daniel.

"Everett Frye left Mrs. Alice Longhorn a sum of one thousand pounds when he passed on February sixth, 1867," he said.

"Did you meet Mrs. Longhorn's husband at the time?" Daniel asked.

Mr. Edgerton considered the question. "I suppose I must have," he said at last.

"But you don't remember him?"

The lawyer shrugged as if he'd already forgotten why they were having the conversation.

"Thank you, Mr. Edgerton," Daniel said.

"I'm not sure that man would remember his own mother," Daniel said once they left the office.

"Given that he's probably been practicing law since Jesus was a toddler, I can't say I blame him," Jason replied.

Daniel tried to cover up his bark of laughter with a cough. It didn't seem appropriate to laugh, but Jason had a knack for putting things in a way no Englishman would ever dare. "Well, we got what we came for. Longhorn was telling the truth," Daniel said as he raised his hand to hail a passing hansom.

"Which doesn't mean that Longhorn couldn't have embezzled the funds. The two events are not mutually exclusive," Jason pointed out as they climbed into the cab and set off.

"I completely agree, but my gut instinct tells me Longhorn is not our man," Daniel said.

"No, I don't believe he is. If a man like Adam Longhorn was driven to murder, it would be an act of passion, a momentary madness brought on by extreme fear or stress. He is not a man to meticulously plan a murder and then go about carrying it out, taking pleasure in his task."

"You think the murderer took pleasure in killing Blake Upton?" Daniel asked.

"I think he must have. It would have taken some considerable time to extract the brain and would require concentration and a steady hand, not to mention a strong stomach. An individual who simply wanted to do away with someone would opt for a quicker method, and probably a less personal one.

"Let us suppose for a moment that the person seen talking to Blake Upton up on deck Monday night was the killer. Once Peter Moffat left, all that person had to do was grab Upton by the ankles and tip him overboard. If someone realized there was a man overboard, the killer could cry for help and pretend it was all a terrible accident. Given the speed at which the vessel was moving, the lack of daylight, and Upton's shock at being pushed overboard into freezing water, even if he'd managed to resurface, chances are he wouldn't have been rescued. By the time enough people were roused and a rescue attempt was mounted, he would have drowned."

Daniel nodded, deep in thought. "So, you are suggesting that although this was a crime of passion, whoever killed him wasn't overcome by emotion, but bent on extracting the maximum amount of pleasure from Blake Upton's death."

"Yes, I am. I think the killer's objective was to punish Blake Upton for some transgression, not merely to kill him and be done with it."

"Which makes this case even more baffling, since I honestly can't see any of the suspects we've spoken to thus far seeking to enjoy the killing. Given Jock Thomas's innate restlessness, he wouldn't have the patience to carry out the procedure, although I think he might enjoy the irony of stuffing Blake Upton into the sarcophagus he'd stolen from the man who found it. If he were to kill Upton, he'd want to be done with it quickly. Adam Longhorn doesn't have the stomach. Peter Moffat has no motive, so far as we know. The two women hardly knew Upton and would have absolutely no reason to wish him dead. Richard Scarborough is the only one who'd have the necessary skill and the patience to carry out such an elaborate killing, but being a man fearful for his reputation, I can't see that he would take the chance of being discovered when he could have disposed of Blake Upton in a much less obvious manner."

"Exactly," Jason said as the hansom came to a stop.

Daniel paid the cabbie and they alighted, ready to question their next suspect.

Chapter 18

Michael Dillane wasn't at home, but they found him at a nearby public house, nursing a jar of ale. Since they'd seen an image of him in Peter Moffat's photograph, he wasn't difficult to pick out in the thin crowd. Jason and Daniel slid onto a bench across from him, much to the astonishment of the man, who stared at them with something akin to fear.

"What do you want?" he demanded.

Daniel showed him his warrant card and introduced himself and Jason.

Michael Dillane relaxed somewhat. "I figured you'd want to talk to me sooner or later."

"And what have you got to tell us?" Daniel asked.

"Not a hell of a lot," Michael Dillane replied. He was about twenty-five, with slanted hazel eyes and dark hair that brushed his collar. Even when seated, it was obvious that he was tall and had the wide shoulders and well-defined arms of someone who frequented a gymnasium. He was well dressed but would never be mistaken for a gentleman, nor did he care to be, given his demeanor. Daniel couldn't help wondering why Lord Belford would send him along with the archeologists. He clearly didn't fit in.

"How long have you worked for Lord Belford, Mr. Dillane?" Daniel asked.

Michael Dillane smirked. "I don't really work for him."

"What is it that you do for him, then?" Jason asked.

Michael Dillane's face tensed, and his gaze slid sideways, watching the passersby through the grimy window. "I'm his son. Born on the wrong side of the blanket, of course," he added bitterly. "I suppose I should be grateful he takes an interest—many men don't acknowledge their bastards—but it'd be nice if he didn't expect me to do his dirty work."

"And what dirty work do you do?" Jason inquired.

"For lack of a better description, I'm the watchman," Michael Dillane said. "Daddy Dearest thinks that as long as I'm present, everyone will be on their best behavior."

"And are they?"

"For the first week or so, but then they pretty much ignore me and get on with the business at hand."

"So, what can you tell us about Blake Upton?" Daniel asked.

Michael Dillane shrugged. "Not a lot. He was a good man, very passionate about his work."

"Was there anything else he was passionate about?" Jason asked.

"You mean, did he have a mistress?" Dillane asked.

"Did he?"

"Not that I know of. He wasn't happy with his wife, though. I think he was glad to be away from her."

"Why do you say that?" Daniel asked, his interest piqued.

"She disappointed him."

"In what way?" Jason asked, leaning slightly forward, also interested in this new angle.

"They never had any children. I think that was his one big regret."

"How do you know? Did he tell you that?"

"No, but it was obvious. He'd change the subject and become irritated whenever one of the other men would mention their offspring. I think—and this is just my opinion, mind—that he regretted not divorcing his wife and marrying someone who could give him the family he wanted."

"A man needs grounds for divorce," Jason pointed out.

"Grounds for divorce can be easily fabricated," Michael Dillane said. "Just ask Peter Moffat."

"What do you mean, Mr. Dillane?" Daniel asked.

"I mean that a compromising situation can be staged and photographed, thereby offering proof of infidelity. I think Peter has been party to several such arrangements. Not that it matters in Blake Upton's case, because he'd never do that to his wife. He was an honorable man."

"What about Adam Longhorn? Is he an honorable man?" Jason asked.

"Why do you ask?"

"Because there are reports of him embezzling funds," Daniel replied.

Michael Dillane shook his head in disgust. "Adam would never."

"Let us say that Adam Longhorn did wish to skim from the pot. How would he go about it?" Jason asked. "Would there be a way to keep the ledgers from revealing his crime?"

"Oh sure," Michael Dillane replied. "There's quite an easy way to do that."

"Do tell," Daniel invited. Whether it was Michael Dillane's resentment toward his father or a desire to clear himself of suspicion, he was clearly willing to talk, and Daniel was willing to listen.

"Let's say Adam Longhorn orders one hundred shovels for the workers, and they cost one hundred quid, for simplicity's sake. He can ask the supplier to give him a receipt for one hundred and fifty quid and pocket the fifty quid difference, since in actuality he only paid a hundred. Or perhaps he'll give a part of the fifty quid to the supplier, for his trouble and silence. So, the ledger matches the receipt, but in reality, Adam Longhorn made a profit no one can account for or prove unless the supplier is willing to grass."

"So, what you're suggesting is that Adam Longhorn can have made hundreds of pounds in profit without any evidence to prove his wrongdoing?" Daniel asked.

"Precisely. But as I said, I don't believe Adam would ever do that. He's not a crook."

"So, if Adam Longhorn is not a thief, who would have motive to kill Blake Upton?" Jason asked.

"The obvious person would be Jock Thomas, because he has the most to gain, but again, I don't think he's your man."

"Because you don't think he's capable of murder?"

"Because he's just not that stupid," Michael Dillane replied, baring his teeth in a smile devoid of amusement. "If Jock were to kill, he'd do it in a way that would never lead the investigation back to him. He's one of the smartest, most resourceful men I've ever met. If he were to take such a drastic step, he'd think it through first, believe me."

"And what about Dr. Scarborough and Peter Moffat?" Daniel asked, feeling deflated. So far, he hadn't heard anything that was helpful to the investigation.

Michael Dillane took a long pull of his ale and set the mug down with a *thunk*. "What possible reason would either of them have to kill Blake? Peter made out quite nicely and got his photographs in the papers, and Dr. Scarborough got to take a holiday from his boring existence and colorless wife."

"Blake Upton believed Dr. Scarborough to be responsible for Henry Ames's death," Daniel said, watching Michael Dillane closely.

The man shrugged. "Blake was very upset by Henry's death, but in time, he came to see that Dr. Scarborough was not to blame."

"How do you know that?" Jason asked.

"Because his attitude toward him became less hostile."

"Did he not threaten to report Dr. Scarborough to the Royal College of Physicians and accuse him of negligence?"

"He did, yes, but that was immediately following Henry's death. As the weeks passed and he came to slowly accept his loss, he saw that he'd been unreasonable."

"Did Dr. Scarborough believe himself to be safe from prosecution?" Daniel asked.

"I don't think any of us ever believed that Blake Upton would be so vengeful. He was very protective of his professional reputation and understood only too well what it means to other men. He would not have made such an accusation lightly, not unless he was one hundred percent sure that Henry Ames could have been saved. What do you think, Lord Redmond?" Michael Dillane asked. "You're a surgeon. Do you believe a man with a ruptured appendix can be saved?"

"That really depends on the circumstances," Jason replied evasively.

"And what about you, Mr. Dillane?" Daniel asked, redirecting the interview to the murder. "You are a suspect as well."

"Me? I have no motive," Michael Dillane said, now clearly amused. "What would I have to gain by killing Blake Upton?"

"Your father wouldn't send you on any more expeditions?" Daniel suggested.

"Wrong. He'd simply pick another horse to back, like Jock Thomas. In truth, Jock is the better bet, if you ask me. He's less interested in fame and fortune and more interested in the actual work. Blake Upton wished to be remembered. And now he will be, only for all the wrong reasons."

"What about the crew of the *Sea Witch* and the two ladies?" Daniel asked, feeling he needed to tick the boxes should John Ransome ask him about the others on board.

"The women kept mostly to themselves."

"Mostly?" Jason asked.

"Mrs. Forster enjoyed talking to Blake and Jock about the dig and the various legends and myths. She's a student of history and plans to visit Italy next year. Lots to see there, according to her."

"And Miss Gibb?"

"Miss Gibb was bored," Michael Dillane said. "There's only so much reading and doodling a person can do, and she doesn't have the patience for either."

"So, what did Miss Gibb do to pass the time?" Daniel asked.

"Peter Moffat taught her to play shesh besh. We all played it."

"And what is shesh besh?"

"It's backgammon, at its core. The tradition of playing shesh besh goes back thousands of years in Egypt. They say they invented it."

"But you don't believe them?" Jason asked.

Michael Dillane shrugged again. "What does it matter who invented it? It's a clever game. I brought a set back the first time I went to the Middle East. I taught my friends to play."

"So, Miss Gibb liked to play?"

"Yes. She played with Peter, and Jock, and even me. She's quite good."

"Did Miss Gibb do anything else?" Jason asked.

"She liked to walk on deck."

"She's a very attractive woman," Daniel said, his gaze pinning Michael Dillane. "Did you try to court her?"

A pained expression passed over Michael's face. "She'd never bother with someone like me. I have nothing to offer her, socially speaking. My father gives me an allowance, but no amount of money can erase my bastard status. No respectable woman would consider me seriously."

"Surely that's not true," Jason interjected.

Michael smiled sadly. "Judging by your accent, I'd say you grew up in America, Lord Redmond. The land of the free," he added somewhat sarcastically. "Maybe the circumstance of one's birth doesn't matter as much in a place where everyone comes from someplace else, but it still matters here. I can have my pick of maidservants and nursemaids, but a woman from a good family will not entertain my suit unless she's desperate."

"And you don't think Miss Gibb is desperate?" Daniel asked.

"I can't speak to Miss Gibb's feelings, Inspector," Michael Dillane said. "I don't know her well enough to offer any salient observations."

"And Mrs. Foster? Was she interested in anyone romantically?" Daniel knew he was grasping at straws, but there had to be something he was missing.

"Not that I noticed. She's rather a cold fish, in my opinion, except when it comes to Miss Gibb."

"Meaning?" Jason asked, watching the man closely.

Michael Dillane's gaze slid away again. That seemed to be what he did when he felt nervous or unsure. "There was something odd about their relationship," he said at last.

"How do you mean?" Daniel asked.

"I don't know. It's just that Mrs. Foster regarded Miss Gibb with a sort of possessiveness, and I got the impression Miss Gibb resented it."

"Is Miss Gibb a paid companion, despite being Mrs. Foster's niece?" Jason asked Daniel.

"I didn't think to ask," Daniel replied. "It wasn't relevant to the case."

"Maybe she's not paid a wage, precisely, but she gets room and board, stylish dresses, her travel expenses are paid, and Mrs. Foster does like to buy her gifts," Michael Dillane pointed out. "She had several trinkets that she said were gifts from her aunt."

"Do you think Miss Gibb is happy with the arrangement?" Jason asked.

"I don't think she's unhappy with it," Michael Dillane said. "It's better than working as a seamstress or teaching the snot-nosed children of the rich their numbers and letters."

"But she may wish to marry at some point," Jason pointed out.

"That she might," Michael Dillane agreed. "I didn't get the impression that Mrs. Foster would encourage an attachment. She guarded her rather jealously. I suppose she is just protective of her. A woman's reputation can suffer after weeks aboard a ship with dozens of men. She tried to make sure Miss Gibb was chaperoned at all times."

Daniel sighed, his own gaze sliding toward the window. The afternoon was slipping away, but they'd learned little of value. Once they finished with Michael Dillane, they'd have to return to Scotland Yard to brief John Ransome, and Daniel had no idea what to tell the superintendent that wouldn't make him look like a blundering idiot.

"And what about the curse of the mummy?" Jason asked.

Michael Dillane shrugged. "Blake and Jock made it all up. People love spooky stories. A painted sarcophagus will draw crowds, but a painted sarcophagus that's been stolen from a tomb guarded by the spirit of a vengeful mummy is so much more exciting. It's no longer just an inanimate object; it now has a life of its own, and terrible things can happen thousands of years after it was buried."

"Was that the story Blake Upton and Jock Thomas meant to present to the British Museum?" Jason asked.

"Yes. That's how the artefacts from the tomb would be promoted to the public."

"So, you saw nothing whatsoever untoward?" Daniel tried again. Michael Dillane was clearly an observant young man who was the outsider in the group. If anyone had seen something off, it would be him.

Dillane looked thoughtful, some memory clearly reconstructing itself behind his eyes. "I think Blake was robbed," he finally said.

"Robbed? In Cairo?" Daniel asked.

"No, on the ship."

"Robbed by whom?" Jason asked.

"One of the sailors."

"Did he tell you he was robbed?" Daniel asked.

"No."

"So, what led you to arrive at that conclusion?" Jason asked.

"Blake had a gold watch. It had belonged to his father and held great sentimental value for him. Blake always wore it, even out in the desert, and consulted it quite often. I noticed he didn't have it on Sunday, either during luncheon or afterwards, at dinner." Michael Dillane looked from Daniel to Jason, his expression quizzical. "Did he have it on him when he was found in the sarcophagus?"

"No," Daniel replied. "He had nothing of value on him."

Michael Dillane nodded, as if his suspicions had been confirmed. "He also asked me just before our final dinner aboard to lend him some money to get home. I think someone stole his purse."

"Did Blake Upton report the theft to Captain Sanders?" Jason asked.

"No. He refused to discuss it when I asked him about the money and the watch and bid me not to tell the other members of the team."

"So, it is your belief that the theft occurred on Sunday?" Daniel asked.

"It is."

"And what makes you think it was one of the sailors?" Jason asked.

"Sunday service was held on deck every week at nine. For lack of a vicar, Captain Sanders or Mr. Crowther took the service, and every member of the crew was expected to attend. The passengers went as well, but attendance wasn't mandatory. That last Sunday, I woke with a sore head, having stayed up late drinking with Blake and Jock, and decided to have a bit of a lie-in.

It was nice to have a bit of peace, since I rarely had the cabin to myself. Well, after a while, I started to feel bilious and thought I should get some air. The service was still in progress. The congregation was in the middle of a hymn; I could hear the singing through the door. When I stepped into the corridor, I saw Mr. Lewis. He seemed to be coming from Blake Upton's cabin. He ignored me and went up on deck, where he joined in the singing."

"Had anything been taken from anyone else?" Jason asked.

"Not as far as I know."

"Do you have any reason to suspect this man, besides seeing him walk past your cabin on a Sunday morning when he should have been at the service?"

"There was something between him and Blake," Michael Dillane said. "I noticed it on the second day we were at sea. Lewis walked past Blake and bumped into him. It was quite intentional, and he didn't apologize. I expected Blake to be outraged and report the man's behavior to the captain or the first mate, but he dismissed it."

"Was that the only time you noticed Mr. Lewis's animosity toward Blake Upton?" Jason asked.

"Yes, but I'm sure Blake went out of his way to avoid the man. I got the impression they'd met before."

"Did you ask Blake Upton about it?" Daniel asked.

"I did, but he denied knowing the man."

"Do you think Mr. Lewis killed Blake Upton?" Daniel asked, his mind awhirl with this new possibility. If Upton had unexpectedly come face to face with someone from his past, whatever had subsequently transpired between them could be the motive Daniel was searching for.

Michael Dillane shook his head, taking Daniel's excitement down a notch. "I'd like to say I do because that would put my mind at rest about the men I've spent so much time with over the past few years, but it would be irresponsible to level such a serious accusation based on the little I know or suspect."

"Thank you, Mr. Dillane," Daniel said, and rose to his feet.

"You seem upset," Jason said once they had left the pub.

"I am," Daniel snapped. "How is it possible that no one saw or heard anything that might give us a clue as to why this murder was committed? They were trapped aboard a ship together for weeks. Surely Blake Upton had an altercation with someone shortly before his death. Something must have happened to incite whoever killed him to murder," Daniel said angrily. "And what was all that about the sailor? What I am to do with that?" he demanded, his frustration boiling over.

"Do you believe Michael Dillane?" Jason asked, watching Daniel closely.

"I honestly don't know. If Blake Upton was robbed the day before he was murdered, we only have Michael Dillane's suspicions to go on, since Upton refused to report the incident or tell the rest of the team about it. Why would he keep something like that to himself? Wouldn't you report the theft of your purse and gold watch?" Daniel demanded.

"I certainly would, unless I had a reason to keep quiet," Jason replied.

"What sort of reason? A sailor named Lewis was seen in the passageway on Sunday, March twenty-ninth, the day before Blake Upton was murdered, and—according to Michael Dillane—had bumped into Upton on deck weeks before the alleged robbery. Did he bump into Upton intentionally, or was it an accident? Might the sailor have been walking past Dillane's cabin for some other reason? Do we even know if anything was stolen if we can't verify it?" Daniel asked, his anger mounting.

"Perhaps Michael Dillane had taken the money and the watch himself and is covering his tracks in case Mrs. Upton suddenly realizes her husband's things are missing from among his belongings."

"Perhaps, but we'll never be able to prove that Michael Dillane is responsible, since no one seems to have seen anything, nor do we know for certain that Blake Upton was robbed. But if Dillane's suspicion that Upton and this sailor had known each other before is true, it begs the question, in what context did they know each other, and why would this man risk robbing Blake Upton? If caught, he'd be flogged at best, turned over to the authorities and hanged for theft at worst. Why would he risk it?"

Jason considered the question. "Because he believed he could get away with it, I suppose. Perhaps he thought Upton wouldn't realize he'd been robbed until he'd disembarked, or maybe he had a hiding place aboard the ship where no one would find his loot until he was ready to retrieve it once he deemed it safe. Without it, no one could prove he'd stolen the watch and the money. It's entirely possible that this wasn't the first time this man had helped himself to the possessions of the passengers."

"That's very possible, I agree, but there's quite a leap between theft and murder. Why would he kill Blake Upton, especially in such a staged way? I can't see a sailor, who might well be illiterate, stealing chloroform, luring Upton into the hold, and using an ancient method he couldn't possibly know anything about to kill the man, and then laying out his body inside the sarcophagus, knowing full well that it would be discovered as soon as the artefact arrived at the museum. It just doesn't add up."

"We need to track down this Lewis," Jason said, his voice firm with conviction.

"Jason, in less than a half hour, I am to sit across from my superior and give him an account of my progress. I have no idea what to tell him," Daniel sputtered.

"You tell him that you're pursuing all possible leads. It's been two days, Daniel. John Ransome can hardly expect you to solve a case in forty-eight hours."

"He's not like Superintendent Coleridge, Jason," Daniel said, his shoulders slumping. "Ransome's men are a means to an end, not valued colleagues."

"You knew things would be different in London," Jason pointed out softly.

"Yes, I did, and I'm up to the challenge, but there are times when I feel a lack of support, and it undermines my confidence. Knowing I was coming home to Sarah at the end of the day made all the difference," Daniel explained. "Now all I do is sit alone in my rooms in the evenings, second-guessing my decision."

"Daniel, may I offer you a word of advice?" Jason asked once they'd hailed a cab and were heading to Scotland Yard to apprise John Ransome of their progress.

"Yes, please."

"Keeping away from Sarah will not solve your problems. The distance will only drive a deeper wedge between you. Why not bring Sarah and Charlotte to London, at least for a time? Talk to her about your work, share a bed again. It will help. Maybe not right away, but little by little, you will find your way back to some sort of normalcy."

"You make it sound so simple," Daniel said, feeling utterly defeated.

"It is simple. You can either try to save your family or you can give up, and years from now, you will find that you not only lost your wife but your daughter as well. Charlotte will not know you, Daniel. You'll be the man who appears from time to time and brings her presents to assuage his guilt, but you will not be a beloved father, and fathers are important. Their successes and failures shape their children's lives. Don't you agree?"

"Yes," Daniel muttered.

"Then fight, man," Jason urged him. "Fight for your happiness, and fight for your place at the Yard. You're a damn good detective. Don't allow minor setbacks to undermine your belief in yourself."

Daniel smiled sadly as he looked at Jason's impassioned expression. "Did I ever tell you that you're very American?"

"Yes, several times," Jason replied, clearly unsure what Daniel meant by the comment.

"I wish I could be more like you, Jason," Daniel said wistfully.

"Being yourself is more than enough, for both your family and the police service."

Chapter 19

Superintendent Ransome was in a meeting, the door to his office firmly shut, but raised voices came from within, and Daniel was sure Ransome wasn't going to be in a good mood once his meeting finished. It took nearly a quarter of an hour for a flustered Detective Inspector Hillier to finally emerge. He murmured something that sounded like a greeting and hurried away.

"Come," Ransome called when he saw Daniel waiting in the corridor.

Daniel and Jason entered the office, settled in the two guest chairs, and faced the superintendent.

"Well?" Ransome demanded, pinning Daniel with his dark gaze. "What have you got for me, Haze?"

"We have three possible suspects, sir: Jock Thomas, Adam Longhorn, and Dr. Scarborough. All had motive, means, and opportunity."

"And what were their motives?" Ransome asked, somewhat mollified to be presented with a list of suspects.

"Blake Upton took credit for Jock Thomas's discovery, adding fuel to resentment that was already motivated by professional jealousy. Adam Longhorn may have been embezzling funds, while Dr. Scarborough was blamed by Blake Upton for the death of a member of the group, a young man whose family Mr. Upton was close to. He threatened Dr. Scarborough with professional ruin."

John Ransome gave Daniel a baleful look that said volumes about Daniel's abilities as a detective. "Anything else?" he demanded, clearly striving for patience.

"We've also just learned that Blake Upton may have been robbed by a member of the crew. If Mr. Upton meant to report the theft, the man would have had a motive for murder."

"May have been robbed?" John Ransome asked, his eyebrows lifting in astonishment. "Was he or wasn't he?"

"This is the first we've heard of this, so we need to speak to the sailor in question and see what we can discover before arriving at any conclusions."

Ransome leaned back in his chair and fixed Daniel with his dark, unblinking gaze. "Haze, first, it's not *we*, it's *you*. You're the detective, and this is your case. Last I checked, Lord Redmond wasn't on the pay roster of Scotland Yard. I take no issue with his offer of help, but I am in no position to make any demands on his time and intellect. Second, and more important, do you have any evidence against any of these men that would stand up in a court of law?" Ransome asked. "Do you have the murder weapon? Witnesses? Bloodstained or brain-splattered clothing? In other words, can you offer me anything besides baseless supposition?"

"Not yet, sir. It's only been two days," Daniel reminded him.

"Yes, two days in which you've learned next to nothing. The public already think we're blithering cretins. It's not enough to suspect someone of a crime. We need evidence to charge them."

"I'm aware of that, sir," Daniel retorted.

"Then go out there and find some. Where do you plan to start?"

Daniel felt as if he'd been punched in the stomach. He had no immediate answer. He needed time to think and analyze the matter before coming up with a next step. He hadn't expected Ransome to ask for a detailed plan, simply to hear his report and demand a quick result.

"I'm going to find and interview the sailor, Mr. Lewis, sir."

"And then?" Ransome demanded. "Is that the extent of your strategy for catching the killer? You're not dealing with a tavern brawl, where a dozen men would have seen the miscreants, or an illegal duel over a woman. Whoever has done this is pragmatic and clever and managed to leave no evidence, either physical or circumstantial, for the police to find. And I'll publicly resign my position as superintendent if you can prove to me that some dolt of a sailor had the wherewithal to pull off a murder that required this level of acumen."

Daniel swallowed hard, humiliation rendering him mute. For a moment, he considered resigning his own position, but then common sense prevailed. Superintendent Ransome was under pressure to deliver results. It wouldn't be Daniel Haze who was ridiculed in the papers or taken to task by the commissioner; it would be John Ransome who'd be raked over hot coals in the court of public opinion and made the scapegoat if the police service failed to solve such a high-profile case. It was up to Daniel to prove to the superintendent that Ransome's decision to take a chance on him hadn't been a colossal mistake. Ransome was absolutely right; Jason was not a member of the service. It was Daniel's responsibility to apprehend the killer, but first, he had to get into the killer's mind, which would require more than a few seconds.

John Ransome's gaze nailed Daniel to the spot as he awaited a reply.

"Sir, if I may," Jason interjected, to Daniel's great relief. He was incapable of coherent thought at the moment and wished only to be released from the hot seat so he could regroup and rethink his approach to the investigation.

"Of course," Ransome said, instantly moderating his tone.

"As I mentioned after the postmortem, I detected an odor of chloroform coming from the victim's lungs. Naturally, this puts Dr. Scarborough in the frame for the murder, but it's not impossible that someone had helped themselves to his supply. It would seem that the cabins were not locked during the day, so anyone could have walked in. Given that Jock Thomas and Adam Longhorn have so readily alibied each other, perhaps they were in on it together. Or, to take this theory one step further, the three men could have planned the murder together, since each one had something to lose."

John Ransome nodded slowly. "That is plausible. But we still require irrefutable evidence to charge them, my lord. How do you propose to get it?"

"First, it's imperative that we reinterview Dr. Scarborough," Jason said. "I would like to hear his own account of Henry Ames's death so that I could determine the extent of his responsibility and fear of repercussions. Second, I think we should examine the sarcophagus and the crate one more time, just in case we missed something the first time around, since we couldn't search the bottom of the crate at the time," Jason said. "And third, I think we should speak to Mrs. Foster and Miss Gibb."

"Why?" Ransome demanded. "Inspector Haze has already interviewed the women and ruled them out as suspects."

Jason nodded in acknowledgement but didn't relent. "The ladies might have seen or heard something without realizing it, especially since their cabin was directly across from Blake Upton's. And not being part of the archeological team, they owe no allegiance to anyone in the group, so would not feel compelled to withhold information."

"And what about this alleged robbery?" Ransome asked, all his attention fixed on Jason.

"The robbery must be investigated as it might have bearing on the case. A lowly position in life doesn't preclude someone from being devilishly clever, Superintendent," Jason said. "I've met many a man who couldn't read or write but had the street smarts to turn a profit just by rubbing two nickels together. I make it a habit to never make assumptions about someone's intelligence based on their station."

"You're right on that score, Lord Redmond. I spoke in haste," Ransome added plaintively. "This case is keeping me up at night," he confessed, his gaze still on Jason, as if Daniel were no longer in the room. Ransome pulled out his pocket watch and consulted the time. "The commissioner has asked to be briefed at six o'clock sharp." He put away the watch and sighed heavily. "Go to it, gentlemen." He gave Jason a slow smile. "Anytime you decide you'd like to join the police service, you just say the word, Lord Redmond. I like the way your mind works. You are a natural-born detective."

"Thank you, sir," Jason said.

"Brief me again at the same time tomorrow," Ransome said dismissively.

"You saved my bacon in there," Daniel said, relieved to be out of Ransome's presence. "What do you hope to find in the crate?"

"I don't know yet, but I think it's wise to examine it now that the sarcophagus has been removed. Perhaps we'll find something we overlooked before."

"I agree. In the meantime, I think we should question Mr. Lewis and try to find out the truth of this robbery and then pay a visit to Lord Belford," Daniel suggested. "He wasn't present during the murder, but he knows these men and might be able to suggest an angle we've overlooked. I'd also like to borrow the ledgers Adam Longhorn had submitted to him and have Mr. Kimball, the Yard auditor, have a look. He might pick up on any irregularities Lord Belford's man might have missed."

"Yes, I think that's a good idea," Jason agreed.

Daniel followed Jason out into the chilly April evening, glad it wasn't pissing down for once. The streets were crowded, countless men in dark coats and bowler hats hurrying home, having just finished work for the day. An omnibus rumbled past, people hanging precariously off the step, and several men disappeared down the entrance to the underground railroad, willing to risk traveling below the surface to arrive at their destination sooner. Boys screamed themselves hoarse trying to sell the evening papers, and numerous vendors had materialized out of the shadows, hoping to catch those who had no wife to return to and might want to buy a hot pie for their supper.

Daniel briefly wondered what it would be like to have the sort of job where he'd leave his office at the same time each day and return to home and hearth instead of traipsing all over the city, making a nuisance of himself to people who had no wish to speak to him. He had to admit that having Jason with him opened doors. Few people dared to refuse to admit a nobleman, but they could easily slam the door in a policeman's face, and had when he'd come to interview potential suspects during previous investigations. At least he was an inspector now and not a constable, but no member of the police was ever really welcome unless their help was required.

"I hope Mrs. Upton has sent over any papers she found in her husband's trunk," Jason said, interrupting Daniel's reverie.

"I'm not holding out much hope for Mrs. Upton," Daniel said. "Perhaps she's too frightened to go through her husband's papers, worried she'll find something that might tarnish his memory."

"Such as?"

"Such as letters from a mistress," Daniel suggested.

"We haven't found anything to suggest Blake Upton kept a mistress," Jason replied.

"No, but that doesn't mean he didn't. He could have been discreet, but a wife always knows, I think. Have you noticed that no one seems particularly saddened by Blake Upton's death? They all say it was a tragedy and he was a good man, but I haven't witnessed any actual grief from anyone but his wife, and I think that's more because of her uncertainty about the future rather than because she genuinely loved the man."

"Yes, I have noticed that," Jason replied. "The real tragedy is to have lived a life and discover at the end of it that no one really cared for you. Let's hope that will never be our fate," Jason said with a wistful smile.

Chapter 20

Evan Lewis lived in Dray Walk in Spitalfields, a dim, narrow alley off Brick Lane that stank of piss, rotting vegetables, and despair. The houses were so dilapidated as to seem unhabitable, but the muffled voices from inside and the candlelight flickering through the holes in the ratty curtains that covered the grimy windows told a different story and gave the place an even more desperate and sinister air.

Spitalfields had once been home to Huguenot silk weavers who'd settled outside the boundaries of the City of London to avoid the legislation of the guilds, but the silk trade had drastically declined since a treaty with France had allowed cheaper silks to be imported to England, leaving London weavers with no choice but to slash their prices. Some had managed to hang on, but others had fled, knowing they couldn't compete and seeking a life elsewhere.

Furniture makers and boot makers had set up shop in the once-stately homes and workshops of the Huguenots, and Jewish refugees had flocked to the area, drawn by the promise of work in the textile trade. But the area continued to decline, becoming one of the most dangerous and poverty-ridden slums in the city. Spitalfields lodging houses were home to thieves, whores, and pimps, and no man who valued his health would set foot in that area without first thoroughly preparing himself. When he'd realized where they were heading, Daniel had taken a pair of handcuffs before leaving the Yard and armed himself with a 622 Beaumont-Adam revolver that was standard issue for the detective branch, but Jason was unarmed. Now that they were here, Daniel thought it might have been wise to bring backup, but it was too late to return to Scotland Yard now.

"Perhaps we should have come in the morning," he mumbled as they stepped into the impenetrable shadow cast by the tumbledown dwellings that lined the alley.

"Let's get this over with," Jason said, his voice reedy with apprehension. He could handle himself, but Daniel didn't think he fully comprehended the dangers that lurked in the shadowy doorways and blind alleys of London's underbelly.

"I'll go first," Daniel said, hoping Jason wouldn't argue. He didn't.

As they approached the doorway, a ragged-looking girl of about thirteen stepped outside, mostly likely being sent to the nearest public house for a pitcher of ale or a hot pie. Daniel turned to her, his very presence making her shrink back in terror.

"Miss, we're looking for Evan Lewis. Do you know him?" Daniel asked. Knocking on every door and asking after Lewis could be hazardous to his health, and he was sure the girl knew everyone in the building.

The girl was trembling, her shoulders hunched, and her head bowed as she drew her ratty shawl tighter about her shoulders as if it were armor. She took a step back, poised for flight.

"First landin' to the right," she mumbled, and took off toward the mouth of the alley.

Daniel started up the stairs but only made it halfway to the landing when a dark shape exploded from the shadows, hurtling toward him like it had been fired from a catapult. Daniel tried to grab for the banister, but it was too rickety to offer stability, and he stumbled backward and lost his footing, falling on his side, the edge of the step digging into his ribs and knocking the air from his lungs. His hat was knocked off, and he felt momentarily stunned by the fall, unable to get his bearings in the dark. As Daniel groped for something to grab onto to pull himself up, he heard a cry of alarm and then the sound of something heavy landing on the floor with a muffled thud.

Scrambling to his feet, Daniel peered into the darkness, but it was impossible to make anything out other than a large, shapeless mass that seemed to be heaving and grunting. Something kicked at the door that was hanging precariously on rusted hinges, and the door flew open, allowing a glimmer of starlight to penetrate the darkness. The mass separated into two parts, and

Daniel was finally able to make out Jason, who appeared to be sitting astride a writhing beast that was spewing curses and demanding to be released.

"Are you Evan Lewis?" Daniel barked once he cuffed the man, who was still down, his cheek pressed to the filthy wood floor.

"What's it to you?" the man snarled.

"I am Inspector Haze of Scotland Yard, and I need to ask you a few questions. Is there a more comfortable place we can talk?" he asked, his sarcasm doing little to mask his unease. This was no place to linger. The man could have friends inside the building who'd descend on Daniel and Jason like a horde of barbarians and use anything they had to hand to take on the two men. Daniel took out the revolver and pointed it at Evan Lewis, making sure he saw its outline clearly. Then he stepped back, the gun still trained on the man.

"You will get to your feet and take us to your lodgings. Is that understood?" he asked. "If you try anything, I'll shoot."

"Understood," Lewis replied.

Jason grabbed him by the arm to help him to his feet, since Lewis had no use of his cuffed hands. He wasn't very tall, but he was solid, with muscular arms and a thick neck exposed by his closely cropped hair. Daniel couldn't make out his features in the dim light from the doorway, but he thought the man was no older than thirty and had even, pleasing features.

Evan Lewis walked up the stairs slowly, leading them to a door on the right, which he pushed open with his foot. In his haste to escape, he hadn't bothered to lock the door. Once inside, Jason lit the oil lamp on the small table, and the golden glow illuminated the shabby room, which was surprisingly clean. There were two narrow, blanket-covered cots, a table and two chairs, and a battered sea chest. Faded curtains covered the window, and a braided rug lay between the two cots.

"Sit down," Daniel said, indicating that the man should take a cot. Evan Lewis sat down, but his posture was rigid, his gaze wary.

Daniel and Jason each took a chair and set them across from the sailor before sitting down. Daniel laid the revolver across his knees and saw the fear in the sailor's eyes as his gaze followed its progress. He remained silent, but his expression was defiant.

"Why did you run?" Daniel asked.

"Because if you're here, that means only one thing. You're going to pin the murder of Blake Upton on me, and I'll hang for a crime I didn't commit."

Daniel studied the man more closely. As he had suspected, Evan Lewis was relatively attractive and well groomed. His face was smooth, and his dark blond hair had seen a pair of scissors quite recently. His clothes had probably been clean before Jason had decided to wipe the floor with him. Daniel tried to hide his smile. The only way Jason could have taken the man down so quickly was by tripping him as he came down the stairs, Jason's reflexes lightning quick, as usual. Daniel returned to his appraisal of the sailor. Evan Lewis had strong white teeth, his gaze was direct, and his speech was way too educated for someone who lived in a hovel in this part of town.

"How did you know we were here?" Daniel asked.

"I heard you asking Sally about me," he replied.

Daniel nodded. He supposed he'd spoken loudly enough for his voice to carry up the stairs. "What was the nature of your relationship with Blake Upton?" he asked.

"We didn't have a relationship."

"Did you rob him?"

"No."

"So, why would you think we'd come for you?" Daniel asked, genuinely curious to understand the man's reasoning.

"Because I figured that weasel, Michael Dillane, would set you on my trail."

"He did," Daniel replied. "He said you helped yourself to Blake Upton's purse and a gold watch."

"Blake Upton gave me the money and the watch."

"Oh, ho," Daniel exclaimed, amused despite himself. "Do you honestly expect me to believe that, Mr. Lewis?"

"There's proof."

"What proof?" Jason asked, watching the man with obvious fascination.

"Richard Scarborough knows he did."

"Richard Scarborough?" Daniel asked, his amusement turning to disbelief.

"That's right."

"Where are the things you took from Mr. Upton?" Daniel asked.

"In that box over there." Evan Lewis jutted his chin toward a cardboard box that sat on a shelf affixed to the opposite wall. There were also several books and a faded photograph in a tarnished pewter frame. Jason walked over and picked up the box.

"Open it," Evan Lewis instructed.

Opening the box, Jason extracted a gold watch, several bank notes, and a stack of folded papers. Jason handed the papers to Daniel, who glanced at them. They were receipts for various items and an invoice from a company called Wrigley and Hobbs, billing an annual fee of five quid.

"So, why would Blake Upton, with whom you claim to have no relationship, give you all this money and his father's watch?" Daniel asked.

"Blake Upton was responsible for what happened to my family," Evan Lewis said, his face drooping like wax in the heat.

"In what way?" Jason asked, beating Daniel to the punch.

Evan Lewis took a deep breath and bowed his head, as if bracing himself for something difficult, then he lifted his head and met Daniel's gaze, his face now set in the hard lines of anger.

"My father, Martin Lewis, worked as a porter at Christ Church College in Oxford. He'd held the job for nearly twenty years," Evan Lewis said. "He was not an educated man, but he was proud to be associated with such an important institution of learning and tried every day to better himself and improve his lot in life. He spent his every free moment reading and taught me to appreciate the value of an education. I attended a local school and hoped to pursue a law degree at university."

"So, what happened?" Jason asked, his head tilted to the side as he listened to the man speak.

"Blake Upton happened," Evan Lewis spat. "He had a reputation for carousing in his student days. Came back to his rooms drunk more often than not and caused such a ruckus the other students in his dormitory complained. There was one time when he was so pissed, he decided to take his clothes off in the middle of Tom Quad and do a victory lap. It was my father's job to remind him of the rules and get him to his rooms."

Evan Lewis looked away, his expression pained. "After my father had been forced to speak to him on several occasions regarding his behavior, the young master accused my father of drinking on the job. He had a few of his cronies back up his statement. Richard Scarborough was one of them," Evan Lewis said bitterly. "My father was sacked without a character. After twenty years on the job, no one bothered to check if the accusations were true or if the little fucker was doing it out of spite." He swallowed hard, his Adam's apple bobbing. "My father couldn't find respectable employment after that. The best he could do was to find work as an ostler at a nearby livery. He was devastated."

Daniel was about to comment but realized there was more to the story and kept quiet, waiting for Lewis to continue.

"My mother became ill shortly after my father lost his position, Inspector, and eventually her heart failed. My father blamed himself. He thought if he'd not caused her such distress, she may have lived. He began to drink heavily and died less than a year later. I was left alone, with nothing to call my own but a few books, my clothes, and the few pounds my mother had managed to put by. My dream of going to university died with my parents, so I went to sea. I thought I'd enjoy seeing something of the world, and, in truth, all I wanted was to get as far away as I could from the place where I'd known such pain."

"I'm sorry for your loss, Mr. Lewis, but what happened aboard the *Sea Witch*?" Daniel asked.

"I might not have recognized Blake Upton on sight, even though I'd seen him before, but I recognized the name, and all the old hurt and anger came flooding back. I didn't confront him right away, but eventually, I found him alone in the hold. He liked to come down to check on the safety of the artefacts he was bringing back. They were in sealed crates, but he liked to make sure they hadn't shifted or come to harm. I told him who I was and what had happened to my parents because of him."

"How did he react?" Jason asked.

"At first, he dismissed me and threatened to report me to Captain Sanders. I was angry, but I let him be. I'd said my piece, and it made me feel better, if only temporarily."

"Did you consider killing him?" Daniel asked.

"I did, yes," Evan Lewis replied without remorse. "I was so angry with his lack of compassion. He'd ruined a man's life and had indirectly killed my mother and destroyed my future, but he didn't seem to care. He saw no reason to take responsibility for his actions."

"So you confronted him again?" Jason asked.

Lewis shook his head. "No, I didn't. I spoke to a friend of mine aboard the ship, and he advised me to leave it. I've been saving my wages so I could open my own shop," Evan Lewis said. "That's why I live in this shithole. It's cheap, and since I'm not here nine months out of the year, all I need is a place to lay my head down when I'm in town. I share it with another sailor. I was afraid Blake Upton would follow through on his threat and report me to the captain. He would destroy my life once again, so I backed off."

"You plan to open a shop?" Daniel asked, looking around the seedy room for evidence of Evan Lewis's prosperity. Opening a shop required ready cash, and Lewis had just acquired that by taking it off Blake Upton.

"Yes," Lewis said. "Those receipts are for goods I purchased abroad, and the invoice is for storing them in a warehouse at Wapping."

"What did you buy?" Jason asked, his curiosity obviously piqued.

"Turkish rugs, ceramics, silver trinkets. Wealthy Londoners are mad for that sort of thing."

"Did Captain Sanders know you were transporting your own goods on his ship?" Daniel asked.

"Yes, he did. He allowed me to bring one crate aboard free of charge."

"This money and proceeds from the sale of the watch would go a long way to bringing you closer to your dream," Daniel said, holding up the gold watch that glinted in the light of the oil lamp.

"Yes, they would," Lewis agreed.

"So, what happened? Did Blake Upton report you to the captain? That would give you a motive for murder."

"He didn't report me. He saw me on deck on Saturday and asked me to come to his cabin the following day at half nine. He didn't want anyone to see us together," he explained.

"Right," Daniel said, shaking his head in disbelief. "So you skipped the service and went to his cabin?"

"I went to the service but stood at the very back and then slipped away halfway through. The men who stood next to me assumed I needed the head and couldn't wait. Blake Upton was waiting for me in his cabin. He said he'd had time to think on what I said and felt awful for what he'd done. He was young and foolish and didn't think for a moment about the consequences of his actions. He apologized and gave me the money and the watch. I was afraid to take either because then he could accuse me of theft and have me hanged, but he said he had told Richard Scarborough what he meant to do and Dr. Scarborough would collaborate my account if need be. Normally, I wouldn't accept charity from any man, but this man had robbed me of my parents and the life I might have had if not for him. So, I accepted what he had to give and left his cabin. I saw Michael Dillane in the corridor but offered no explanation for why I was there."

"So, why would Michael Dillane think Mr. Upton was robbed?"

"He saw me coming out of Blake Upton's cabin. What other reason would I have to be there but to steal something?" Evan Lewis asked bitterly.

Daniel studied the man. He might be telling the truth, or he could be lying through his teeth. One thing Daniel knew for certain—as soon as he removed the cuffs and turned his back, Evan Lewis would disappear, never to be seen again.

"How do you wish to proceed, Daniel?" Jason asked. He was probably thinking along the same lines but didn't want to influence Daniel's decision.

"We're going to take Mr. Lewis to Scotland Yard and keep him in the cells until we can either verify his story or charge him, either with theft or with murder. I've yet to determine which."

Lewis didn't look surprised. "Please take the box with you," was all he said. "If you leave it here, it'll be gone before we reach the downstairs door."

"Oh, I will," Daniel replied. "That's evidence against you, Mr. Lewis."

Daniel smiled despite himself. Whether Evan Lewis had killed Blake Upton or not, at least now Daniel had something to show Superintendent Ransome. Fifty pounds and a gold watch were evidence aplenty.

Picking up his hat on the way out the door, Daniel brushed it off and put it on, thankful it hadn't been stolen. He was tired and hungry, but this day was nowhere near over. Once Evan Lewis had been locked up and the evidence logged in, he and Jason would stop by Lord Belford's residence, as planned. They had a suspect in custody, but it was too soon to abandon the investigation into the archeological team. The method of murder precluded Daniel from growing too comfortable with the idea that he had his man.

Daniel was anxious to speak to Richard Scarborough, but that conversation could wait until tomorrow. Evan Lewis wasn't going anywhere.

Chapter 21

Lord Belford's home in Belgravia was as opulent as it was tasteful. A dignified butler with silvered temples and shrewd dark eyes greeted them as if he had been expecting a visit from the police and showed them directly into the drawing room, which was an oasis of taste and comfort. Decorated in shades of cream and gold, the room smelled delicately of the fresh flowers that were artfully arranged in an ornamental urn. The master of the house was clearly a lover of art, as the room boasted several very fine paintings and sculptures. There were no Egyptian artefacts, however, which Jason found strange, given the man's love of anything Egyptian and his willingness to spend thousands of pounds to fund his own archeological excavations.

Lord Belford, when he entered the room, proved to be younger than Jason had expected, early forties if he were to guess. He was of middling height and weight but had rather arresting green eyes and a warm smile that lit up his face. Try as he might, Jason couldn't see any resemblance to Michael Dillane and wondered if the man had lied about his parentage.

"Gentlemen, do sit down. Can I offer you some refreshment?" Lord Belford asked, as if they were welcome guests instead of uninvited callers.

"Thank you, no," Daniel replied. "We won't take too much of your time."

Lord Belford looked briefly at Daniel, but then his gaze settled on Jason. "Lord Redmond, it truly is a pleasure to meet you. I heard about you from Arthur Barrett, Esquire. You investigated the murder of his sister-in-law, Elizabeth Barrett," Lord Belford reminded him, but Jason needed no reminders. He remembered the case quite clearly, as well as the lovely young woman who'd been savagely murdered.

"An American Civil War surgeon who hasn't allowed a noble title to prevent him from getting his hands dirty. I do admire you, sir," Lord Belford said, his expression earnest. "I've always been fascinated with the science of crime, if such an expression can be applied to something so common and brutal. To gather viable clues from a dead body is marvelously clever, and not so very different from my own area of interest. There's much a historian can learn from the rituals of death and the manner in which a person was buried. Egyptian funerary practices are a passion of mine. I was giddy with excitement to hear about this most recent find. Thanks to Peter Moffat and his photographs, I felt like I was there in person."

"Have you never considered going on a dig yourself?" Jason asked. "Surely it would be very exciting to be there at the moment of discovery."

Lord Belford's face fell, as if Jason had picked at a newly formed scab and made it bleed. "I have, but I'm afraid my wife is in delicate health, and I would hate to leave her and the children. My responsibilities are here, but I don't allow the impediments to keep me from my life's work."

"What can you tell us about Blake Upton, your lordship?" Daniel asked, eager to redirect the conversation toward the murder.

"Blake Upton was more than a historian; he was a friend. His passing saddens me greatly, but I think he would have taken great pleasure in the manner of his death."

"How so?" Daniel asked, shocked by the man's callous observation.

"Just as a captain will go down with his ship and a great thespian might wish to die upon the stage, so a passionate historian might wish to die in dramatic circumstances. It's certainly more gratifying than dying of some terrible illness and watching one's body waste away day by day. Blake's death will be remembered and forever linked to his life's true passion. If this sarcophagus weren't so precious, I would offer to have Blake buried in it so that he could repose in splendor for eternity."

"That's very poetic, my lord, but the reality is not nearly as romantic," Daniel said, trying hard to keep the disdain from his voice. "Blake Upton was murdered in the prime of his life and at the pinnacle of his career, and I intend to find out who's responsible."

"As well you should, Inspector. I have the utmost confidence in the abilities of Scotland Yard. How can I assist with your inquiry?"

"How well did you actually know Blake Upton?" Jason asked.

"Very well. Blake and I go back a long way. We first met at the British Archeological Association when we were both fresh out of university. We both read history, Blake at Oxford, me at Cambridge. We were also both members of the Royal Archeological Institute."

"Are you a historian as well, your lordship?" Daniel asked.

"In my own right. It has always been a dream of mine to contribute something of value to academia. That's why I sponsor excavations and donate all the finds to the British Museum."

"You don't keep any of the artefacts for yourself?" Jason asked.

"I don't feel it would be right to appropriate articles that belong to all of mankind."

"What about the archeologists? Do they take anything for themselves?" Jason asked, recalling Mrs. Upton's scarab necklace.

Lord Belford smiled sadly. "I fear they help themselves when no one is looking. They like to keep souvenirs of their time in Egypt. I think that's only to be expected. Blake kept several pieces of jewelry he found over the years. I believe Jock took a small statue of Bastet, the cat goddess," he explained.

"Lord Belford, how closely do you monitor expenses, given that the money is coming directly out of your own pocket?" Daniel asked.

"Very closely. And I have my own man there, Michael Dillane," he replied. "If you've interviewed Michael, you already know he's my natural son."

"You must have been very young when he was born," Jason observed.

"I was. Seventeen. My father wasn't very happy with me, since Michael's mother was his mistress. She was ten years my senior," he explained with a proud smile. "We had developed quite a bond, you see. She was so often here."

"How did you know the child wasn't your father's?" Daniel asked, clearly scandalized.

"My father had ended things with the lady several months before we started to spend time together. I have no doubt Michael is my son," Lord Belford said, a hint of defensiveness creeping into his voice. "I have always looked after him, and always will."

"Do you have other children, Lord Belford?" Daniel asked.

"Yes. I have two beautiful daughters. Twelve and fifteen years of age." Lord Belford smiled quizzically. "But what does that have to do with Blake's death?"

"Nothing," Daniel said gruffly. "I'm only trying to get a clearer picture of the relationships between the members of the dig."

"Well, Michael and I have a very cordial relationship. I trust him implicitly," Lord Belford said.

"But you clearly didn't trust Blake Upton," Jason observed.

Lord Belford shook his head. "Not so, my good man. Not so. I trusted Blake to do the job he was hired to do, and he did it admirably. Jock Thomas as well. A clever man and a knowledgeable historian. The reason I sent Michael along is because he's somewhat rootless, this son of mine. Never taken an interest in anything. He had the best tutors growing up. I had offered to send him to university, but he simply wasn't interested. I thought being part of the digs might ignite a love of learning in him. It hasn't," Lord Belford added ruefully. "We don't have much in common, I'm afraid. I do think that being there as my representative made him feel trustworthy and appreciated."

"Can you think of any reason someone would want to kill Blake Upton?" Daniel asked.

"No, I really can't."

"What about Jock Thomas? He was the one to discover the burial chamber," Daniel pointed out. "Yet it was Blake Upton who'd get the credit for the find, being the lead archeologist."

Lord Belford shook his head. "Jock and Blake were well matched, which is why I thought they'd get on well together. And they did. They found dozens of artefacts over the past few years. Quite admirable what they've been able to accomplish. And everyone at the Archeological Society knows it was Jock that discovered the chamber; I made sure of that."

"Does Mr. Thomas know that?" Jason asked.

"I haven't spoken to him since he got back, but I'm sure he'll find out as soon as he attends a meeting of the society."

"Will you fund another expedition?" Daniel asked.

Lord Belford looked thoughtful. "I'd like to, but no definite plans have been made."

"Will you consider Jock Thomas for the position of lead archeologist?"

"Of course. He's the prime candidate now that Blake is gone."

Daniel nodded. "My lord, we'd like to borrow the ledgers Adam Longhorn submitted for your perusal."

"What? Why?" Lord Belford asked, clearly surprised by the request.

"It has been intimated to me that Adam Longhorn might have been fiddling the numbers," Daniel said.

Lord Belford let out a guffaw. "Never. Adam is one of the most strait-laced men I've ever met. I have my own man go over the ledgers after every dig, and he's never once questioned anything Adam has listed as an expense. If anything, the numbers come in less than what I expect. Adam keeps…kept Blake in check, despite his penchant for the finer things in life."

"Such as?"

"Blake enjoyed good wine, twelve-year-old Scotch, and fine cigars. He also spent quite a bit on hashish. It was a weakness of his. He indulged nearly every night. Said it helped him relax."

"What about the other members of the team?" Jason asked. "Surely the method of the murder is indicative of the perpetrator. Any suspicions?" he prodded.

"None," Lord Belford stated with stony finality. "Dr. Scarborough doesn't have the imagination, or frankly the bollocks, to pull off something so fantastical, and Peter Moffat has too much to lose by killing the man who'd offered him steady employment and an all-expense-paid trip to Egypt. Peter's photographs hang in the halls of the Archeological Society and have been printed in the newspapers. He's made quite a name for himself, thanks to me and Blake."

"And what of your son?" Daniel asked carefully.

Lord Belford remained unfazed. "Michael doesn't have it in him to kill somebody. Squeamish as a girl. Besides, what reason would he have to kill Blake? They got on well. I know that from both their letters. Who had the most to gain by Blake's death?"

"That's what I have yet to figure out. It seems that no one would profit significantly, but several people might have perceived Blake Upton as a threat, one of them being a sailor who's in procession of fifty pounds and Blake Upton's gold watch."

"Then he's your man!" Lord Belford cried. "It's your duty to see that he hangs."

"And he will, if he proves to be the murderer," Daniel replied.

"You doubt his guilt?" Lord Belford gaped at Daniel as if he'd lost the use of his faculties.

"I do, yes."

"Why?" Lord Belford demanded, still looking at Daniel as if he were daft.

"The method of the murder precludes me from jumping to a hasty conclusion, my lord," Daniel replied.

Belford considered his answer. "I suppose you do have a point there, Inspector. I can't see a lowly sailor going to such lengths to dispose of somebody." He shook his head in dismay. "I won't be able to rest until I know who the culprit is. I can't imagine that any man I put my trust in would be capable of such an outrage. It boggles the mind."

"Yes, it does," Daniel agreed as he pushed to his feet. "If we can have the ledgers, please," he reminded Lord Belford.

"Of course. I would like them back once you've finished examining them," he said as he stood.

"They will be returned to you in a few days," Daniel promised.

With the two ledgers under his arm, Daniel and Jason left Lord Belford's house.

"Let's go home," Daniel said. "I'm famished."

Mrs. Pimm was waiting for them, her face wreathed in a smile of welcome. "I'll serve supper now, shall I?" she asked as Daniel and Jason removed their outer garments and moved into the parlor.

"Yes, please, Mrs. Pimm," Daniel replied. "Did anything come for me?"

"Why, yes." Mrs. Pimm beamed. "There's a letter from Mrs. Haze, and a parcel, brought this afternoon by messenger. Shall I fetch it now, or would you prefer to dine first?"

"I'll take it now," Daniel replied.

Mrs. Pimm left and returned a few moments later with the letter and parcel. Daniel put the letter in his pocket to read later, then tore the brown paper from the neat parcel. Inside were a leather-bound journal and a stack of letters, all written by Blake Upton to his wife, with the first one dating back to September of the previous year. It had been mailed from one of the ports en route to Alexandria.

"Let's read these after supper," Daniel suggested. "I always think better on a full stomach."

"You won't get an argument from me," Jason said. "Whatever is in that journal will keep for another hour."

Having eaten a good meal, they settled in the parlor, a bottle of brandy at the ready, with Jason leafing through the journal and Daniel reading the letters.

"Anything?" Daniel asked once he refolded the last letter and sighed with disappointment.

"Not a damn thing," Jason said. "Blake Upton made an entry every day, but most of the entries are no longer than a few sentences, except for the days when something was discovered. Then he goes on at length. The rest of the time he talks about the locations, the weather, the frustration of not finding what he'd hoped to find, but there's nothing at all of a personal nature, and he made no entries during the voyage home, so there's no mention of Evan Lewis."

"What about Henry Ames?" Daniel asked.

"No. Not a word."

"I really hoped we'd find something," Daniel said, his shoulders slumping in defeat. "An accusation in his own words would go a long way toward proving someone's guilt."

"Blake Upton never alludes to any arguments or ill feeling between the members of the team, so it's quite possible that Evan Lewis is your man after all. He's clearly intelligent and has a rudimentary education, as well as ambition. He could have read up on Egyptian funerary practices simply out of curiosity and used his knowledge to throw the police off the scent and point the finger at the members of the archeological team. Had Michael Dillane not noticed the absence of Blake Upton's watch, Lewis would have gotten away with it, and the money and the proceeds from the sale of the watch would go a long way toward setting up his business that much sooner."

"I suppose we'll know more once we speak to Richard Scarborough." Daniel drained the rest of his brandy and stood. "Well, I'm off to bed. I hope tomorrow will prove more productive."

"So do I," Jason said. "So do I."

Chapter 22

Friday, April 3

The day dawned sunny and bright, the sky a dazzling blue that was not to be taken for granted in a city where every chimney was belching out coal smoke, the thick plumes rising like volcanic ash. Having finished breakfast, Jason and Daniel decided to start the day by revisiting the British Museum, since it was too early in the day to call on Dr. Scarborough.

Mason Platt came hurrying toward them, his face wreathed in an anxious smile. "Inspector Haze. Lord Redmond. Is there any news?" he cried. "Do you know who killed Blake?"

"Not yet, Mr. Platt, but we'd like to take a look at the crate and the sarcophagus one more time," Daniel said.

Mr. Platt sucked in his breath as if Daniel had just asked him to disrobe in the middle of the Egyptian Hall. "Is that really necessary?" he asked, his gaze growing more hopeful. "You can examine the crate, of course, but the sarcophagus is nearly ready to go on display. All those newspaper stories about the curse of the mummy have whipped the public into a frenzy. People are coming in droves, asking when they can see the ill-fated sarcophagus. I would really rather—"

"Mr. Platt, this is police business," Daniel cut across him. "We will be most careful. You have my word."

"I can't imagine you'll find anything," Mr. Platt replied sulkily, trotting behind them as they headed toward the door to the storage area.

"Be that as it may, we still need to look at it one more time," Daniel replied patiently.

The storage area looked vastly different than it had only a few days ago, when it had been full of unopened crates and resembled the cargo hold of a ship. There were still several crates in the room, but they were stacked high against the walls, the central space devoted to the artefacts that had been unpacked, cleaned, and relegated to the display cases, which would be moved into the Egyptian Hall just before the exhibit opened next week.

Daniel looked around, searching for the sarcophagus, but it wasn't displayed along with the other artefacts that had come off the *Sea Witch*. He spotted an elongated shape laid out on a sturdy pedestal by the far wall, the artefact covered with canvas and most likely padded for protection, since the shape resembled a disturbingly large cocoon more than the sleek coffin they'd seen on Tuesday.

"We're just waiting for the display case," Mason Platt explained. "It will be delivered tomorrow. It's being specially made to accommodate the sarcophagus."

Jason turned to him. "Do you have cotton gloves I can use, Mr. Platt?"

"Are you going to touch it?" Mr. Platt demanded, his gaze flaring with outrage.

"I'm afraid I must," Jason replied.

"But you'll damage it further," Mr. Platt moaned.

"Is the sarcophagus damaged?" Jason asked. "I hadn't noticed that when I examined Mr. Upton's remains."

"The damage is not clearly visible to the naked eye, but when you study an artefact the way we do, you see every nick and flake of paint."

"And are there many areas of damage?"

"There are some, but there are bound to be. The wood warped somewhat over time, so the paint cracked in several places."

"Would you say any of the damage is recent?" Daniel asked.

Mr. Platt pursed his lips. "I think so. There are several infinitesimal scratches on the hands, the nose, the tip of the snake headdress, and the toes," he replied, his anger bubbling just below the surface. "I think the workers didn't use a deep enough crate to start with and damaged the topmost points when attempting to nail down the lid. Such carelessness," Mr. Platt fumed. "Such disrespect for the priceless article within."

"Who would have overseen the packing of the crates?" Daniel asked.

Mr. Platt sighed heavily. "Blake Upton. I don't suppose I can berate him for his carelessness now, can I? The poor man is dead," Mr. Platt said softly, as if reminding himself what this was all about. He pulled two pairs of cotton gloves out of his pocket and handed them to Jason and Daniel. "I always carry gloves with me in case I need to touch an artefact unexpectedly," he explained.

Jason pulled on the gloves and turned to Mr. Platt. "May I see the damage you're referring to?"

"Of course." He had obviously resigned himself to his prized possession being manhandled and walked over to the padded coffin.

Mr. Platt carefully lifted the canvas, then peeled away the layers of padding that swathed the sarcophagus to prevent further damage. Lamplight fell on the lid, setting the newly cleaned colors ablaze and making the gold accents gleam as if they'd been painted on just yesterday and not several thousand years ago. The black-painted eyes shone so bright, they seemed to be moving, examining their surroundings and the men who bent over the lid, staring at it intently.

"Here, here, and here," Mr. Platt said, pointing out the barely visible imperfections.

"Was the sarcophagus not wrapped in cotton wool when it was packed in Cairo?" Daniel asked, leaning down to get a closer look.

"Yes, it was, but the padding might not have been thick enough," Mr. Platt said with disgust. "Or it might have shifted on the journey to the port of Alexandria."

"Was the padding there when you first opened the crate?" Jason asked.

Mr. Platt paused, considering the question. "It was. To be honest, I was so excited to see this beauty's face, I pushed it aside without examining it too closely."

Jason gently ran his gloved fingers over the scratches. They felt rough beneath his fingers, the scars still fresh.

"Might these scratches have been made when the workers removed the sarcophagus from the burial chamber?" he asked.

Mr. Platt shook his head. "No. I've seen the photographs of the chamber, and the doorway was both wide and high enough that the workers were able to pass through without incident. Also, the letter I received from Blake described the coffin in detail, and he said it was absolutely perfect, untouched by time except for a few miniscule cracks in the paint that would have occurred naturally. These knicks are manmade," Mason Platt said angrily. "Someone inflicted damage on the lid between the time it left the burial chamber and arrived at the museum."

Jason carefully lifted the lid of the coffin, ignoring Mr. Platt's sharp intake of breath.

"Shall I help you take that off?" Daniel asked. Mr. Platt suffering an apoplexy in response to their actions would not sit well with John Ransome.

"Yes, please," Jason replied distractedly.

Together they lifted the lid and placed it on a nearby display table. "The lid would require two people to lift out of the crate as we just did, but only one person if they were to push it backward," Jason said. "It's quite possible that when the killer opened the crate, he shoved the cotton wool out of the way and pushed the lid backward, sliding it along the back of the crate, which was now devoid of padding. The topmost points of the figure on the lid would come into contact with the wood, and that would account for the fresh scratches."

Mr. Platt looked shocked and impressed in equal measure. "Yes, I believe you're correct in that assumption, your lordship. That hadn't occurred to me. I simply assumed the damage was inflicted when some clumsy oaf tried to nail down the lid."

"Did you find anything inside after the body was removed?" Daniel asked, peering into the now-empty cavity.

"Not a thing. Just particles of sand and dust from the mummy. Oh, but I completely forgot," Mr. Platt cried, now excited as a child on Christmas. "We found the mummy in one of the other crates. It's intact and will be displayed inside the sarcophagus."

"How can you be sure that's the same mummy that was inside the sarcophagus?" Daniel asked.

"Because there were no other mummies listed on the inventory Blake Upton sent me," Mason Platt explained. "Every article is now accounted for."

"Is there any damage to the mummy?" Jason asked.

"No. It must have been removed prior to lowering the corpse into the coffin. There wouldn't have been enough room for both. The coffin must have been crafted to accommodate its occupant rather snugly, so the mummy had to go. Had Blake been a bigger man, he wouldn't have fit inside," Mr. Platt observed.

"I suppose the killer must have taken that into account, given that he'd seen the sarcophagus up close before it was crated and had known Blake Upton well enough to determine whether he would fit," Daniel said.

"Actually, nearly every member of the team would have fit, except for Michael Dillane," Jason said. "He's too tall and wide in the shoulders, but the rest of the men were all of average height and weight."

"Curious, that," Mr. Platt said.

"Why do you say that?" Daniel asked, turning to the curator.

"Well, it's only that I wonder if Blake Upton would have been killed in the same way had he been too big to fit into the coffin."

"I don't suppose we'll ever know the answer to that," Daniel said.

"Do you know why Blake was killed, Inspector?" Mason Platt asked, looking up at Daniel as if he'd only just thought to ask.

"I'm afraid we still don't have a clear motive, Mr. Platt," Daniel said, embarrassed to admit the truth.

"Then how can you figure out who did it?" Mason Platt asked. It was an obvious question, but it irritated Daniel, and he wished the little man would just stand aside and let them do their job.

"If the motive and the identity of the killer were obvious, there'd be no need for an investigation, Mr. Platt," he answered, more gruffly than he'd meant to. "But we will get to the bottom of this," he added, with considerably less conviction.

Daniel and Jason examined the interior of the sarcophagus carefully, despite Mr. Platt's protestations that there was nothing to find, then replaced the lid and allowed Mr. Mason to wrap the coffin in cotton wool and pull the canvas over it. He looked relieved that the examination was over.

"May we see the crate now?" Jason asked.

"Of course." Mr. Platt led them to the other side of the room, where the empty crates were stacked.

"What do you do with the crates once they've been emptied?" Jason asked.

"We use them to store various paintings and artefacts that are no longer on display."

"Have the crates that came in on the *Sea Witch* been cleaned?" Daniel asked.

"No, they haven't. We've only just finished unloading them. You will find that nothing has been removed, not even the padding used to wrap the artefacts."

"Good," Daniel said, relieved that the crate hadn't been emptied out. They hadn't been able to search beneath the sarcophagus, since it had filled the space almost completely, but perhaps something had fallen inside. Would it be too much to hope that the murder instrument had been carelessly tossed inside the crate once the killer was finished with it?

"It was this one," Mr. Platt said, checking the number on the side of a crate. It was the longest and widest crate in the storage area, so there was no doubt that Mr. Platt was correct. There were two smaller crates stacked atop, but Jason and Daniel had no difficulty removing them. They set the empty crates aside and focused on the one the coffin had arrived in.

Daniel lifted the top of the crate and set it aside after examining the underside closely for any evidence of scratches or paint. There were none.

"Mr. Platt, might we borrow a magnifying glass?" Jason said as he looked into the frustratingly empty crate.

"Of course." Mr. Platt pulled a small magnifying glass out of his pocket.

"Do you have anything else in there?" Jason asked, a smile tugging at the corner of his mouth. "Some sandwiches, perhaps?"

Mr. Platt smiled. "I always carry certain items on my person, so that I don't have to return to my office if I need to examine an artefact closely."

Jason held the magnifying glass up to his eyes and leaned as far into the crate as he could without falling in. The crate wasn't deep, so he was able to see the bottom and the sides clearly.

"Look here, Daniel," Jason said, pointing to the back panel of the crate. Daniel squinted at the planks of wood.

"Here, take this." Jason handed Daniel the magnifying glass and pointed to several spots on the wooden planks.

With the aid of the magnifying glass, Daniel finally saw what Jason had spotted. There were several spots where the wood was scratched and there were miniscule flakes of colorful paint and gold dust. Daniel reached in and traced his finger over the spots, mentally measuring the distance between them. Sure enough, they would correspond with the snake in the headdress, the tip of the nose, the folded hands, and the tips of the toes.

"You were right," he said, handing the glass back to Jason. "Whoever did this pushed the lid backward, which leads me to believe that the killer didn't have an accomplice and wasn't strong enough to lift the lid on his own."

"I think this also exonerates Jock Thomas," Jason said. "He has too much reverence for the artefacts to knowingly inflict damage on something as precious as that sarcophagus."

"That's an interesting point," Daniel said. "I do wish we had found the murder weapon."

"Had we found a bamboo stick or a scalpel, we'd be no closer to identifying the killer," Jason said. "They could have been wielded by anyone."

"Yes, that's true," Daniel agreed. "Did you find anything inside when you lifted out the sarcophagus, Mr. Platt?" he asked, still hoping for a clue.

"Only Mr. Upton's handkerchief. It must have fallen out of his pocket," Mr. Platt replied.

"Do you still have it?" Daniel asked.

"Yes. I'll get it for you," Mr. Platt said, and walked away.

Jason suddenly raised the glass to his face and bent low over the crate.

"Do you see something?" Daniel asked, following his gaze. Sure enough, there was a glint of something in the far-right corner. They would not have spotted it had it been a cloudy day, but the sunlight illuminated the inside of the crate, reflecting off whatever it was they were looking at. Jason reached in and lifted the object out.

"What is it?" Daniel asked, squinting at the find.

Jason dropped the object into his palm and held it up for Daniel to see. "It's a section of a chain," he said.

He handed the magnifying glass to Daniel, who studied the links closely. The segment glowed in the sunlight, the links larger and sturdier than he'd first thought.

"This came from a fairly thick chain," Daniel said. "The kind a man would wear."

"That could have been there for months, if not years," Mr. Platt said, having returned with the handkerchief and joined them by the crate.

"I don't believe so," Jason replied. "Had it been there for a long time, it would have tarnished, especially when exposed to air and damp. The links are as good as new."

"Do you think that's significant?" Mr. Platt asked, peering into Daniel's gloved palm.

"It's difficult to say," Daniel replied, still staring at the chain and trying to figure out where it might have come from.

Jason held out his hand for the handkerchief and examined it. It was a plain square of lawn, the edges untrimmed, loose threads hanging off the sides. Jason lifted the cloth to his nose and sniffed at it, then folded the square and dabbed it on his tongue.

"What are you doing?" Daniel asked, wrinkling his nose in disgust. He'd touch anything at a crime scene and had handled the corpses many times, but he'd never willingly put anything in his mouth, not even something as innocuous as a square of lawn.

"Thank you, Mr. Platt," Jason said, ignoring Daniel's question.

"Anytime, my lord. Anytime. I hope you found what you were looking for."

"Possibly," Jason replied. "I think we're done here."

"Thank you, Mr. Platt," Daniel said as he handed the links to Jason, who wrapped them in the handkerchief and put it in the pocket of his coat for safekeeping.

They left the storage area and reentered the museum, which had just opened to the public. There were people everywhere, some walking slowly and examining each artefact with care, others glancing at the offerings in a perfunctory way, probably looking for that one display that really caught their fancy. A well-dressed man led a girl of about six by the hand and was talking to her quietly. He lifted her into his arms when they reached a display that was too tall for her to see, the little girl chattering excitedly as they examined the various pieces of ancient jewelry.

Daniel felt a pang of longing for Charlotte. He hadn't seen her in a few weeks, and it was as if a part of him was missing. He allowed himself a brief fantasy of bringing her to the museum once she got older and showing her the exhibits. It was only a few minutes later, as he followed Jason outside into the glorious April morning, that he realized Sarah had not been a part of his daydream.

"Why did you taste the handkerchief?" Daniel asked as he refocused his mind on the investigation. "It must be filthy."

"I needed to be sure," Jason said. "The handkerchief had a mere trace of an odor, which might have been chloroform."

"Are you able to taste chloroform?" Daniel asked, wondering how long the substance retained its properties.

"Chloroform has a particular sweet taste and a rather pleasant odor. I became familiar with the taste and smell while working at the hospital in New York. We used it to put the patients to sleep before major surgical procedures."

"And the minor ones?" Daniel asked, wondering if the patients were simply told to brace themselves and hold on.

"For the less invasive procedures, we used a local anesthetic. Mostly cocaine based. It numbs the area, but it's also highly addictive if applied to the mouth or nose, so it was administered by injection."

"So this is the handkerchief that was used to anesthetize Blake Upton?"

"Yes, but it's not his handkerchief," Jason said.

Daniel nodded. "I agree. Someone tore the trim off the handkerchief to make sure it couldn't be traced back to him if found. Perhaps it had a distinctive pattern or a monogram."

"This handkerchief might belong to a man, but it could just as easily belong to a woman," Jason said. "It may have been trimmed with lace."

"That doesn't prove anything, though, does it?" Daniel argued. "Everyone has handkerchiefs, and the men could have even used a handkerchief they'd taken from their wife as a keepsake, not wishing to ruin their own."

"Yes, unfortunately that's true."

"What about the chain?" Daniel asked as they continued to walk. "Any ideas?"

"It's too thin to be from a watch chain," Jason theorized, voicing Daniel's own thoughts. Wherever this had come from, it wasn't from Blake Upton's watch. "If one of the men was known to wear a gold chain around his neck, we might be able to connect him to the crate," Jason said. "Perhaps Blake Upton had grabbed at him when the chloroform-soaked handkerchief was held to his nose and tore it." Jason turned to Daniel. "Do you still have the group photograph?"

"I left it at the Yard," Daniel said. "Ransome wanted it included in the file, and I didn't think I'd have need of it. Peter Moffat has another copy. I can stop in later today. He might also remember seeing someone wearing a chain. Perhaps the men had taken off their jackets and ties while out in the desert, exposing their necks."

"We're not too far from Dr. Scarborough's residence. Let's go speak to him first," Jason suggested. "I'd like to hear his version of events that led to Henry Ames's death and see if he knows anything about the business with Evan Lewis."

"Yes," Daniel agreed. He checked his watch. "He must be up by now. It's nearly half ten. Let's go."

Chapter 23

It was a fine day, so they walked over to Dr. Scarborough's house. The same maidservant as last time opened the door, looking a bit anxious when she recognized them.

"We'd like to speak to Dr. Scarborough, miss," Daniel said.

"I'm afraid 'e's not receiving yet, sir," the maid replied.

"He'll receive us," Daniel said somewhat forcefully.

He wasn't in the mood to be trifled with, not when this was the biggest case he'd been entrusted with since joining Scotland Yard. This case would make or break him with Superintendent Ransome, and he needed it to be the former, since losing Ransome's respect could result in scraping the bottom of the proverbial barrel when it came to the assignment of cases.

From what Daniel had heard from the other detectives, John Ransome had a long memory and wasn't likely to give someone another chance once they'd let him down, or worse, allowed him to be humiliated in the press or before his superiors. But ambitious as Ransome was, he wouldn't charge someone without compelling evidence just to satisfy the public and the powers-that-be, so even though he had a suspect in the cells, Daniel had yet to prove conclusively that Evan Lewis had killed Blake Upton and the members of the archeological team were in the clear before the case could be considered closed.

"Yes, sir," the maid replied sourly. "If ye'll just wait 'ere a moment."

She left them in the foyer and went to summon her master, who must have been at breakfast, if the sound of cutlery on plates coming from the room the maid had entered were anything to go on. Dr. Scarborough appeared a few minutes later, obviously annoyed by the interruption.

"It's rather early to be paying calls, gentlemen," he said. "Mrs. Scarborough and I were at breakfast."

"This is not a social call, Doctor," Daniel pointed out.

"No, I don't suppose it would be," Dr. Scarborough grumbled. "Come into the drawing room," he said ungraciously, and strode through the door without waiting for them. He sank into a wingchair and crossed his legs, his expression one of impatience. He gestured for Jason and Daniel to have a seat.

"I'm afraid I don't have anything to add to what I've already told you," he said by way of opening volley.

"Don't you?" Jason asked, tilting his head to the side as he studied the doctor, whose eyebrows lifted in incomprehension. He didn't appear nervous, just anxious to be rid of them. "Dr. Scarborough, you didn't mention the stolen chloroform," Jason said conversationally. Given his medical knowledge, they'd decided that he would take the lead when questioning the doctor.

"Sorry?" Dr. Scarborough asked, clearly knocked off balance.

"When last we spoke, I mentioned that I had detected an odor of chloroform during the postmortem. The chloroform must have come from you, as you were the only medical man on board."

Dr. Scarborough looked instantly contrite. "Yes, it did, but I didn't know that at the time of our conversation. After you left, I went through my supplies and discovered that a vial was missing."

"Or perhaps it wasn't missing at all, and you'd used it to incapacitate Blake Upton before excerberating him," Jason suggested.

"What possible reason would I have to murder Blake Upton?" Dr. Scarborough demanded, the color rising in his pale cheeks. "And why would I go to such lengths?"

"Blake Upton blamed you for the death of Henry Ames," Daniel interjected. "He threatened to destroy your career and reputation."

"Yes, he did," Dr. Scarborough admitted with surprising candor. "But he wouldn't have followed through on the threat."

"How can you be so sure?" Jason asked.

"Because when Blake accused me, it was his grief talking. And guilt. Henry was the son of Blake's godparents, and he felt responsible."

"Yet you never mentioned Henry Ames at all when we last spoke," Jason reminded him.

"You never asked about Henry, and given that he wasn't aboard the *Sea Witch* and couldn't have killed Blake Upton, I didn't see the relevance," Dr. Scarborough replied defensively.

"You also didn't see the need to draw attention to your possible motive," Daniel replied.

"I have no motive," Dr. Scarborough retorted. "Henry's death was tragic, but there's nothing I could have done to save him."

"What did he die of?" Jason asked, watching the man intently.

Dr. Scarborough looked like a cornered rabbit but didn't avert his gaze. "He died of a burst appendix."

"So you concur with the findings of the local surgeon?"

"I do. I was present during the autopsy, and it was obvious to us both."

"Which was precisely why Blake Upton held you responsible for Henry's death," Daniel pressed.

"He had no right to," Dr. Scarborough cried, clearly exasperated. He looked at Jason, seemingly appealing for his understanding. "Do you know what a hypochondriac is, Lord Redmond?" he asked.

"I do. Is that what you think Henry Ames was?"

Dr. Scarborough nodded, clearly relieved that Jason was familiar with the term. "I met Henry Ames for the first time when I came aboard in Southampton the day we set sail. He wasn't at our farewell dinner, so I never got the measure of him, which would have been helpful, since we were to share a cabin on the voyage out. I knew by the second day that he was the sort of person I needed to tread carefully with. The list of ailments he believed himself to have seemed endless and completely unfounded. I heard him out and offered the least harmful forms of treatment, since I didn't think he was truly ill. The only thing he'd suffered from was a bout of seasickness during the first few days of the voyage, but he wasn't the only one. The sea was choppy, and the boat rocked from side to side morning, noon, and night. Our poor steward spent most of the day cleaning up vomit and taking out puke-filled chamber pots. But then the weather turned, the sea stilled, and everyone instantly felt better, including Henry. There was nothing wrong with him."

"But he died," Jason reminded the man.

"He did, but through no fault of mine."

"Please outline his symptoms and the course of treatment you prescribed for him," Jason demanded, watching the doctor closely. "And I would like to study your case notes."

Dr. Scarborough nodded, seemingly eager to cooperate. "Henry was miserably uncomfortable from the start. Once he recovered from the seasickness, he developed persistent constipation, which is not uncommon, since there are few fresh fruits or vegetables served at table when at sea. I brought a generous supply of castor oil and gave him a spoonful every day to relieve his symptoms."

"Did the castor oil help?" Jason asked.

"Yes. It did the job admirably," Dr. Scarborough said with a sarcastic smile.

"Then what happened?" Daniel demanded.

"Then, once we arrived, Henry immediately got a terrible sunburn, because he wouldn't heed my advice and took off his hat during the hottest time of the day. His face was as red as a lobster, so I offered him a soothing lotion to relieve the discomfort. The sunburn became less painful and began to fade in a few days. It went on from there, gentlemen. It was something new every day, the ailments ranging from bug bites that he believed to be fatal to a sore head after a night of drinking that he was convinced was a terminal tumor of the brain. When Henry began complaining of stomach pains, I asked him some basic questions and prescribed more castor oil, since I believed something he ate hadn't agreed with him and it was best to purge the irritant from his system. It seemed to help," Dr. Scarborough said, his eyes pleading with Jason to concur with his diagnosis.

"But the pain returned," Jason said. "Did you even examine him?"

"I did, but his symptoms didn't fit with an inflamed appendix. He was not vomiting, had no fever or abdominal swelling, and his appetite was unaffected. Most men, myself included, suffer moderate to severe gastric discomfort upon arriving in a foreign land. The unfamiliar food, strong spices, and the insufferable heat, which leads one to drink water that comes from God only knows where, all require a period of adjustment. Most men feel better within a fortnight; Henry didn't. I advised him to refrain from eating anything spicy and keep his portions small in order not to overwhelm his digestive system. I also suggested he drink less beer and wine and stick to milk or tea to soothe his stomach. I thought, under the circumstances, that those were reasonable measures Henry could easily implement."

"They were," Jason agreed. "So, why did Blake Upton blame you?"

"Blake thought I should have sent Henry back to England as soon as he began complaining of abdominal pain."

"Would sending him home have saved his life?"

"I don't believe so. By the time Henry would have found a ship bound for England, he'd already be a dead man walking, since his appendix would have without doubt ruptured on board. Besides, Henry had no wish to leave. He was enjoying the adventure, if not the actual work."

Dr. Scarborough sighed in resignation. "I admit that I didn't take his complaints as seriously as I should have because of his history, but in truth, there was nothing I could have done differently, even if I had diagnosed his symptoms correctly. I'm not a surgeon, Lord Redmond, so any attempt to operate would have killed him regardless. And Henry would never have permitted a local surgeon to go anywhere near him. He made that clear when Blake suggested taking him to a local hospital the day he died. What happened was unfortunate, but Henry's fate was sealed as soon as he decided to come to Cairo."

"Did you explain all this to Blake Upton?" Jason asked.

"Yes, of course. And once his grief dulled somewhat, he acknowledged that I was right."

"Did he actually say so?" Daniel asked.

"He did, if somewhat grudgingly. Blake understood the risks of traveling to a place like Egypt. We all did. Things can very easily go wrong, and there's always the possibility of losing a member of the team. Blake had explained all that to Henry, but he insisted on coming. He had a highly romanticized view of what Blake did and wanted to be a part of it."

Dr. Scarborough bowed his head, his gaze fixing on his clasped hands. "I think Blake would have felt less guilty had he been able to at least ship Henry's body home for burial. But given the heat and the length of the journey, that was never a real possibility. Henry was given a Christian burial. That's the most Blake could have hoped for in a predominantly Muslim country."

"Dr. Scarborough, who had access to your medical supplies?" Jason asked.

"Anyone who entered my cabin."

"Did you see anyone entering your cabin?" Daniel asked.

"No, but there were plenty of times when I wasn't there, so anyone could have slipped in and helped themselves. We didn't bother locking the doors. And, of course, the steward had access."

"Is anything else missing?" Jason asked.

"No, nothing." The man looked up, his eyes filled with misery. "Henry Ames's death will haunt me for the rest of my days, but I did not kill Blake Upton," Dr. Scarborough said, his voice resonant with conviction.

"I'd like to see your medical journal please," Jason said.

"I will get it for you."

Dr. Scarborough left the room and returned a short time later with a brown leather-bound book, which he handed to Jason. Opening it to the day of the team's departure from Southampton, Jason studied the entries. There weren't that many, and most of them pertained to Henry Ames. Dr. Scarborough's answers corresponded with the entries that detailed Henry's complaints and the doctor's advice for treating them. Unless Dr. Scarborough had intentionally left out the more serious symptoms, his course of treatment was mostly correct.

"Thank you, Dr. Scarborough," Jason said as he closed the journal and handed it back to the doctor.

"Do you agree with my assessment?" Dr. Scarborough asked.

"I agree that you didn't have a choice," Jason replied vaguely.

Dr. Scarborough nodded, willing to accept that. "Is that all, then?"

"Not quite," Daniel said. "Do you recall a man named Martin Lewis?"

Richard Scarborough didn't appear surprised by the question. "Yes. He was a porter at Christ Church College in Oxford."

"Had Blake Upton mentioned him at all on the voyage back?" Daniel asked.

"Yes."

"In what context?"

"Blake had the man dismissed from his position by accusing him of being drunk on the job."

"And was that true?" Jason asked.

"No, but Blake held a grudge against him and would accept nothing less than dismissal."

"Did you back up Blake Upton's accusation to get the man sacked?" Daniel asked.

"I did, and I have regretted it ever since. Which was why, when Blake came to me and told me that Martin Lewis's son had confronted him in the hold, I advised Blake to make amends."

"And was he willing to take your advice?"

"Blake knew that what he'd done was awful. Martin Lewis had only been doing his job. Hearing that the man had lost his wife and then drank himself to death came as a shock, and Blake wanted absolution."

"How did he hope to attain it?" Jason asked.

"He thought about what to do for a while, but, in the end, he decided that money was always the best antidote to any illness. He gave Evan Lewis all his money and his father's gold watch. He loved that watch and felt that giving it away was appropriate penance for destroying this family."

"So, Blake Upton gave the money and the watch to Mr. Lewis willingly?" Daniel asked. "He wasn't threatened or coerced?"

"No. It was his decision," Dr. Scarborough confirmed.

"Did he have any intention of reporting Evan Lewis to Captain Sanders?" Jason asked.

"No. Why would he do that?" Dr. Scarborough asked, clearly confused by the question.

"Perhaps he wanted his pound of flesh for being thus accosted while on board," Daniel said. "He might have felt remorse for what he'd done to Mr. Lewis Senior, but perhaps he still wanted to punish is son for putting him in such an awkward position."

Dr. Scarborough shook his head. "No, Inspector. Blake regretted what he'd done and wanted to make amends. He had no intention of reporting Evan Lewis, nor did he wish to punish him for anything. He asked the man to come to his cabin on Sunday and gave him the money and the watch and told him to go with God. That was the end of it."

"Why didn't you tell us about this when we questioned you the first time, Doctor?" Daniel asked.

"Because it never occurred to me that it was relevant to the investigation. Why? Do you think Evan Lewis killed Blake?" Dr. Scarborough asked, the thought clearly never having entered his mind. "Why would he?"

"To teach him a lesson?" Daniel asked, but the wind had gone out of his sails.

"I never got the impression that Evan Lewis sought to harm Blake. He hadn't expected to get anything. I think all he wanted was an acknowledgement that what Blake had done was thoughtless and cruel. The money and the watch were a bonus."

"But he took it," Daniel pointed out.

"And why wouldn't he? That doesn't make him a killer," Dr. Scarborough said.

"No, I don't suppose it does," Daniel grumbled as he rose to his feet. "Thank you, Doctor. We'll see ourselves out."

They stepped out into the sunshine and walked toward a small park, where several nursemaids were pushing unwieldy prams containing their charges. Daniel and Jason settled on a bench and sat in silence for a moment, each lost in his own thoughts.

"He confirmed Lewis's story," Daniel said at last. He had a hard time masking his disappointment. Had Richard Scarborough not confirmed Blake Upton's willingness to make amends to Evan Lewis, Daniel's task would have been a lot simpler. He'd charge Lewis with theft and murder and be done with this case, but as Dr. Scarborough had pointed out, Evan Lewis had no earthly reason to kill the man who'd just given him fifty pounds and a gold watch. For a man like Lewis, it was a fortune. Even for Daniel, it was a sum he'd have to work as an inspector for years to earn. And the watch was worth a considerable amount. But Lewis had no motive and would have to be released, and Daniel would have to explain to John Ransome why he was no closer to finding Blake Upton's killer than he had been yesterday.

"How do you mean to proceed?" Jason asked.

"I mean to investigate this case until I know for certain who killed Blake Upton," Daniel said stubbornly. "Is what Dr.

Scarborough said about Henry Ames's death true? Could he have done anything differently?"

"Short of strongarming Henry Ames into seeing a local surgeon when the pains continued to grow in intensity, I don't believe so. I think he's genuinely upset by Henry's death, but each doctor walks through his own graveyard in his mind. As much as you want to, you can't save every patient. There will always be those who die, sometimes due to a mistake in treatment and sometimes because there's simply nothing you could have done. Henry Ames may have lived had he been in England at the time of his appendix attack, but since he was in Cairo, his chances of survival were drastically reduced, more so because the Englishmen refused to bring in a local surgeon until it was too late."

"Would you entrust someone you care about to a local surgeon?" Daniel asked.

"I really couldn't say. I've never been to Egypt and know nothing about the level of their medical care, but if I had chosen to travel there and remained for six months, I'd probably have no choice but to put my faith in a local man if I wasn't in a position to help."

"But Dr. Scarborough made a grave mistake in his diagnosis," Daniel pointed out, not ready to let the matter drop.

"Given the circumstances, the symptoms could have easily been mistaken for indigestion caused by an intolerance of local products. I also agree that to perform surgery in those conditions and with a complete lack of skill would have killed the patient."

"Do you suppose a local surgeon would have saved him had he got to Henry in time?" Daniel asked.

"Possibly."

"Do you think Dr. Scarborough could have killed Blake Upton to preserve his reputation?"

"No, I don't."

Daniel sighed heavily, his shoulders sagging in defeat. "We seem to have reached a dead end, Jason. Neither Jock Thomas, Adam Longhorn, nor Richard Scarborough had a good enough reason to kill Blake Upton, and if they had, I can't see them resorting to such a gruesome way of doing it. They're levelheaded, intelligent men. Had they wanted Upton dead, they would have found a quicker, cleaner method that would never lead back to them. This murder was committed by someone who's ruled by emotion and was driven by a desire for revenge. There are the two younger men, but again, I don't see why they'd want to kill Blake Upton. Since we found the money and watch, we know for certain Michael Dillane did not take them, and I've heard nothing to arouse my suspicions regarding Peter Moffat. Neither one of them seem to have anything to gain by committing murder. Peter Moffat benefited both professionally and financially from his association with Blake Upton, and Michael Dillane could have ended his relationship with Upton at any time by refusing to go on any more excavations. What am I missing?" Daniel exclaimed, lifting his hands in his frustration.

"I don't see any discernable pattern either," Jason replied. "My instincts tell me that we're on the wrong track, but for the life of me, I can't see where we took a wrong turn."

Daniel stared straight ahead, his gaze fixed on the house just across the park, where a young woman exited using the servants' entrance and set off down the street, a wicker basket slung over her arm.

"This doesn't make any sense, Jason. We've interviewed all the suspects, and I haven't noticed a glimmer of guilt or a flicker of fear in anyone's eyes. Some people are skilled liars, but an experienced copper can always tell when someone is trying to hide the truth. No one can keep up the façade indefinitely. There's always just that little something that gives them away. A shifty look, a moment of panic when they think they've made a mistake, an attempt to discredit someone else or to point the finger toward a possible scapegoat. Evan Lewis is the only one who panicked, possibly because he didn't believe Dr. Scarborough would confirm his account, but it seems he was telling the truth, so we're back to the members of the team. They all have their vices, but killing Blake Upton doesn't appear to be one of them."

Jason nodded in understanding. "It's only been a few days, Daniel. We have to be patient and keep at them until they slip up. Someone always does and then that one mistake is the key that opens Pandora's box. One of those people killed Blake Upton, and we will find out which one."

"The steward," Daniel suddenly said.

"What?"

"The steward. The servants always know what goes on in a household, no matter how jealously the masters guard their secrets. And although the employers realize this, they still treat the servants as if they were invisible. Same goes for a ship's steward. Dr. Scarborough said so himself. The steward was in and out of the cabins. He might have seen or heard something without realizing its importance." Daniel took out his notebook and flipped back to the list of crew members. "Here we are. Mr. Keith Mulligan, Steward. He lives near the Poplar docks."

"Let's go speak to Mr. Mulligan, then," Jason said, already rising to his feet.

Daniel nodded, and the two men left the park in search of a hackney.

Chapter 24

The area where Keith Mulligan lived could only be described as a slum. It looked gray, the shadowy alleyways murky despite the bright sunshine. Ragged children roamed the narrow streets in packs, and grim-looking men and women went about the business of surviving from day to day, their attention focused solely on the task at hand. Piles of horse shit, decaying fruit, and countless unwashed bodies filled the air with an unhealthy miasma, the stench strong enough to make Daniel wish he could cover his nose and mouth, afraid that whatever was festering in the rotting refuse was catching.

Jason sucked in his breath but made no comment as they searched for the right address. When they found it, the door was opened by an elderly man who was missing several teeth and whose hair hung in limp gray curtains around his face. He squinted at them as if unsure they were really there.

"What d'ye want, then?" he finally asked.

"We're looking for Keith Mulligan," Daniel said.

"What's 'e meant to 'ave done?" the man demanded, peering at Daniel's warrant card.

"He hasn't done anything. We only want to talk to him," Daniel said patiently. "May we come in?"

"Suit yerselves," the man said, and stepped aside to let them enter.

"Who is it, Da?" a voice called from somewhere inside the house.

"Two fancy coves to see ye, lad," the man called back. His voice was thick with phlegm, and he coughed loudly before disappearing down a dark corridor.

A man of about twenty stepped out to greet them. He was lean to the point of being gaunt and had wooly hair and whiskers that reminded Daniel of a sheep. His clothes were worn but looked fairly clean, and his dark gaze was open and welcoming.

"Good day to ye," he said. "I'm Keith Mulligan."

"Is there somewhere we can talk, Mr. Mulligan?" Daniel asked, eager to get out of the dark, narrow corridor.

"This way." Keith Mulligan led them into a small, dim room that faced the back of the house and appeared to serve as parlor, dining room, and storage area all at once. There were only two chairs, which their host generously offered to Daniel and Jason, saying he preferred to stand.

Daniel and Jason sat down, while Keith Mulligan leaned against the door jamb for support.

"What can I do for ye, gents?"

"Mr. Mulligan, are you aware that Mr. Blake Upton was murdered while aboard the *Sea Witch*?" Daniel asked.

The man's eyes widened in shock. "Wha'? Murdered, ye say?"

"Haven't you seen the papers?" Daniel asked.

"I can't read," Mulligan said matter-of-factly. "Never learned me letters. 'Ow were 'e murdered?"

Daniel briefly outlined the details of the murder, watching as Keith Mulligan grew more amazed.

"They took out 'is brains? Who'd do a wicked thing like that?"

"That's what we're trying to discover," Daniel replied. "And we need your help."

"Sure. 'Course. Anything I can do."

"Mr. Mulligan, how many of the passenger cabins were you responsible for?"

"Why, all of them," Mulligan replied.

"And what were your duties?" Daniel asked, his pencil poised to take notes.

"Clean the cabins, make the beds, take out the chamber pots, and see to any washing as needed doin'."

"Did you do the washing yourself?" Daniel asked.

"Nah. It were not me job."

"Mr. Mulligan, did you ever hear anyone arguing?"

Keith Mulligan shrugged. "Not really. I were there when they wasn't," he rushed to explain.

"Did you ever go through anyone's possessions?" Daniel asked carefully.

The man shook his head. "Never. I could lose me place for doing that."

"Did you ever see or hear anything out of the ordinary?" Jason asked, as frustrated as Daniel with the lack of progress.

Keith Mulligan suddenly smiled, revealing surprisingly good teeth. "I smelt a lady in Mr. Upton's cabin."

Both Daniel and Jason sat up just a bit straighter. "You smelled a lady?" Daniel asked, wondering what exactly Keith Mulligan was referring to.

"A lovely scent," Keith Mulligan said dreamily. "Like fresh gardenias."

"Whose scent was it?" Daniel demanded.

"It could'a been either of the ladies," Keith Mulligan said. "They wore the same scent. 'Ad just the one bottle."

"How many times had you smelled the scent inside Mr. Upton's cabin?"

"A few times," Keith Mulligan said, maddeningly vague.

"Did you smell it in any of the other cabins?" Daniel asked.

The man shook his head. "Nope. Just there."

"Mrs. Foster and Miss Gibb's cabin was right across from Mr. Upton's cabin. Might it have simply wafted there when the doors were opened?"

Keith Mulligan's smile answered for him. "The scent were on the bedlinens, Inspector. Most specially on the pillow where the lady 'ad lain 'er 'ead."

"Are you saying Blake Upton had a romantic relationship with one of the ladies?" Daniel asked, needing to clarify Keith Mulligan's comments.

"I'm sayin' I smelt their scent on Mr. Upton's bed. I ain't never seen 'em abed together."

"Did you ever see Mr. Upton with Miss Gibb together outside the cabin?"

Keith Mulligan shook his head. "I seen 'im with Mrs. Foster. She liked talking to 'im. If ye ask me, she 'ad feelings for 'im."

"Is there anything else you can tell us, Mr. Mulligan?" Daniel asked.

"Nothin' at all," Keith Mulligan replied. "That's all I know."

"Thank you," Daniel said. "Will you be sailing on the *Sea Witch* when it goes out on its next voyage?"

"I surely will, Inspector. Can't wait to leave this 'ere shithole. I love the sea," he said, his expression dreamy again.

"There ain't nothin' like it. It's a big world out there, and I mean to see as much of it as I can. If it weren't for me da, I'd not come back at all. 'E were a sailor too, when 'e were a young man, but 'e's old and frail now, and 'as no one to look after 'im 'sides me. Fifty, 'e is," Keith Mulligan added confidentially.

Daniel had thought the man was seventy if a day, but he supposed these living conditions would age anyone prematurely.

"Well, I wish you luck, Mr. Mulligan," Daniel said. "Please find me at Scotland Yard if you remember anything else."

Keith Mulligan nodded and walked them to the door. "Good day to ye both," he said cheerfully. "I do 'ope ye catch the sly bugger as done for Mr. Upton."

There were no cabs to find in Poplar, so Daniel and Jason walked as quickly as they could, eager to leave the smelly slum behind. It took nearly a half hour until they finally spotted a hansom and flagged it down.

"If what Keith Mulligan says is true, then we have a whole new angle," Daniel said as he settled more comfortably on the cracked leather seat.

"Which is?" Jason asked, turning to look at Daniel.

"Blake Upton was having an affair," Daniel exclaimed, eager to pursue this new lead.

"But that still doesn't explain why someone wished to kill him," Jason replied.

"Jealousy. Perhaps one of the men was in love with the same woman."

"All right, let's go with that," Jason said. "Say Blake Upton was having an affair with Amelia Foster. Who would care enough to kill him? It's not as if Amelia Foster would immediately switch her affections to someone else. And which of the men would it be? I hadn't noticed a twinge of affection in any of the men when they referred to Mrs. Foster. If anything, they all remarked on her lack of approachability."

"All right. Miss Gibb, then."

"Do you think Miss Gibb would risk lying with a married man in a cabin directly across from the one she shared with her aunt? That would be pretty brazen. And when would these assignations take place?"

"Perhaps she sneaked out at night," Daniel suggested.

"Say she did, and Mrs. Foster found out. Do you think she would lure Blake Upton down to the hold and remove his brain? That seems a bit extreme, don't you think?"

"You're right," Daniel admitted. "She would be furious, I'm sure, and worried about Miss Gibb's future prospects, but I highly doubt she'd murder the man."

"What would a devoted aunt do in such a situation?" Jason asked.

"She would try to find a suitable match as quickly as possible for fear that the young woman was already with child."

"Did you get the impression that Mrs. Foster was looking to secure a match for her niece when you spoke to her?"

"No, can't say I did."

Jason shook his head in dismay. "Something doesn't add up, Daniel. How do you wish to proceed?"

"I've already spoken to Mrs. Foster and Miss Gibb. Perhaps you'll have better luck and ask a different set of questions now that we suspect one of the women was carrying on an illicit affair with Blake Upton. Why don't you head over to Cavendish Square while I stop by Peter Moffat's house to ask for a copy of the photograph. Figuring out whom the chain belonged to might help us narrow down the list of suspects."

"All right."

"There's a tavern a few streets away. The Queen's Ransom. Meet me there once you're done. I'm starving," Daniel said.

"That sounds like a good plan."

Daniel gave the cabbie Peter Moffat's address and asked to be dropped off before he proceeded to Cavendish Square.

Chapter 25

Daniel hoped Peter Moffat was at home as he knocked on the door. Now that he had a new lead, he was eager to explore it further and hoped the photographer would be able to either confirm or rule out an affair between Susanna Gibb and Blake Upton. Daniel didn't think either would have confided in Peter, but perhaps the young man had seen or heard something that would help Daniel verify Keith Mulligan's supposition.

If Peter Moffat couldn't comment, Daniel would have to speak to Michael Dillane one more time. He was an observant man and owed no allegiance to Blake Upton. He might refuse to comment out of some misguided desire to protect Miss Gibb, but Daniel would be able to tell if the man were lying. It was one thing to not divulge something; it was quite another to be asked a direct question and lie outright.

The door was once again opened by Mrs. Moffat, who looked frightened at the sight of Daniel. To question her son once was only natural, given the tragedy that had taken place, but a second visit didn't bode well, her fearful gaze seemed to say. Despite her apprehension, she invited Daniel in and offered him a cup of tea, which Daniel accepted gladly, since Peter Moffat was in the darkroom and would be a few minutes yet.

Daniel settled on a settee and looked around the room for lack of anything better to do. Everything looked much as it had before, except for one thing. Daniel stood and walked over to the mantel, reaching for the delicate silver frame. In it was a photograph of Susanna Gibb, her gaze direct as she stared into the camera. A small smile played about her lips, and there was a softness in her gaze that Daniel hadn't noticed when he'd interviewed her two days ago. He peered into the background, trying to make out where the picture had been taken. It was hard to tell, but Daniel thought Miss Gibb was standing in front of a wall. He could make out the pattern of the wallpaper, which had a dark background. Making a mental note to ask about the photo, Daniel set it back on the mantel and resumed his seat.

He was finishing his second cup of tea by the time Peter finally walked into the parlor.

"Hello, Inspector," Peter said as he sat down across from Daniel and lifted the pot to see if there was any tea left. He poured himself a cup, added sugar and milk, and reached for the last almond biscuit. "How can I help you today?" He didn't appear nervous, only mildly curious about why Daniel had come back so soon.

"Did any of the men wear a gold chain around their neck?" Daniel asked without preamble.

Peter Moffat paused, the cup suspended in midair. "Eh, no. Why do you ask?"

"A segment of a gold chain was found inside the crate that held the sarcophagus."

Peter Moffat shrugged. "Sorry, no one wore a chain, and I would have noticed. But everyone except for Michael Dillane wore a pocket watch," he offered.

"No, the links are too small to belong to a pocket watch."

"In that case, I can't help you," Peter Moffat said, looking at the empty plate of biscuits with obvious disappointment.

"Perhaps you can," Daniel said. "I just noticed the new addition to your mantel."

The young man colored, his gaze sliding guiltily toward the photograph. He clearly hadn't expected Daniel to return or he wouldn't have put it on display.

"I thought you said you didn't take any pictures of the ladies," Daniel said, setting his cup back on the tray.

"I didn't."

"This isn't a candid photograph. She posed for you," Daniel observed.

"Yes, she did."

Daniel was growing exasperated. "Mr. Moffat, unless I'm much mistaken, the cabins aboard the *Sea Witch* were not papered but plain wood. This photograph was taken elsewhere."

"You are very observant, Inspector," Peter Moffat replied, faint color staining his cheeks.

"How well do you and Susanna Gibb know each other?"

"We met on the ship," Peter Moffat said, but something in his furtive gaze told Daniel that wasn't quite true.

"Don't lie to me," Daniel snapped. "Or would you prefer to have this conversation at Scotland Yard, with you in handcuffs?"

The panic in Peter's eyes was as good as an admission of guilt. "This photograph was taken before," he said, his voice barely audible.

"When?"

"About a year ago. When at home, I work at a photo atelier in Oxford Street, plus I do some discreet freelance work. Miss Gibb came in to have her picture taken."

"Did you keep a copy of the photograph?" Daniel asked.

Peter nodded guiltily. "I thought she was beautiful. I never showed it to anyone. I only kept a copy for myself."

"And did Miss Gibb tell you what the photograph was for?"

"It was to be a present. She didn't tell me for whom. I assumed it was for her sweetheart."

"Tell me what happened when you met Miss Gibb aboard the *Sea Witch*," Daniel invited.

"She remembered me, but I could tell she didn't want to make that obvious to Mrs. Foster. I wasn't sure why and didn't ask. I thought maybe Mrs. Foster didn't know about Miss Gibb's sweetheart, but given that she was still unmarried, I assumed the relationship hadn't worked out and the man was no longer in the picture."

"Did you try to court Miss Gibb?" Daniel asked, his tone softer now. Peter gave an almost imperceptible nod.

Daniel felt a pang of sympathy for the man. He'd fallen in love with Susanna Gibb when he met her a year ago, that was obvious, and suddenly he'd met her again, quite by chance, but their encounter hadn't turned out any better than the first.

"Mr. Moffat, I have it from the steward, Mr. Mulligan, that Miss Gibb had visited Mr. Upton's cabin on more than one occasion. Did you know that?"

Daniel was watching Peter Moffat closely, but the only emotion he could identify was wry amusement.

"Mr. Moffat?" Daniel prompted. "The woman you are in love with was carrying on an affair with a man who was murdered. And now you have a strong motive to want him dead."

"You've got the wrong end of the stick, Inspector," Peter said at last. "Blake Upton was an honorable man. Not a very happy one, but a decent one, nonetheless. He would never have been unfaithful to his wife."

"And how do you know that?" Daniel asked, his frustration mounting.

"I know that because it's my business to know. The camera lens is like a third eye that allows the photographer to see all manner of secrets. I've photographed hundreds of couples, in the same room, posed the same way, and each one of them is different. There's so much you can tell by the look in their eyes, the set of their shoulders, and the softness or hardness about the mouth. The woman sits in a chair, the man stands behind her. They're not looking at each other but at the camera, but you see their whole world in that gaze, in the way the man places his hand on the wife's shoulder, affectionately, indifferently, or possessively. You see how close he stands, and if she leans back, relaxed, or forward to avoid touching him, her entire body tense, ready for flight.

"Same goes for portraits. There's so much you can see in a person's face, in their stance. Blake Upton was intelligent, confident, and driven, but he wasn't fulfilled. He loved his wife, or had done, but he mourned the family they would have created had things turned out differently for them. They were united in their disappointment and grief, and he would never have added to his wife's heartbreak by taking a mistress. He never met Susanna in his cabin. I did."

"You and Susanna Gibb met secretly in Blake Upton's cabin?" Daniel reiterated, just to be sure.

"We did. She didn't want her aunt to know, so when Mrs. Foster went down for her afternoon nap, Susanna and I would meet in private. A half hour stolen from an autocrat who treated Susanna as if she were her handmaiden."

"And were you two intimate?"

"Not in the way you think," Peter Moffat replied.

"But you made use of the bed," Daniel pressed.

"Susanna suffered with seasickness, so I advised her to lie down for a bit to let the sickness pass. I never lay down with her."

"And did Mr. Upton know you were using his cabin for your assignations?" Daniel demanded.

"Yes, he did. Aside from Dr. Scarborough, who was to have bunked with Henry, Blake Upton was the only one of us to have a private cabin, and I would never have approached Richard Scarborough. He's too much of a pompous prig to feel any sympathy for two people who only wanted to spend a few minutes alone. Blake didn't mind. He went for a walk up on deck and let us use his cabin. All we did was talk." Peter's gaze implored Daniel to believe him.

"What about?" Daniel asked, wondering if there might be a connection to Blake Upton's death after all.

Peter Moffat looked like he hated to betray a confidence but knew he had little choice in the matter. "Susanna is lonely and bored. She rarely gets to meet new people and doesn't have any friends who aren't also her aunt's friends. Mrs. Foster doesn't even give her an allowance, so she has no money of her own and must depend on her aunt for everything. And then I saw the photograph I had taken in Mrs. Foster's book. It hadn't been for a sweetheart; it was a present for her aunt. There was never a sweetheart, Inspector, so I knew I stood a chance."

"And how did you leave things with Miss Gibb?" Daniel asked.

"I want us to be married, but she said we must wait a while."

"Why?"

"Because her aunt will not want to let her go. We're making plans to elope."

Daniel took a moment to absorb this. Peter Moffat and Susanna Gibb's relationship had nothing to do with Blake Upton. Surely they'd had nothing to gain by murdering the man. If they chose to elope, that was their business. They were both of age. But something was niggling at him.

"Mr. Moffat, what did you make of Mrs. Foster, or is it only when you photograph someone that you can see them clearly?"

Peter shook his head in dismay. "I saw a frightened, controlling woman who desperately tries to keep the situation from changing."

"What situation?"

"She is afraid of being left alone, Inspector. Aren't we all, to some degree? She lost her husband, and now she's going to lose Susanna as well. She wishes to prevent that from happening."

"But Susanna is her niece. Surely she wants her to be happy."

"I don't know about that," Peter replied sadly. "There's a possessiveness in the way she treats her. She wishes to control her every move, her every thought. She guards her so jealously. Susanna and I would have happily made our feelings known, but it was obvious her aunt would stand in our way, so we had to improvise."

"Do you think your secret is still safe?" Daniel asked.

"We were very careful not to be seen. No one knew except Blake, and he wouldn't have told anyone. As I said, he was an honorable man, someone you could trust."

"Thank you for your eventual candor, Mr. Moffat," Daniel said, pushing to his feet. "I wish you much happiness in your marriage."

"Thank you, Inspector."

Daniel left the Moffats' lodgings and walked down the street, lost in thought. Peter Moffat had no obvious motive for killing Blake Upton and had seemed sincere in his admiration for the man. Blake Upton had been willing to help him win the one thing he truly wanted, a selfless gesture Peter clearly appreciated. And he and Miss Gibb were making plans to run away together, or so Peter had said.

But what if Blake Upton, despite his admirable decency, had decided he wanted Miss Gibb for himself? Might the lovely Miss Gibb have been stringing both men along? If she was so desperate to get away from her controlling aunt, the voyage could have been her one opportunity to hatch a plan that would lead to freedom. Peter Moffat was offering marriage, a more respectable but less profitable option. He would no doubt give his wife all he had, but it wasn't much. Even if he opened his own photo atelier, he would never be wealthy or well-known and would probably spend the rest of his days living in rented lodgings with his widowed mother. They didn't even have a servant. Mrs. Moffat appeared to look after the household all by herself.

Blake Upton, on the other hand, had been comfortably off and would savor the accolades that came with this new discovery of the tomb. There was sure to be financial gain aside from the publicity. He might have offered Miss Gibb freedom of a different nature. As his mistress, she'd have her own home and be able to come and go as she pleased. And if he had so desperately wanted children, he could have had progeny with Miss Gibb, who was still young enough to give him a dozen children. Of course, the children would be born illegitimate, but there were ways around that. For one thing, Blake Upton could leave everything he owned to the children he had with Miss Gibb. Or he could have married Miss Gibb if he were to become a widower, therefore legitimizing his children.

If Peter Moffat had discovered that Blake Upton was working against him, he'd have a damn good reason to be rid of him, and his desire to kill the man would be fueled by passion, not reason. The method of murder would then make perfect sense.

Daniel hastened his steps in agitation as he recalled Miss Gibb's demeanor when he'd spoken to her. She hadn't struck him as heartbroken or even particularly upset. Had her meal ticket been stolen from her, there'd be some emotion that ruled her. Anger. Disappointment. Frustration. But she had seemed calm and a little sad, as one was when someone they knew had died, but with no obvious sense of loss. Perhaps she was simply prepared to move on to plan B because she didn't harbor any genuine feelings for any man and they were simply a means to an end.

But something was niggling at him, unease creeping up his spine as he replayed the interview with the ladies in his mind. He came to such an abrupt halt, the man behind him nearly collided with him and swore viciously before bypassing Daniel, who hardly noticed. His heart was racing, his breath coming in short gasps.

"Of course," Daniel muttered under his breath. And then he was on the move, weaving his way through the crowd, his gut instinct urging him to hurry. He had no reason to suspect anyone was in immediate danger, but some primitive part of his brain was firing off alarm signals, and Daniel had learned never to ignore the knot of fear that sometimes formed in the gut before the mind knew anything was amiss.

Chapter 26

It took Jason longer than expected to get to Cavendish Square. It seemed that all of London was in motion, everyone going somewhere, either on foot, by omnibus, or in a carriage or hackney cab. The streets were congested, and the hansom moved at a snail's pace toward his destination, slowing down every few minutes to allow someone to pass or to avoid colliding with another conveyance. Jason sighed with irritation when a crossing sweep no older than eight or nine years old materialized before a handsome carriage just in front of them and went to work, sweeping a pile of horse droppings with his twig broom. The driver tossed him a coin when he was finished, and they were finally moving again, the cabbie cursing under his breath in frustration. Jason decided then and there that next time he would attempt the underground railroad. He didn't much like the idea of traveling below ground, but if it got him to where he was going in a fraction of the time, he'd try to overcome his reservations.

The hansom finally rolled into Cavendish Square, which was a pleasant place with newly greening trees and imposing homes, the windows facing the square lit up by the afternoon sun, and the doors and window frames gleaming with fresh paint. This was a wealthy area, an oasis of peace and calm in a city that was like a bubbling cauldron of humanity. Here, there were no crossing sweeps or vendors calling out their wares. A pregnant hush fell over the square, as if the air itself were holding its breath for fear of disturbing the residents. A beautifully dressed middle-aged couple strolled past, the man glaring at the hansom as if it had no right to be in the square.

As Jason alighted in front of number five, he wondered how Amelia Foster truly felt about another family residing in her house when she was relegated to the top floor, even if it was by her own choice. Or perhaps it wasn't. Maybe she wasn't as well off as she had led Daniel to believe and couldn't afford to forgo the rental income from the property. Could she have spun a story that had no basis in the truth and hoped Daniel would accept it as fact?

Jason looked up at the impressive façade. They only had Amelia Foster's word that she owned the house or even that she had been married. She was in her late thirties, possibly a few years older. Miss Gibb was around twenty, Daniel had said. It wasn't beyond the realm of possibility that Miss Gibb wasn't Mrs. Foster's niece at all, but her natural daughter, a clandestine relationship that would explain Mrs. Foster's protectiveness toward the younger woman. If Mrs. Foster had found herself with child by a man who'd lied to her or left her unexpectedly, she'd do everything in her power to prevent her daughter from going down the same path and would accept nothing less than a respectable marriage, not something Miss Gibb could have found aboard the *Sea Witch*. The well-to-do men were already married, and the two unmarried men had little to offer in the way of wealth or status.

Perhaps she had hoped to meet someone on their travels. Mrs. Foster was still of marrying age, and an attractive woman, according to Daniel, as was Miss Gibb. But two women traveling alone would have to be very careful, especially in places where women weren't always treated with the same consideration they would expect in the West. Mrs. Foster would be aware of the danger, both to herself and to her ward, which would make her that much more likely to have seen or heard something she might have found threatening. Given the close quarters on the ship, Jason was sure the two women had been witness to more than they had initially let on, and he meant to discover what they knew.

Jason used the heavy brass knocker to announce his presence. A prim-looking servant answered the door, her eyes widening when Jason gave his name and asked to see Mrs. Foster. The maid stared up at him as if she'd suddenly found herself in the presence of royalty, her entire body wobbling in something resembling a curtsy.

"Mrs. Foster resides on the top floor, my lord," the maidservant said. "Shall I show ye the way?"

"No need," Jason replied, already heading toward the staircase. As he ascended the steep stairs, Jason wondered if the servants' quarters had been converted into a separate apartment.

He didn't imagine that many people who had the means to live in Cavendish Square would feel the need to seek an extra income from dividing their residence in this way.

"Good afternoon, miss," Jason said to the young red-headed maidservant who opened the upstairs door to his knock. She was neatly dressed in a pale-blue dress with a crisp white apron tied around her narrow waist, her gaze full of curiosity as she studied him. Jason didn't think Mrs. Foster and Miss Gibb received many visitors.

"Lord Redmond to see Mrs. Foster and Miss Gibb," Jason said, relying on his title to gain entrance. He noted with some displeasure that he was out of breath after walking straight up to the top floor. He'd grown soft during the long winter.

"Mrs. Foster ain't at 'ome, sir," the maid said, her eyes opening wider once she realized she was speaking to a member of the nobility.

"And Miss Gibb?"

"She's 'ere," the maid replied hesitantly.

"Then please announce me," Jason prompted, still feeling a bit breathless.

"Yes, sir."

A few moments later, having taken his things, the maid led Jason into the parlor, which was surprisingly spacious and tastefully decorated. He was relieved to note that the sash window was open, filling the room with the fresh, earthy scent of spring. He was still a bit warm from the climb and glad the room wasn't stuffy.

Miss Gibb came forward to greet him. She was a beautiful young woman, her smile warm and genuine, as if she were truly pleased to see him and not just feigning an expression of welcome. She wore a stylishly cut gown of periwinkle silk with a delicate ecru lace collar and matching lace at the cuffs. The color accentuated her eyes and dark hair and put Jason in mind of a summer twilight. Teardrop pearl earrings drew attention to her long, pale neck, and a pearl and diamond ring sparkled on her right hand. If Mrs. Foster was struggling financially, Jason saw no evidence of her difficulties.

"Good afternoon, your lordship. Please, do sit down," Miss Gibb invited. Her gaze was inquiring, but she was too polite to ask him the purpose of his visit.

"Miss Gibb, I'm assisting Inspector Haze in his inquiries pertaining to the death of Blake Upton. I'd like to ask you a few questions, if that's all right."

Jason wasn't sure why he'd chosen to downplay the severity of the act and refer to it simply as a death rather than the violent murder it had been, but some part of him wanted to spare Miss Gibb the gruesome details, though he was sure she was well aware of what had happened to Mr. Upton. Anyone who stepped outside from time to time and walked past a newspaper boy was bound to.

"I'm afraid my aunt is not here, but I'll be happy to answer any questions you have," Miss Gibb said. "Would you care for some refreshment?"

"Thank you, no," Jason replied. "I'll try not to take up too much of your time."

Miss Gibb laughed softly. "Please, take as long as you need. We don't get many visitors," she said, her cheeks coloring with embarrassment. "And I get so restless being here on my own. Amelia doesn't like it when I go out."

"Why?" Jason asked, although he already knew the answer. Few well-bred young ladies wandered the streets alone, even in the more affluent neighborhoods.

"She worries about me," Miss Gibb replied with a smile. "She barely let me out of her sight during our travels, but there I didn't mind. I was too frightened to go anywhere on my own. It's so easy to get lost in those winding streets that all look the same and seem to have no names. But in London, I feel safe. I'm at home."

"Did you enjoy Damascus?" Jason asked.

"I enjoyed some things, like the souks. They are street markets," she rushed to explain. "They have such beautiful things. I would have liked to buy an embroidered scarf or a cuff bracelet, but Amelia said they would look out of place in London. She was right, I suppose," Miss Gibb said, sounding disheartened.

"Did she let you do anything you wanted to do?" Jason asked, feeling sorry for the woman. She reminded him of a young doe, all innocence and curiosity.

"Not really. Amelia had our every day planned to the last minute. She likes to be in charge, so I just go along. It's easier that way." Miss Gibb tilted her head, studying Jason openly. "You have a charming accent, your lordship. Are you from America?"

"I am. I grew up in New York. Have you ever been to the United States?"

"No," Miss Gibb said sadly. "Amelia has no interest in America. It's too new. She's drawn only to dusty ruins and smelly camels."

Jason chuckled. Her candor was refreshing. "And what interests you?"

"I like things that are new and modern. I have ridden on the underground railway," she confided, lowering her voice should anyone overhear. "Amelia would be furious if she knew."

"Did you go alone?" Jason asked.

"No, a friend accompanied me. It was a little scary, because it's underground, but quite exhilarating. I mean to do it again. Have you tried it?"

"I haven't had the pleasure," Jason admitted. "But I mean to."

"You must," Miss Gibb said, grinning happily. "It really is extraordinary how quickly it moves. Faster than any carriage or omnibus. And definitely faster than a ship," she said, wrinkling her nose in distaste. "I hate boats. They take forever, and I get seasick."

"Miss Gibb, your cabin was directly across from Blake Upton's. Is that correct?" Jason asked.

"Yes."

"What did you think of him?"

"I thought he would make a lovely father," she replied.

Jason paused, unsure how to take that. "You mean to your child?" he asked carefully.

"No, to me. I don't remember my father, but I thought it would be so nice to have a kind, patient man like that to look after me. It would make me feel safe and loved, and I would have someone to see to my future."

Jason was dumbstruck. Daniel had described Miss Gibb as detached and aloof, but this young woman was sharing her innermost thoughts with him. Was it because he was American and she thought he was freer in his ways or because her aunt wasn't at home and she was desperate to talk to someone about how she really felt? He wanted to keep her talking.

"Do you not feel safe and loved now?"

"On, no, I didn't mean that at all. I am safe, and Amelia loves me very much. We all wish for a different life sometimes, don't we?" she asked wistfully.

"Yes, I suppose we do."

"Is that why you came here, to have a different life?" Miss Gibb asked.

"Yes," Jason replied truthfully. "Life in New York had become…" He let the sentence trail off, unwilling to elaborate.

"Become what?" Miss Gibb asked.

"Unhappy," Jason said at last. "I lost the people I loved, one by one."

"I'm very sorry to hear that. Are you happy here?"

"I am," Jason replied, smiling despite his best efforts to remain serious. "I have a baby daughter. Lily," he said proudly.

Miss Gibb's eyes misted with tears. "How I would love to have a family," she whispered. "I adore children."

"There's still plenty of time. You are very young," Jason said, hoping to reassure her.

"I don't meet many eligible men, my lord," Miss Gibb said sadly. "Amelia sees to that."

Jason heard the bitterness in her voice, but as much as he wanted to cheer her up, he wasn't there to talk about her future prospects. Daniel had a murder to solve, and Jason's purpose for calling on Mrs. Foster and Miss Gibb was to help him.

"Miss Gibb, did you get the impression that someone might have meant Mr. Upton harm?" Jason said, hoping she wouldn't see the change in subject as indifference on his part.

"Not at all. The members of the group argued, rather loudly at times, but there was no malice in it. They were passionate about their work and eager to express their views."

"You noticed no animosity between anyone?" Jason prodded.

"Not really. They all respected Mr. Upton and wanted his approval."

"Even Michael Dillane?"

"Even Mr. Dillane. I think he would have liked Mr. Upton for a father as well. He's the natural son of Lord Belford, you know," Miss Gibb said.

"Yes, he did tell us that."

"I felt sorry for him. He is lonely, and a bit lost."

"What about the other members of the team?" Jason asked, hoping she'd keep the observations coming.

Miss Gibb turned toward the window, her gaze thoughtful. "Mr. Longhorn is very nice. Chivalrous," she added. "I didn't much care for Dr. Scarborough. Too rigid for my taste, but he always treated me with the utmost civility. And Mr. Thomas is a firebrand," she said, smiling. "I liked him. I think we'll be hearing his name a lot in the future."

"What about Mr. Moffat?" Jason asked. He couldn't help noticing the softening of her gaze.

"Mr. Moffat is very kind," Miss Gibb said, opting for the most innocuous of descriptions.

"He taught you to play shesh besh," Jason said, watching her.

"Yes. He loves that game. We all played to pass the time. There's not much to do aboard a ship like the *Sea Witch* that's not a passenger vessel."

"Did your aunt play too?"

"No. Amelia kept to a strict schedule. It made it easier for her to manage the time."

"Miss Gibb, tell me about that last dinner," Jason invited. "Were there any disagreements or barbed comments exchanged between any of the diners?"

"No. Everyone was in high spirits. Even Amelia was in a good mood and drank two glasses of wine."

"Did you see Mr. Upton after dinner, or perhaps hear something after you had retired?"

"I'm afraid I didn't," Miss Gibb said. "I drank rather a lot of wine at dinner and went straight to bed after returning to the cabin. Amelia says I sleep like the dead," she said, coloring slightly.

"Did Mrs. Foster return to the cabin with you?"

"She did, but only to retrieve her coat and hat. She went up on deck for a breath of air."

"Was this something she did every night?" Jason asked.

"No, but she said she wasn't ready for bed and needed to take a walk."

"Were you still awake when she returned to the cabin?"

"No. I fell asleep right away."

"Did you sleep through the night?" Jason asked.

He knew he was grasping at straws. If Susanna Gibb had gone straight to bed and slept through the night, she wasn't likely to have heard anything, even unwittingly. Jason wished Mrs. Foster would come home. She sounded like the more observant of the two and, having been up on deck, might have seen something either there or on her return to the cabin. Perhaps she could identify Blake Upton's companion.

"Yes, I did. I woke early, but all was quiet until the crew began to prepare for our arrival in Southampton. Amelia and I had breakfast in our cabin and finished packing. It took a long time to actually disembark," Miss Gibb said.

Jason looked around the room, his mind working furiously. Was there anything else he could ask her? It seemed pointless to keep going over the same ground, since she hadn't told him anything she hadn't already shared with Daniel. She clearly hadn't seen or heard anything and had been bored during the voyage and eager to get back home. As his gaze traveled around the room, it settled on a book lying on a side table next to a comfortable leather wingchair.

"Were you reading when I arrived?" Jason asked, leaning sideways in an effort to see the name of the volume, which was partially obscured by the pence-nez resting atop, the gold chain pooled on the red morocco leather of the cover and reflecting the sunlight pouring in through the open window. He tilted his head to get a better view but could only make out one word—*Sappho*.

Jason had never read Sappho, but he'd heard of her poetry while at medical school in New York. At one of their student gatherings, a friend of his had regaled them with tales of Sappho's unashamed love of women, deriving great pleasure from their obvious shock that such radical sentiments went all the way back to nearly a thousand years before the birth of Christ, when Sappho had lived on the island of Lesbos. That same friend had educated them about what it meant to be of the sapphic persuasion, or a lesbian, as he'd called it. Until then, it had never occurred to Jason that such a relationship could even be possible, much less romanticized so openly in ancient poetry.

"No, that's Amelia's book. It's something hideously boring. It always is," she replied, but bright spots of color bloomed in her cheeks, confirming to Jason that she knew exactly what the book was about.

"I quite like poetry," Jason said, but his mind was no longer on the conversation. His gaze returned to the gold chain, its links exactly like the ones they'd found inside the crate. He turned back to Miss Gibb. "That's a lovely chain. I wonder where Mrs. Foster got it. My wife is always misplacing her spectacles. I should get her a chain just like it so that she can start wearing them around her neck."

Miss Gibb glanced at the chain, as if noticing it for the first time. "You'll have to ask Amelia. She just had it replaced. Her old one broke when she snagged it. Good thing it happened just before we arrived back in England, or she would have had to carry her pence-nez in her hand all through the voyage home or use that hideous black ribbon she's been wearing for the past few days."

"What did she snag it on?" Jason asked. "The chain doesn't look very delicate."

"I have no idea. She didn't say."

Jason took a deep breath, considering his options. It was no coincidence that Amelia Foster had just replaced the chain for her pence-nez, given that she'd broken the one she'd had, either when she snagged it on the crate or when Blake Upton grabbed for her as she tried to administer the chloroform-soaked handkerchief. Perhaps she'd had an accomplice, perhaps not, but it was clear that she had been involved in the man's death, and it most likely had nothing to do with either the excavation or the artefact she had used to hide his body. The method of murder and the use of the sarcophagus had been a clever misdirection to divert suspicion toward the members of the archeological team.

Amelia Foster's motive was personal, her need to kill arising either out of fear or rage. And both those emotions had been stoked by Susanna Gibb. Having made note of the book Amelia Foster was reading, Jason thought he might have an inkling of what he was dealing with, but he needed to be sure. Even if Amelia Foster preferred women, it didn't mean that Susanna Gibb was her lover. She could still be her niece, or even her daughter, and if Blake Upton had made overtures to Miss Gibb, Mrs. Foster would have been furious, given that the man was already married and could do nothing but hurt the woman she loved.

"Miss Gibb, were you romantically involved with Blake Upton?" Jason asked bluntly, taking the young woman by surprise.

"No! Why would you ask me that, Lord Redmond?" she asked, looking genuinely perplexed.

"Because I believe you are the motive we've been searching for," he said, wondering if he should be this frank. But he needed answers and hoped Miss Gibb would slip up in her innocence and share something vital.

Susanna Gibb's head jerked back, as if he'd slapped her. "I had nothing to do with Blake Upton's death," she cried, the color rising in her face. "He barely noticed me. He was always talking to Amelia, since she showed such an interest in his work."

For a fraction of a moment, Jason thought that he'd got the wrong end of the stick and it had been Mrs. Foster who'd been involved with Blake Upton. Perhaps he'd rejected her or had forced himself on her. But this theory didn't feel right. Amelia Foster would not have murdered a married man for rejecting her advances. Not after knowing him for only a few weeks and knowing all along that there could be no future for them. Nor was there any evidence of sexual violence, unless Blake Upton had lured Mrs. Foster into the hold under some pretense. But if he had, she wouldn't have had the chloroform ready, or the tool she had used to scoop out his brain. No, she had been the predator, not Blake Upton, and Jason still believed she'd been motivated by anger, or possibly a terrible jealousy.

"And who was talking to *you*, Miss Gibb?" Jason asked softly.

Miss Gibb looked frightened, cornered even, but then raised her chin defiantly, as if she no longer wished to keep her secret. "Peter. Peter Moffat," she said at last. "We love each other, and we're going to be married."

Had she been facing the other way, she would have seen Amelia Foster appear in the doorway, but it was Jason who saw her first. She stood rooted to the spot, the expression on her face difficult to categorize. He would have said it was fury, but that would be too simple a description. She looked stunned, heartbroken, and deranged all at once, her eyes blazing with emotion, her mouth open in shock.

Following his gaze, Miss Gibb spun around, her hand going to her breast. "Amelia, I didn't hear you come in," she said, her lips stretching into a watery smile.

"Clearly not. And who is this?" she hissed. "Another one of your admirers?"

"No. Amelia—" Miss Gibb began, but Amelia Foster didn't allow her to finish.

"You will never see Peter Moffat again. Is that understood?" Mrs. Foster looked dangerously manic, a woman who'd brook no argument.

Something came over Susanna Gibb then, and suddenly she was no longer the delicate young woman but a lioness ready to fight to the death.

"You don't own me," she said, enunciating her words as her eyes narrowed in anger. "I'm not one of your books or artefacts to be kept in a safe place and examined lovingly whenever you feel like it. You're suffocating me," Miss Gibb said, her voice steely with resolve. "And I'm leaving."

Jason glanced from one woman to the other, unsure what to do. This was clearly a private moment, and he shouldn't be a witness to their confrontation, but something told him he needed to remain. He was sure what was happening was relevant to the case, and he could hardly leave Susanna Gibb with a woman who'd already killed once. *As far as we know*, Jason's mind added unhelpfully.

Amelia Foster unbuttoned her coat, her movements jerky in her distress. She glared at him, as if deciding what to do, then turned away, all her attention focused on Miss Gibb. Her nostrils flared, and her breaths came in short gasps, her fury seemingly building rather than ebbing. She lifted her arm and pulled out an exquisite onyx and amethyst hatpin before yanking off her hat and tossing it on a chair.

Seeing the deadly intent in her gaze, Jason exploded out of his seat, but he was too late. Amelia Foster buried the hatpin in Susanna Gibb's chest, plunging it in just above the bodice and driving the sharp needle downward, toward the heart. Miss Gibb cried out, her eyes widening with shock and pain as she stared at Mrs. Foster, whose face was contorted with rage.

"You cheap whore," she spat out. "I lifted you out of the gutter. You'd have been dead in another few months if not for me, and now you will go back into the earth, where you belong." Her voice was low, the expression in her eyes vicious. She wanted to watch Susanna Gibb die, and she didn't care who knew it. Amelia Foster was driven by an emotion so deep, Jason's presence was a mere distraction, an inconvenience she'd deal with later.

Jason had about a second to decide what to do. He could help Miss Gibb or apprehend Amelia Foster before she attempted to flee. He didn't know if he could help her, but he had to try, so he turned his back on Amelia Foster just in time to catch Susanna. Her knees buckled as she began to plummet, her fall not the abrupt collapse one would expect of a person who was fatally wounded, but a slow descent, like a snowflake settling gently on the snow-covered earth, with very little fuss. A bloody flower bloomed on her breast as her hand instinctively went to the wound. Jason caught her by the wrist just as she was about to pull out the pin and maneuvered her toward the settee, laying her gently on it.

"Susanna, I'm a doctor. I will look after you," he said, but she didn't seem to hear him, her eyes glazed as her mind distanced itself from what was happening.

An instinct for self-preservation Jason had developed during the war years forced him to jerk his head back to look at Amelia Foster even before his brain registered the danger. She was not a woman to turn one's back on, not even in a dire situation such as this. Jason froze, his gaze meeting hers.

She was standing in the same spot but no longer trembling with rage. The look in her eyes was speculative, her hand steady as she held a small handgun trained on Jason. She must have pulled it out of her reticule. Did she always carry a gun, or had she feared that the investigation was progressing, suspicion circling above her like a murder of crows that would peck her eyes out as soon as she let down her guard? Strange what thoughts went through one's mind when faced with death, Jason mused as he stared down the barrel of the gun that was pointed at his chest. At such close range, the shot wouldn't go astray. If Amelia Foster pulled the trigger, he was a dead man.

An image of Katie with Lily in her arms swam before Jason's eyes, and he felt a visceral pain in his heart. The thought of never seeing Lily again, of not watching her take her first steps or hearing her first words, of never holding Katie in his arms again or seeing the look of love in her eyes, was more painful than any gunshot wound. How had things spiraled out of control so quickly?

Amelia Foster's gaze narrowed as she brought up her other hand to steady the gun. This was it. She was about to fire. Jason knew that just as surely as he knew that nothing would save him now. Or Miss Gibb. He drew in a shaky breath, his entire being focused on the barrel of the gun.

Somewhere in the background, he heard a noise, and then Amelia Foster fired. The gunshot sounded like a pop, like a bottle of champagne being opened on New Year's Eve. Jason braced for impact, but it seemed Amelia Foster had heard the noise as well, and it had broken her concentration. Jason's body jerked back as the bullet entered his shoulder, a searing pain tearing through him and forcing him back. He nearly fell atop Susanna Gibb, who lay perfectly still on the settee.

Jason sank into a chair, his hand going to his wounded shoulder and coming away wet with blood. Would she shoot again? How many bullets did she have? Amelia Foster raised the gun again, but at that moment, Daniel exploded into the room, his eyes wild with fear.

"Jason," he cried when he saw the blood on Jason's hand. Daniel's gaze slid to Susanna Gibb, who moaned softly.

The four of them were like some tableau in a play that was billed as a tragedy and would end badly, to the great satisfaction of the audience. Jason felt dizzy with pain.

"Get her," he whispered as his gaze trained on Amelia Foster, who looked like a cornered rabbit.

She didn't waste any time on recriminations or explanations. Instead, she dropped the gun on the floor and turned toward the door, but her escape was blocked by Daniel. There was nowhere for her to go but deeper into the room. Jason thought she'd give up the fight and allow Daniel to arrest her, but Amelia Foster was made of sterner stuff. She wasn't about to be arrested and spend what was left of her life in jail before being publicly led to the scaffold and hanged, to the great delight of the spectators who'd come to watch her die. She had lived life on her own terms, and her resolute expression said she would die on her own terms as well.

Before Daniel could stop her, she charged toward the window. Balancing her weight on her hands on the windowsill as she leaned out, she pitched herself forward, going over headfirst. For a moment, Daniel remained frozen, but then he rushed to the window and looked out. A terrified scream pierced the quiet afternoon as someone came upon the body of Amelia Foster.

Daniel swore under his breath and turned to Jason, clearly hesitant. He had to get down there, to summon a constable, who'd fetch a wagon and help Daniel remove the body to the dead house. There'd be no autopsy, only a hasty burial arranged by the police if no one bothered to claim the body.

"Go on," Jason rasped. "It's a flesh wound. I'll be fine," he promised. He pushed to his feet and staggered into the dining room, where he grabbed several linen napkins off the table. He carefully removed his coat and pressed the napkin to the wound, then returned to the other room to see to Miss Gibb.

"Is Amelia—?" Susanna Gibb asked weakly.

"I'm afraid she's gone, Miss Gibb," Daniel said. "May the Lord have mercy on her soul. I must see to her." He looked at Jason, his face tight with concern. "Jason, shall I summon a physician?"

"I am a physician," Jason reminded him. "Go, Daniel. You're needed."

Jason heard cries of shock and calls for a constable through the open window. A small crowd must have gathered down below, the residents of Cavendish Square rushing outside to see what had happened in their peaceful haven.

Daniel thundered down the stairs, while Jason sat down on the settee next to Miss Gibb.

"I'm so sorry," she whispered. "I should have known." Tears slid down her temples and into her hair as she lay there, the tip of the hatpin protruding from her chest. "I never suspected," Miss Gibb murmured.

"Susanna, I'm going to pull out the pin. It will be painful, but given that you're still with us, I think it missed any vital organs. You were very lucky," Jason said softly.

"Was I?" Susanna Gibb asked, her gaze filled with pain.

"Yes, you were," Jason assured her as he grabbed hold of the pin and pulled it out very carefully. Blood flowed into Susanna's bodice as soon as the tip was removed, and Jason pressed a napkin to the wound, then lowered his head to listen to Susanna's chest. Her breathing was ragged, but he thought it was due to her emotional state rather than the injury.

"Take a deep breath for me," Jason instructed.

Susanna did. She was shaky but managed to do it several more times. Jason listened intently, holding his own breath so as not to miss a gurgling sound in the vicinity of the heart or a hissing in the lungs. Miraculously, the pin had missed both the heart and the lungs.

"You will be in pain for a few days, but unless there's an internal hemorrhage, you will recover quickly. I will make sure you're comfortable and return to check on you tomorrow," he assured her.

"You're bleeding," Susanna said weakly.

Had Jason been alone, he would have slumped down on the settee and closed his eyes, allowing the nausea that threatened to overwhelm him to pass. He hoped he wasn't going to be sick, not when Susanna Gibb needed reassurance that all would be well. Jason could feel the bullet lodged in his shoulder, the pain excruciating every time he moved his left arm. He pressed the napkin more firmly down on the wound and staggered toward the wingchair, sitting down and leaning back before he allowed himself to close his eyes and drift.

He barely heard the frightened cry of the maid who'd come into the room and come face to face with the carnage, or the return of Daniel, who'd brought a middle-aged man with him, a medical bag gripped in his gloved hand.

"Jason, can you hear me?" Daniel demanded as he squatted before him. "Jason?"

"I'll be fine. I just need a few minutes," Jason muttered.

"You need considerably more than a few minutes," Daniel argued.

Daniel helped Jason to Amelia Foster's bed while Dr. Palmer and the maid looked to Susanna. There was really nothing the doctor could do for her save clean and bandage the wound. Susanna was put to bed and instructed to rest. Then Dr. Palmer came to attend on Jason. He examined the wound and shook his head as if his worst suspicions had just been confirmed.

"The bullet will need to come out," he announced. "I'm going to give you some laudanum for the pain and then extract the projectile. Inspector Haze tells me you're a physician yourself," Dr. Palmer said conversationally as he searched in his bag for the right instrument.

"Yes," Jason replied.

"American, eh?" Dr. Palmer said. "Fought in the war, did you?"

Jason nodded miserably. He really wasn't in the mood to make small talk. The pain had dulled somewhat, but he felt weak and nauseated and wished the doctor would just get on with it. He hadn't eaten in hours, and the weakness and lightheadedness were exacerbated by the lack of food. However, had he eaten, he would have vomited, so perhaps this was for the best. Jason drew in deep, even breaths to combat his anxiety.

He was always the doctor, rarely the patient, and he hated the feeling of helplessness, as well as the knowledge that he was lying in the bed of a woman who'd just killed herself and had tried to kill him and Susanna Gibb. Despite his impaired condition, he couldn't help but wonder if he could have handled the situation differently. It was his fault Susanna Gibb had been attacked and Amelia Foster was probably now lying on a slab in the dead house. Not a place he'd ever wish to end up. What a waste of her life, Jason thought as he tried not to watch the doctor make his preparations.

He knew what Dr. Palmer would do and braced himself. The extraction would be the worst part. Then he'd just need some time to heal. Katie would be incensed once she found out what had happened, and rightly so. He'd blundered into danger without once considering that he might not come out alive.

Dr. Palmer mixed some laudanum into water and held the glass to Jason's lips, urging him to drink.

"There now. You'll feel better in a moment," he said, nodding with satisfaction as Jason's eyelids began to droop,

Daniel's solid form dissolving into a dark silhouette as the laudanum took effect.

Chapter 27

When Jason woke, the sky beyond the window was dark, silvery moonlight washing the room in its pale glow. Dr. Palmer must have given him a strong dose of laudanum to keep him insensible for this long, but he probably would have done the same in order to give his patient an opportunity to rest undisturbed as the body began the natural healing process.

Jason shifted his shoulder experimentally. A slow burn spread from the wound toward his chest and upper arm, but the pain wasn't sharp, nor could he feel the bullet lodged in his soft tissue as he had before. He tried to sit up, but a wave of dizziness and nausea assaulted him, so he lay back down, wondering when someone would come to check on him. He needed to see to some basic needs and ask for something to drink. His mouth was dry, and his belly felt alarmingly empty, reminding him of his days at Andersonville when he was always starving. He didn't think he could stomach anything more substantial than broth and maybe a piece of bread, but he needed to eat something before too long.

A dark shape that proved to be Daniel materialized in the doorway a few minutes later, his face tight with anxiety as he advanced further into the room and into the beam of moonlight. He breathed a sigh of relief when he saw Jason was awake.

"How do you feel?" Daniel asked.

"Not too bad, all things considered. Please tell me you didn't send a wire to Redmond Hall."

"I didn't, but I did consider it. Katherine will be very angry with me when she finds out you've been shot and I didn't send for her right away."

"I was in good hands," Jason replied. "I could use some help, actually."

Once Jason was back in bed, Daniel brought him some water and settled in a chair next to the bed. "I asked the maid to heat some beef tea," he said. "You should eat something."

Jason nodded. "How's Miss Gibb?"

"She was in a lot of pain before, but she's sleeping now. Best thing for her. She's still in shock."

"I'd say," Jason agreed. "She never saw that coming. If not for your timely arrival, Amelia Foster might have fired off another shot. Did you know she was Blake Upton's murderer?"

"I realized it after speaking to Peter Moffat."

"I guessed when I saw the chain from her pince-nez and Miss Gibb confirmed Mrs. Foster had just had it replaced, but I still don't quite see her motive for killing Blake Upton. Miss Gibb had no interest in the man."

"No, but she is in love with Peter Moffat, who's about the same height, fair and blue-eyed like Blake Upton. A woman with impaired vision might have mistaken one for the other in a dim corridor, and Peter Moffat admitted to me that he and Miss Gibb met in Blake Upton's cabin to snatch a few moments of privacy while Mrs. Foster went down for her afternoon nap. Perhaps seeing her niece emerging from Blake Upton's cabin had been enough of a provocation."

"Have you questioned Miss Gibb?" Jason asked.

"No. She wasn't in any condition to answer my questions, but I did send a boy to the Yard to deliver a message to Superintendent Ransome so he would know the case has been solved and the killer is no longer on the loose."

"Terrible way to die," Jason said, recalling the sight of Amelia Foster hurling herself out the window.

"Are there good ways to die?" Daniel asked, looking wary.

"In bed of old age with your family at your side," Jason replied, smiling wryly.

"But if you were to be murdered, how would you prefer to go?"

Jason thought about that for a moment. "I don't know. Shot through the heart, I suppose. That's the quickest way. What about you?"

Daniel shook his head. "All I ask is that I don't know I'm about to die. Drowning or hanging or burning or stabbing all take time for the victim to die, so he faces the realization that there will be no eleventh-hour rescue. He knows these are his final moments. I think that moment is probably worse than the death itself."

"The loss of hope is its own type of death," Jason agreed.

"What do you think Miss Gibb will do now?"

"She'll marry Peter Moffat and hopefully lead an uneventful and respectable life. I don't think she was Mrs. Foster's niece," Jason said, watching Daniel's face to see if he'd come to the same conclusion.

"Do you think she was her daughter?" Daniel asked.

"The possibility had crossed my mind, but I don't think that was the nature of their relationship."

Jason was about to explain when the maidservant arrived with the food.

"Eat and go to sleep," Daniel said, rising from the chair. "I'm going to bed down in the parlor. I'm exhausted. We'll speak to Miss Gibb tomorrow. I don't think she's going anywhere."

"Goodnight, Daniel," Jason said, glad of the interruption. He wanted to hear what Miss Gibb had to say before voicing his own suspicions.

"What's your name?" Jason asked the maidservant as she sat down next to him, looking a bit frightened.

"Tess," the girl said. She held the cup of broth to Jason's lips as he raised his head to drink. "What will happen to me, sir?" the girl asked, her voice cracking with desperation. "Where will I go?"

Tess clearly didn't think Miss Gibb would be staying on in the apartment. Perhaps she knew something.

"Was Mrs. Foster a good mistress?" Jason asked as he took a bite of the bread and chewed slowly, hoping he'd be able to keep it down.

"I s'pose," the girl replied, averting her gaze. "She took me on without a character," she added.

"Perhaps Miss Gibb can write a reference for you so you can get another position."

Tess nodded miserably. "It's 'ard to find employment, 'specially with the summer comin'. The rich go to their country 'ouses. Must be nice," she said with a deep sigh.

Jason finished the broth and gently pushed away her hand as she held out more bread. "I don't want any more. Thank you."

Tess stood to leave. "Sleep well, m'lord."

"And you," Jason replied, fatigue and the remnants of the laudanum in his system already dragging him back into darkness.

Chapter 28

Saturday, April 4

The next time Jason woke, bright sunlight was streaming through the window, the smell of coffee wafting into the room and making his stomach rumble with hunger. Daniel appeared as if by magic, looking a bit rumpled, his jaw dark with stubble, but relatively well rested.

"Seems Mrs. Foster enjoyed coffee as much as you do," Daniel said, his gaze appraising Jason's appearance.

"I'm all right," Jason reassured him. And he was. His shoulder pained him, as expected, but his skin was cool to the touch, and he felt stronger and more alert. "Is Miss Gibb awake?"

"Yes. Tess is just feeding her breakfast. Shall I bring you some coffee and buttered toast?" Daniel asked.

Jason smiled. "You know I'll never say no to coffee."

Once Jason had eaten, Daniel helped him dress, and together they went to see Miss Gibb, who was lying in bed, propped with pillows. Her dark hair cascaded over her shoulders, and her face was nearly as white as the pillowcase her head rested on, but she seemed alert. Dr. Palmer was due to come check on her within the hour.

"How do you feel, Miss Gibb?" Jason asked as he sat down in a chair Daniel had pulled up for him.

"It hurts," Miss Gibb said sadly. "But I'm grateful to be alive. Poor Amelia," she whispered. "I still can't believe she met with such a dreadful end."

"It was her choice to die the way she did," Daniel pointed out.

"It was either that or the noose," Miss Gibb replied.

"That was her choice as well," Daniel said. "Did you know she had killed Blake Upton?"

Miss Gibb glanced toward the window, her lip quivering with emotion. "I was beginning to suspect."

"Miss Gibb, what exactly happened out there?" Jason asked, tilting his head toward the parlor.

"I don't really know," Miss Gibb murmured.

"Susanna, you are not in any trouble," Daniel said gently. "Anything you share with us will remain confidential, except for the facts of the murder."

Susanna Gibb nodded, her gaze sliding away from them as if she were looking at something neither of them could see, recalling a place where no one else could go.

"Amelia wasn't really my aunt," Susanna said at last. "She found me on the street, seven years ago."

"Were you an orphan?"

"My parents had died, one after the other, and I had nowhere to go. I had no family to turn to or any skills someone might be willing to pay for. I tried to find employment, but no one would have me. I had nothing to recommend me save my willingness to work, and no one was feeling particularly charitable that autumn. I was eating what I stole or found in the gutter and sleeping in doorways. If I hoped to survive, I'd have to either go into a workhouse or start selling myself. Given those choices, I wasn't sure I wanted to live. What was there for me to aspire to? The best I could hope for was to become another whore, who'd be lucky to make it to twenty-five before succumbing to disease or despair. I gave up and waited for hunger and cold to claim me.

"Amelia spotted me on one of her walks and asked if I wanted to go home with her. I don't know why she chose me or what had taken her to Spitalfields that day, but I had nothing to lose, so I went. It was never too late to die, I decided. Amelia brought me here," Susanna said softly. "It looked like a palace to me. I'd never seen such finery in all my days. She fed me and then had her maid prepare a bath. I'd never had a bath before," she confided. "When my parents were alive, we washed in parts, using a rag and a basin of cold water. I soaked until the water grew cold, and then Amelia wrapped me in a soft towel and helped me dress in her castoffs. The skirts were too long, and I couldn't hope to fill out the bodice, but for the first time in my life, I was truly clean and wearing fine things. After supper, she put me to bed. This bed," Susanna added softly, as if she could still feel the awe she'd felt that day. "It was soft and clean, and I was warm. I'd never slept in a room by myself before. We had one room when I was growing up, and I'd shared a cot with my sister before she died." A silence settled on the room as Susanna's voice trailed off, her gaze clouded with memories.

"What happened the next day?" Daniel asked at last.

"Amelia asked if I'd like to stay. There would always be food and a warm bed for me to sleep in and clothes and trips abroad. She said we could tell everyone I was her niece, come to live with her."

"Did she ask for anything in return?" Daniel inquired.

Susanna shook her head. "Only that I be her companion. Her husband had died the year before, and she was lonely."

"Did she not have any children?"

"She had two stillborn sons early in the marriage, and then they stopped trying. Amelia said she and her husband were good friends but nothing more."

"So you stayed?" Jason asked. He could almost see that desperate young girl who'd been presented with what must have seemed like a miracle.

"Of course. I couldn't believe my luck. I thought God had sent an angel to look after me."

"And was Amelia Foster an angel?"

"Yes. She was very kind to me. She bought me clothes, took me out in her carriage, and even took me to the seaside that first summer. I had never seen the sea," Susanna said dreamily.

"Then what happened?" Daniel asked.

"After the first few weeks together, Amelia started teaching me to read and write and bought me a sketchbook and pencils because she noticed I liked to draw. We settled into a routine, and I felt happy and secure."

Susanna drew in a shuddering breath and went on, now at the point where it seemed she needed to get everything off her chest. "One night there was a terrible thunderstorm, and I was frightened. Amelia came to my room and got into bed with me. She comforted me and slept with me and made me feel safe. She came back the next night, and the night after that. At first, she only slept next to me, but then she began to touch me. She said she wanted to give me pleasure."

Susanna turned away again, leaving them to stare at her delicate profile. "I let her do whatever she wanted because I wasn't going to go back out there. It'd be like stepping off a cliff after the life of comfort I had led for the past few months. Anything she did to me was preferable to that."

"Did she hurt you?" Jason asked softly.

"No. No one had ever touched me before. Not even my parents. I had never been hugged or kissed or cherished. I'd had very little physical contact with anyone since my sister died and I was left to sleep alone. The things Amelia did made me feel good, and loved. And in time, I learned how to give her pleasure in return. I was her companion in the true sense of the word. I was her wife," Susanna said without rancor. "And she was my husband.

She kept me, loved me, indulged me, and spoke to me of our future."

Jason noticed the look of distaste on Daniel's face. What he was hearing disgusted and appalled him, and Susanna noticed.

"Don't judge Amelia harshly, Inspector," she said. "Life can never be easy for someone like her. She had endured years of marriage to a man before she was brave enough to tell him she didn't desire him and wished to be left in peace. He could have divorced her or had her locked up in an asylum. It's not a difficult thing to do if you set your mind to it. And then, once she was free, she was lonely and frightened, a woman living on the fringes of polite society. There are others like her, there always have been, but unlike homosexual men, who have secret clubs and safe places where they can meet, women are left on their own, locked in a prison of nature's making with no means of escape. Amelia had no notion how to go about finding a mate, so she created one."

"By making you beholden to her," Daniel said with disgust.

Susanna's analogy had brought Frankenstein to Jason's mind, a creature created by its master with no regard for anything but his own needs and desires.

"Are all women not beholden to their husbands, Inspector?" Susanna asked. "Or the men who pay them for their favors? We all make compromises in order to survive."

"Did you resent this future Mrs. Foster had planned for you?" Jason asked.

"Not at first. I was happy to have a home and someone who cared for me. Returning her love was a small price to pay for everything she'd given me and would continue to give in the future. She owns this house, you know," Susanna said softly. "Among other things. And she left everything to me in her will. She made sure I'd be provided for once she was gone."

"And you were willing to throw it all away?" Daniel asked, a note of disbelief creeping into his voice.

"I met Peter Moffat. It was about a year ago. I had gone to a photographer's studio to have my picture taken. It was to be a gift for Amelia's birthday. Peter was so handsome and charming, and he made me feel at ease. Living with Amelia, I had virtually no exposure to men, other than the men we met on our travels, but those encounters were casual, and we hardly ever saw them again. I was intimidated by anyone who showed an interest in me. That day was the first time I felt drawn to a man as a woman might. Peter wanted to see me again, but I refused and hurried back home like a frightened rabbit. I had Tess collect the photographs for me because I was too afraid to see him again."

"And then you met again aboard the *Sea Witch*," Daniel said, watching Susanna intently.

"What were the chances of that happening?" Susanna asked. "It had to be fate. I was given a second chance, and I wasn't going to waste it. I realized that although I loved Amelia, I loved Peter in a different way. I wanted a life with him, a family. I couldn't imagine growing old with Amelia, carrying on as we have for the past seven years. We cared for each other, but our life was barren. We'd always have to hide and keep our relationship secret from other people. That's why we had no friends and were never invited anywhere."

"But with Peter Moffat, you would no longer need to hide," Daniel said. "You would be accepted by society."

"Yes, but that wasn't the reason I was attracted to him. I fell in love, Inspector. I had never chosen the life Amelia had forced on me. I simply went along in order to survive."

"Did you know Amelia's reaction would be so violent?" Daniel asked.

"I never imagined she'd kill her rival. But Peter and I were discreet. I knew she'd be angry if she caught us together, so I made sure to only see Peter when Amelia was asleep."

"But she learned your secret," Daniel said. "Or thought she did. She saw you coming out of Blake Upton's cabin, and because her vision was poor, she mistook Peter Moffat for Blake Upton. They were of similar coloring and build, and she would have done anything to keep you from leaving her."

Susanna nodded miserably.

"Can you surmise what happened next?" Daniel asked. He'd already figured it out, but he wanted to hear Susanna Gibb's version of events, since she'd been the one person to truly know Amelia Foster.

"That last night, Amelia returned to the cabin after dinner to fetch her coat and hat. She went up on deck and met with Blake Upton. I think she asked him to show her the sarcophagus. She'd been so inquisitive and impressed with his accomplishments, he wouldn't have thought it strange. I suppose he was eager to see it again himself. He was obsessed with it," Susanna added.

"Go on," Daniel prompted.

"Amelia was clever and brave. The only thing she truly feared was loneliness. I can only assume that she stole the chloroform from Dr. Scarborough's cabin and used it to incapacitate Blake Upton. That was the only way she could have overpowered a man his size."

"Do you know what she used to extract his brain?" Jason asked.

"Amelia bought a wooden flute in a souk in Damascus. She had no need of it, but the flutes were sold by a small boy and his blind grandfather, and Amelia felt pity for them and wanted to help. The flute was long and narrow and had a narrowed end where the mouth went. I haven't seen it since we returned, so I think she might have used that. I expect she thought that murdering him that way and stowing his body in the coffin would divert suspicion away from her and toward the members of the team."

"Did she realize she'd killed the wrong man?" Daniel asked.

Susanna shook her head. "I don't think so, which was why I didn't see Peter or attempt to communicate with him after returning to London. I didn't want Amelia to guess. She was watching me and gauging my reaction to the news, so I cried for Blake Upton and carried on as if I'd suffered an unbearable loss. I did it to keep Peter safe."

"But you and Peter Moffat were planning to elope," Daniel said. "How did you hope to accomplish that?"

"We hatched a plan before leaving the ship. Of course, we didn't know then that Blake Upton was going to be murdered. Once I began to suspect Amelia had a hand in the murder, I realized I'd have one chance to get away, and I had to make sure she never found me, or Peter."

"Did Peter Moffat know the truth of your relationship with Amelia Foster?" Daniel asked.

"No. I never told him. I simply said that my aunt wouldn't approve of the match and I'd rather tell her after the deed was done. I would have written to her in time," Susanna added. She looked imploringly from Daniel to Jason. "You won't tell Peter, will you?"

"No," Jason said before Daniel had a chance to respond.

All anyone needed to know was that Amelia Foster had been trying to protect her niece and had killed the man who'd led Susanna astray. Her true motive had died with her, as had her love.

"Will you mourn Amelia?" Jason asked, taking Susanna's hand in his.

She looked at him, and her eyes misted with tears. "Yes, I will. She became my jailer toward the end, but she had been my savior. I don't know if I'd still be here if it weren't for her. I don't blame her for being the way she was. It was never a choice for her. She only wanted to love and be loved, like any other person, and she lost her reason when she realized she was about to lose me.

She simply couldn't bear it," Susanna said softly. She looked drawn, her mouth drooping with fatigue.

"Get some rest," Jason said.

"I must send a message to Peter," Susanna said as she sank deeper into the pillows. "Can you please send Tess in?"

"Of course," Jason replied as he pushed to his feet. He was tired as well but had no desire to remain in the apartment a moment longer.

Chapter 29

Jason felt vastly better by that evening, having rested and been fussed over by Mrs. Pimm, who fed him roast beef and potatoes and supplied endless cups of tea because evidently that was the cure for all ailments, even a gunshot wound. Now, settled before the fire in the parlor, Jason tossed back a brandy and held out his glass for more. Daniel silently poured, likely too tired to question the wisdom of getting drunk.

"Are you going to tell Katherine the truth of what happened?" Daniel asked. "About the relationship between Amelia Foster and Susanna Gibb, I mean."

"Of course."

"You don't think she'll be shocked?" Daniel asked, studying Jason with obvious admiration.

"She might be, but I don't think women should be lied to. Katherine is a strong, intelligent woman. I won't insult her by treating her like a child."

"Do you think Susanna Gibb will be happy with Peter Moffat?" Daniel asked.

"I hope so. She deserves to be happy, but I'm sure it will take time for her to come to terms with everything that's happened. Susanna Gibb was unwittingly responsible for two deaths."

"It wasn't her fault," Daniel argued.

"No, it wasn't, but she'll still have to live with the consequences for the rest of her life. Had she been honest, things might have turned out differently."

"Doesn't seem like she had much choice," Daniel pointed out. "If she had confronted Amelia Foster and informed her of her intention to marry Peter Moffat, she might have killed him instead of Blake Upton." Daniel shook his head in dismay. "I can't imagine spending my life with a partner who's so jealous and possessive, but love often turns ugly, doesn't it?" Daniel's gaze was unbearably sad. He wanted Jason to think he was speaking of Amelia Foster and Susanna Gibb, but Jason thought Daniel was reflecting on Sarah's love for Felix and her inability to accept his death, a love that was destroying their lives.

"But it's still worth the risk," Jason said.

"Even if that love breaks your heart?"

"Even then."

"Jason?" Daniel's face turned a mottled shade of pink, a sure indication that he was about to ask Jason something he found extremely embarrassing. "How does a lesbian relationship work? In the practical sense, I mean."

"The relationship has a sexual component, much like a heterosexual marriage."

"But how do they…" Daniel became silent, clearly trying to visualize the logistics of such a union and failing utterly. "Never mind," he said. "It doesn't matter."

"Suffice it to say, they give and receive sensual pleasure," Jason said. "A male appendage is not necessary to achieve climax."

Daniel nodded. "I do feel the ignoramus at times," he confided.

"Alternative forms of love have been around for as long as the human race itself," Jason said.

"As has murder," Daniel replied quietly.

"As has murder," Jason agreed. "Well, I'm off to bed. I'm more than ready to leave this day behind."

"I will accompany you to Birch Hill tomorrow," Daniel announced.

"There's no need. I'm perfectly all right, Daniel."

Daniel smiled shyly. "I'm going home to see Sarah."

Jason raised his glass in a toast. "To love."

"To forgiveness," Daniel added quietly.

Epilogue

June 1868

Jason washed his hands and pulled off the linen cap he used when performing surgeries. The operating theater had been nearly full, the surgical students at St. George's Hospital always eager to watch one of Jason's operations. Today he'd performed a tonsillectomy on a four-year-old child, a simple enough procedure as long as the child was in a deep sleep with the aid of chloroform. The child's parents had not been allowed to be present, despite the fact that the father was a member of Parliament and wielded considerable weight with the College of Surgeons. He saw them now, waiting just outside, their faces tight with worry.

"Is Tommy all right?" the boy's mother cried. She was wringing her hands and was as pale as the overcast sky beyond the window.

"He's absolutely fine. You will be able to sit with him once he's been settled on the ward," Jason replied.

"Thank you, my lord," the father said, holding out his hand.

Jason shook it and continued down the corridor. He had a patient to check on whose appendix he'd removed yesterday.

"My lord?"

Jason turned to find a young constable running after him. Jason had seen him before and thought his name was Napier.

"Constable Napier, how can I help?" Jason asked.

Constable Napier stopped and drew in a deep breath. He looked as if he'd run all the way to the hospital. "Inspector Haze requires your assistance, sir. There's been a murder."

"Where?"

"In Half-Moon Street. A woman was found dead inside a locked room, sir," the constable explained breathlessly. "Stabbed in the throat."

"Might it have been a suicide?" Jason asked.

"Inspector Haze doesn't think so, sir."

Jason didn't bother to ask any more questions. He'd find out more once he arrived at the scene of the crime. He asked Constable Napier to wait while he changed out of his surgical smock and put on his coat and hat.

"Lead the way, Constable," Jason said, and they walked out into the gray September morning.

The End

Please turn the page for an excerpt from Murder Half Moon Street
A Redmond and Haze Mystery Book 8

Notes

I hope you've enjoyed this installment of the Redmond and Haze mysteries and will check out future books. Reviews on Amazon and Goodreads are much appreciated.

I'd love to hear your thoughts and suggestions. I can be found at:

irina.shapiro@yahoo.com, www.irinashapiroauthor.com,

or https://www.facebook.com/IrinaShapiro2/.

If you would like to join my Victorian mysteries mailing list, please use this link.

https://landing.mailerlite.com/webforms/landing/u9d9o2

An Excerpt from Murder in Half Moon Street
A Redmond and Haze Mystery Book 8

Prologue

Valerie Shaw carefully balanced the tray in her hands as she walked up the stairs, careful not to spill the scalding tea. The only item on the tray besides the cup and saucer was a plate of lightly buttered toast spread with orange marmalade. Her mistress requested the same thing every morning and usually left half her breakfast untouched, mindful of preserving her figure. Valerie was all for keeping a trim waist, but if she were ever served breakfast in bed, she'd ask for soft-boiled eggs, toast smothered in butter, strawberry jam, and a pot of chocolate, which she would drink down to the last drop. She was sick of the milky tea and porridge Mrs. Taft served below stairs.

Dragging her mind away from food, Valerie set the tray on the hall table and knocked on her mistress's door before turning the handle. The door failed to open. Puzzled, Valerie tried again. Miss Grant never locked her door at night. Valerie called out, asking Miss Grant if she was all right, but received no answer. In fact, the silence inside the room was ominous. Valerie looked around to make sure no one was about and pressed her face to the door, peering into the keyhole. She wasn't one to listen at doors or spy on her mistress, but this was unusual, and she was concerned. In place of light, Valerie saw impenetrable darkness. The key was still in the lock, blocking it entirely.

As Valerie straightened, she thought she smelled something wafting from beneath the closed door. She inhaled deeper, taking an involuntary step back as her nose registered what her mind had already acknowledged. She'd grown up above a butcher's shop and recognized the odor instantly.

What she smelled was blood. And death.

Chapter 1

Monday, June 8, 1868

Gentle rays of summer sunlight bathed the city of London in a golden glow, the wide ribbon of the Thames glittering playfully as it wound its way through the sprawling metropolis. On mornings like this, London looked magical, a fairytale place where nothing ugly ever happened and everyone lived a life filled with meaning and purpose, but Jason Redmond was on his way to examine a body, a task he performed all too frequently, and only when the deceased was a victim of sudden and violent death.

Alighting from the hansom, Jason followed Constable Napier into the house on Half Moon Street, where Inspector Haze was waiting for him, his continued presence necessary to preserve the crime scene. Jason and Constable Napier were greeted by a churchlike hush, the sort of silence that was often the result of shock and disbelief. There wasn't a servant in sight, the staff most likely too unsettled to do anything but congregate in the servants' hall and talk in soft tones over cups of strong tea, their morbid curiosity outweighing their grief for the dead.

Jason glimpsed the master of the house. He was in the library, sitting by the cold hearth, a glass in his shaking hand. They'd speak later, once Jason had completed his examination and left the body to the tender mercies of the undertakers. Constable Napier led him upstairs, toward a room at the end of the carpeted corridor. The door was ajar, hanging askew off the frame. Daniel Haze was inside, his hands clasped behind his back as he gazed out the window, his face set in grim lines, his spectacles reflecting the shimmering morning light. He turned as soon as he heard them enter, relief clearly showing in his face.

"At last!" he exclaimed when he saw Jason. "What took you so long?"

"My apologies. I was in the operating theater," Jason replied, wondering exactly how long Constable Napier had been forced to wait for him. "I came as soon as I could. Tell me what happened," he invited.

"Miss Sybil Grant was found dead this morning. The room was locked from the inside, and there's no sign of the murder weapon."

Jason nodded. This promised to be another corker of a case. "Let's have a look," he said as he set his medical bag on a chair and approached the bed.

"Miss Grant's brother has forbidden an autopsy, so you will have to base your conclusions on an external examination."

Jason sighed heavily as he took in the woman on the bed. She was young, probably still in her twenties. Her face was pale where it wasn't streaked with blood, her dark hair in disarray, the curls fanned out on the pillow like Medusa's snakes, and her eyes closed as if she were still asleep. She was clad in an expensive nightgown, silk or satin, with delicate embroidery at the neckline and hem. Her trim ankles peeked from beneath the fabric, her bare feet no bigger than those of a child. To say that someone had slashed her throat would have been an understatement. At first glance, it looked as if her throat had been ripped out by a savage beast, not any weapon known to man. The wound looked like a grotesque smile, the jagged lips pulled wide to reveal bloodied gums. The woman's bloody hands were folded on her chest, but Jason was certain that wasn't how the body had been found.

"Did anyone touch her?" he asked Daniel.

"I believe Mr. Grant might have moved her hands and closed her eyes."

"Shut the door," Jason said before taking off his coat and rolling up his shirtsleeves.

He feared Mr. Grant might burst in during the examination to express his outrage at Jason's handling of the body. The cause of death was obvious, but there were many things a dead body could tell a knowledgeable surgeon, and Jason meant to hear what the victim had to say.

Daniel approached the door and pushed it shut, but the panel wouldn't fit properly into the frame due to its twisted hinges.

"I'll make sure you're not disturbed," Daniel said, pulling up a chair and setting it by the door. He lowered himself into it, clearly relieved not to have to watch Jason probe the body. For a police inspector, Daniel was a bit squeamish and preferred to leave the corpse to the experts.

Jason spent the next half hour carefully examining every inch of Miss Grant's remains. He examined the wound carefully, probed her every orifice, and then performed a pelvic exam before finally covering her with a sheet.

"Well?" Daniel demanded impatiently as Jason washed his hands in the basin, the water blooming red with the victim's blood.

"Miss Grant appears to have been in fine health prior to her death. She was well nourished, had excellent teeth, her skin was clear, and her hair lustrous."

"What's the cause of death?" Daniel asked, pulling his gaze away from the figure on the bed.

"There's considerable bruising to the neck. I think the killer tried to strangle her first, then used a long, narrow object, possibly a dull knife, to stab her in the neck. I believe the hyoid bone is fractured and the larynx is crushed, but I would need to perform a postmortem to be certain of the extent of the damage."

"Can you explain that in layman's terms?" Daniel asked. He wasn't familiar with the inner workings of the body or the nomenclature.

"Sorry. Of course. The hyoid bone is situated right here," Jason said, pointing to an area above his Adam's apple. "And the larynx is the voice box, which is a bit lower. Whoever strangled her had powerful hands and pressed down hard with the thumbs to inflict the maximum amount of damage. I'm not sure why they felt the need to stab her as well, since she was probably nearly dead by the time they reached for the weapon. Given the amount of blood on the victim's hands and beneath the nails, I think she fought for her life, but once the carotid artery was severed, death would have come almost instantly."

Jason exhaled deeply and continued. "There are indentations in the mattress on either side of her hips, which leads me to conclude that the killer straddled the victim before going for her throat. Once she was dead, they laid her out and closed her eyes."

"Could a woman have done this?" Daniel asked.

Jason considered the question. "A strong woman could have done this, yes."

"Was the victim violated?"

"There are no signs of sexual assault, but the victim was not a virgin."

"Do you think that's relevant to the case?" Daniel asked.

Jason shrugged. "Depends on the motive for the killing."

"Could she have been with child?"

"If she were, she would have been in the early stages of pregnancy. I would need to perform a postmortem to know for certain."

"Time of death?"

"Before midnight. She's been dead for close to twelve hours."

Daniel nodded. "This was a very personal, almost frenzied attack. The killer didn't simply want to kill Miss Grant, he or she wanted to watch her die. Given that the killer had brought a knife, I think we can safely assume that the murder was premeditated."

"I agree," Jason said. "The murderer had the presence of mind to lay the victim out, remove the murder weapon, and escape from a locked room."

"Since there were no signs of forced entry, it must be someone who was already in the house," Daniel mused.

"Or someone who'd gained access without needing to break in."

"You're saying they had an accomplice?"

"Possibly. Or perhaps the person had managed to get in during the day when the doors were unlocked and remained hidden until everyone had retired."

Daniel removed his spectacles and cleaned them thoroughly with his handkerchief, something he did when he needed a moment to organize his thoughts. "I'd like to begin by speaking to everyone in the house. Do you need to return to the hospital?"

"I don't have anything scheduled for the rest of the day," Jason said as he unrolled his sleeves, donned his coat, and picked up his medical bag.

Mr. Grant, who was still in the library, had left instructions with the butler that they use the drawing room for the interviews. It was a pleasant room with large windows and comfortable furnishings upholstered in aquamarine blue and silver. Several occasional tables dotted the room, and there were arrangements of silk flowers, china figurines on the mantel, and stuffed birds taking flight beneath a glass cupola on a pedestal placed between two tall windows.

Daniel settled in an armchair and took out his notebook, while Jason took the opposite chair and crossed his legs, his gaze fixed on the door. They probably made for an intimidating pair, but sometimes fear made people babble and reveal details they might otherwise have kept to themselves, so Daniel and Jason made no effort to appear friendly or relaxed.

The first witness was Valerie Shaw, Miss Grant's maid. She was about thirty, with light brown hair and nut-brown eyes in a round, friendly face. She was of average height and weight, and her black dress was neatly starched and adorned with a modest white collar that matched her cap. The woman looked utterly bewildered as she entered the drawing room and sat on the edge of the settee at Daniel's request.

"How long have you worked for Miss Grant?" Daniel asked. It was always good to know how far back a relationship went when interviewing a witness.

"Just over two years, sir."

"Miss Shaw, can you tell us what happened this morning," Daniel said, giving Miss Shaw an encouraging smile.

She nodded stoically but looked like she was just barely holding back tears. "I went to wake my mistress at eight o'clock, as I did every morning. She liked to keep to a schedule. I set down her breakfast tray on the hallway table and tried the door, but it was locked. Miss Grant never locked her door, so I found this odd. I peered into the keyhole, but the key was still inside."

"What did you do then?" Daniel asked.

"I knocked and called out to her, but when she failed to answer, I summoned Mr. Hamilton. He's the butler."

"What did Mr. Hamilton do?"

Miss Shaw took a shuddering breath. "He called out and knocked, same as I did. It was at this point that we decided something was wrong. Miss Grant was not a heavy sleeper, nor would she ignore us if she were able to respond. Mr. Hamilton was going to ask Mrs. Taft for a spare key, but I told him the key was still inside the door, so he called Steven—that's one of the footmen—and together they broke down the door."

"Were you the first person inside?" Daniel asked.

Miss Shaw nodded. "I was. I needed to make sure my mistress was decent before I let the men in. That's when I saw…" Her voice trailed off as a sob escaped her chest. "There was so much blood," she whispered, her eyes wide with the horror of what she'd found.

"Did you notice anything out of the ordinary besides the victim?" Daniel asked.

The woman shook her head. "No. Everything looked just as it should. Nothing had been taken."

"Was the window open or closed?"

"It was closed, sir. Locked."

"And the key?" Jason asked.

"The key fell out when the door was broken, sir. It was lying on the floor, just inside the room. I picked it up. I still have it." She reached into her pocket and pulled out a brass key, which she handed to Daniel.

"Miss Shaw, who else has rooms on that floor?" Daniel asked.

"Only the master, sir. But his room is on the other side."

"And are there any places in the house where someone might remain undetected for a long period of time?"

"Why, yes, sir. There are several empty rooms where someone might bide, since no one goes inside after they've been cleaned. Do you think the intruder had been in the house all along?" Miss Shaw asked, her eyes widening in shock.

"There is that possibility," Daniel replied. "Miss Shaw, is there anyone you can think of who might have wished to harm your mistress? Did she say anything in the days leading up to her death? Was she frightened?"

"No, Inspector. She was in reasonably good spirits and looking forward to her trip."

"Where was she going?" Jason asked.

"She was going to the seaside and was going to stay for a fortnight."

"Was she going alone?"

"I was going with her. We were to stay at the cottage."

"What cottage is that?" Daniel asked.

"The family owns a cottage in Southend-on-Sea. There's a couple that looks after it. The Marches," Miss Shaw explained. "Miss Grant loved going there. It was her peaceful place, she called it."

"Had you accompanied Miss Grant to this cottage before?" Jason asked.

"Yes, I've been there twice before."

"Did she meet with anyone while in Southend-on-Sea?" Daniel asked. "Did anyone call on her at the cottage?"

"No, Inspector. She did attend church, of course, but she had no friends there. Not ones who'd come to call, at any rate."

"Did Miss Grant have any suitors?" Jason asked.

"No, sir. Why do you ask?"

"I'm only trying to get a clearer picture of her life," Jason replied. "It wouldn't be unusual for an unmarried young woman to have admirers."

"No, it wouldn't," Miss Shaw agreed.

"But there was no one?" Daniel asked, clearly unsatisfied with the answer.

"No."

"Miss Shaw, what did your mistress do?"

"Do, sir?"

"Where did she go? Whom did she meet with? Surely she must have done something to fill the hours," Daniel said.

"She was involved in charitable works and acted as hostess for her brother when he entertained. He's a judge, you know," Miss Shaw said reverently. "A very important man."

"Thank you, Miss Shaw. Please send in Mr. Hamilton," Daniel said.

Miss Shaw shot to her feet and was out the door in seconds, clearly relieved to be dismissed. It was understandable that she might need time to come to terms not only with what she'd seen but how it would alter her immediate future in a household where there was no other female who might require her services.

Only this morning, she'd had steady employment, but now her future was uncertain. Even if she received a glowing character reference, there'd be those who'd be wary of employing a woman whose last mistress had been brutally murdered, as if Miss Shaw herself were tainted by association. Jason had seen many a servant left out in the cold in the wake of a murder inquiry. He wished he could help them, but he could hardly go hiring staff he didn't need.

Jason dragged his thoughts away from Miss Shaw, ready to hear what the butler had to say.

Chapter 2

Mr. Hamilton was a man of late middle age with a full head of silver hair and pale blue eyes. He was stocky and tall, filling the room with his presence as soon as he entered. He declined to sit and stood before the two men, shoulders back, feet apart, as if facing a firing squad. Daniel couldn't help wondering if the man felt responsible for what had happened. Miss Grant had been murdered on his watch, and he would face the wrath of his employer whether it was his fault or not.

"Mr. Hamilton, I know we spoke when I first arrived, but can you take us through what happened one more time?" Daniel invited.

Mr. Hamilton replied with a curt nod. "Miss Shaw rightly suspected that something was wrong and came down to the servants' hall to fetch me. We returned upstairs, where I called out to Miss Grant repeatedly. When the lady didn't respond, I decided to force the door, since I wouldn't be able to use the spare key to enter Miss Grant's bedroom on account of her key being already in the lock."

"Did you notice anything out of the ordinary while still in the corridor?" Daniel asked.

The butler winced. "Miss Shaw thought she smelled blood, and once she pointed it out, I could smell it as well."

"What did you see when you entered?" Jason asked.

"Miss Shaw went in first, to make sure her mistress wasn't in a state of undress. It was only when she screamed that I entered the room. I bade the footman to remain outside." Mr. Hamilton took a deep breath, as if recalling that awful moment. "Miss Grant was on the bed. Her eyes were open, and her throat looked like it had been savaged by a wild beast. There was blood on her face, hands, nightdress, and bedclothes. The bed was in disarray, as if a struggle had taken place. It was clear she was dead."

"Did you notice anything else about the room?" Daniel asked.

"Other than the smell? No, sir."

"Did you personally check the window and search the room before calling for a constable?"

"I did, sir. The window was locked, and nothing appeared to have been taken."

"You did not find the murder weapon?" Jason asked.

"I did not, sir, although, in truth, I'm not sure what the murder weapon would be, given the nature of the injury."

"What time do you lock up for the night, Mr. Hamilton?" Daniel asked.

"Ten o'clock. I check all the windows and doors before retiring."

"Was everything as you had left it last night?"

"Yes, it was, Inspector. Both the front and back doors were locked when I first came downstairs, as were all the windows."

"Mr. Hamilton, could someone have entered the house earlier in the day and hidden in one of the empty rooms?" Jason asked.

"No, my lord. We had two callers yesterday, but I saw them out myself. And the tradesmen left by the tradesman's entrance after making their deliveries."

"When was the last time you saw Miss Grant alive?"

"Just before ten, sir. She said goodnight to me as she headed upstairs."

"And Mr. Grant?" Jason asked.

Mr. Hamilton's lips compressed in obvious disapproval. "*Judge* Grant," he said, placing undue stress on the title, "was still in the drawing room when I retired." For a moment, the mask of stolid professionalism slipped, and Mr. Hamilton suddenly looked old and tired. "I'd like to add that I have questioned the staff, and no one saw or heard anything untoward last night, your lordship," he said, his attention fixed on Jason.

Daniel felt an irrational stab of annoyance. The butler should be addressing him. This was his investigation, he thought petulantly, and instantly felt ashamed of his churlishness. Any man in service was conditioned to show respect to the highest-ranking personage in the room. It was only natural that Hamilton would single out a nobleman over a mere inspector.

"Mr. Hamilton, is there anyone you can think of who might have wished to harm your mistress?" Daniel asked, forcing the man to redirect his attention to him.

The butler's eyebrows lifted in astonishment. "Of course not. Miss Grant was well liked and respected by everyone."

"And yet someone murdered her in her own bed," Jason pointed out.

"I wouldn't know anything about that, sir," the butler said, his gaze growing anxious, his fear of being blamed obviously returning.

"Thank you," Daniel said. "You've been most helpful."

Daniel was about to summon the next servant when Mr. Grant entered the room, making a gesture of dismissal to the butler. "Inspector Haze, I really need to get out of this house for a short while or I'll go mad. If you'd like to speak to me, please do so now."

"Of course, sir. Please, have a seat," Daniel said, gesturing toward the settee. He felt somewhat foolish for inviting the man to sit in his own drawing room, but Oliver Grant didn't seem to notice and sank onto the settee, facing the two men and looking from one to the other. His eyes were red-rimmed and his shoulders stooped, as if sitting up straight were too much of an effort. Daniel introduced Jason and the man nodded, as if having a member of the nobility examine his sister's remains after she was brutally murdered were the most normal thing in the world.

Oliver Grant was about forty, with hazel eyes and wavy brown hair untamed by pomade. He wore a neat beard, and his gray suit was exquisitely tailored and of the latest fashion. A paisley waistcoat of silver on burgundy silk and a burgundy puff tie provided a splash of color. Following Daniel's gaze, he seemed to realize that he wasn't dressed in mourning attire.

"I really must change," he muttered. "I dressed before I knew what had happened to poor Sybil."

"We're very sorry for your loss, Judge," Jason said.

"Thank you, your lordship." Oliver Grant turned his attention to Daniel. "How could this have happened, Inspector?" he asked, his voice shrill.

Even in a state of shock and grief, Oliver Grant was the sort of man who expected answers and needed someone to blame. He had an air of authority that couldn't be tamped down by tragedy or personal loss. His gaze was angry and accusing, as if Daniel were personally responsible for every crime committed in the city.

"Had Sybil been attacked elsewhere, it'd be shocking and tragic, but feasible. But to be murdered in her own home, a place of safety and comfort, is incomprehensible. I keep going over what happened, and I simply can't understand it. How did the killer get in? How did he get out? Why did he target poor Sybil? She was such a kind soul, so generous with her time and affection."

"We're going to do everything in our power to discover who murdered your sister, but first, we need to ask you some questions," Daniel said. He felt for the man. For lack of a father or a husband, it had been up to him to protect Miss Grant and look after her interests. The knowledge that he'd failed his sister clearly weighed heavily on him.

"How long have you lived in this house?" Daniel asked.

"These past twenty years."

"And how many people do you employ?"

"Well, there's the butler, obviously, a housekeeper, a cook, kitchen and scullery maids, two footmen, a parlormaid, Sybil's maid, my valet, and a groom, who also acts as coachman."

"Are there any recent hires?" Daniel asked.

"No. Everyone's been with us for years," Oliver Grant said. "Except I think there's a new boot boy."

"Judge Grant, unless someone managed to enter the house undetected, this was done by someone on the inside. Do you suspect anyone in your household?" Jason asked.

Oliver Grant thought about that briefly. "No, I don't," he finally said. "Not for a moment. This terrible thing was done by an outsider."

"But how would an outsider get in?" Daniel asked. "Mr. Hamilton claims to have locked up for the night and said he found nothing to suggest that anyone had broken in."

"I really don't know. But why would anyone in this house murder Sybil? She was a kind and considerate mistress. Too kind, some might say."

"You room is on the same floor. Did you hear anything last night?"

Oliver Grant shook his head. "No. I retired around half past ten and went straight to bed."

"What time did you get up?" Daniel asked.

"I'm normally up by seven. I walk in Green Park every morning from seven-thirty until eight-thirty. I had just returned from my walk and sat down to breakfast when Hamilton…" Oliver

Grant's voice trailed off as he recalled the moment he'd heard the news.

"Judge Grant, did Miss Grant have any suitors?" Daniel asked.

"Suitors?" Oliver Grant reacted as if he hadn't quite understood the question.

"Yes. Had she received any gentleman callers within the past few months?"

"Not that I know of," Oliver Grant said sadly. "Sybil had no interest in getting married."

"Why was that?" Jason asked.

Judge Grant sighed heavily. "Because she still fancied herself in love with David Ellis," he said bitterly.

"And what happened with Mr. Ellis?" Daniel asked.

"He was killed during your war," Oliver Grant said angrily, pinning Jason with a belligerent stare. "He was a journalist, you see. He went to America to cover the war and was murdered for his pains."

"I'm sorry to hear that," Jason said.

"Miss Grant may not have been interested, but were there any gentlemen who'd tried to court her?"

"Are you suggesting one of them killed her under my roof?" Oliver Grant exclaimed.

"I'm suggesting that we need to question anyone who might have had a grudge against her," Daniel explained patiently.

"There was Captain McHenry. He pursued Sybil for months, but she rejected him in the end."

"Where's Captain McHenry now?" Daniel asked.

Oliver Grant shrugged. "I really don't know."

"Judge Grant, whom did your sister spend time with? Did she have any particular friends?"

"She was in close contact with her school friends. Annabel Finch, Dorothea Parker, and Eleanor Gladstone-Smith. They saw each other regularly."

"Do you have addresses for them, sir?" Daniel asked.

"Ask Phillip."

"Who's Phillip?"

"The coachman. He'll know the addresses."

"I will," Daniel said, surprised the man couldn't be bothered to provide the addresses of his sister's friends. "Judge Grant, do I have your permission to interview the rest of staff? I need to know everyone's movements, starting with dinner last night."

"Yes, of course," Judge Grant said absentmindedly. His shoulders sagged again after his bout of anger, and his head drooped, possibly because he was tired of answering questions, or maybe because the reality of his loss was finally beginning to set it. "May I go now?" he asked desperately. "I really need some air."

"Certainly."

"Keep me informed of your progress, Inspector. And give my regards to Commissioner Hawkins. He's a close friend," he said, reminding Daniel that failure to solve the case would cost him dearly.

Chapter 3

Once Oliver Grant left the room, Daniel turned to Jason. "Are you absolutely certain Miss Grant's death couldn't have been an elaborate suicide?"

Jason's eyebrows lifted comically. "Do you?"

"No," Daniel conceded, recalling the degree of savagery with which the poor woman had been killed. "I just can't figure out how the killer got out. If we are to assume that it was someone who was in the house at the time, then they must have left the room after killing Miss Grant. How did they lock the door from within, and how on earth did no one notice a blood-drenched person walking past? Surely there would have been a lot of blood, given the blood spatter on the headboard and sheets."

"Yes, there would have been a great deal of blood, but perhaps the person wore something to protect their clothing and removed it as soon as the deed was done. Did you search the wardrobe and the trunk at the foot of the bed?"

"I did," Daniel replied.

"We should search the rest of the house as well as the surrounding area in case they discarded the bloodstained garments once they left."

"But how did they lock the room?" Daniel asked again. "Had the room been locked from the outside, it would have been easy enough to comprehend, but how did the killer lock the room from within? And how on earth did they get out of the house if all the windows and doors had still been locked this morning?"

"Might there be a connecting door to an adjoining room?" Jason asked. "Or perhaps a back door no one had bothered to check?"

Daniel sighed. "I highly doubt there's a back door no one is aware of. And do you think this house is riddled with secret passages? It's not that old."

"What does its age have to do with it?" Jason asked, reminding Daniel that he wasn't well versed in British history.

"Many houses built in previous centuries were equipped with priest holes and secret passages, which were used to hide Catholic priests and to escape capture should the family's Catholicism come to the notice of the authorities. However, this house looks to have been built quite recently, so I doubt anyone had thought to add secret hideaways to the original plans."

"I see," Jason said. "Well, that's a shame because a secret passage would explain much in this case."

"Let's ask Mrs. Taft. She's bound to know if this house holds any secrets," Daniel suggested.

Mrs. Taft was in her mid-forties. She had dark hair liberally threaded with silver, shrewd dark eyes, and a thin nose that was pink at the tip. She was tall for a woman, and thin, her black bombazine gown making her appear even more gaunt and forbidding. A dainty lace cap covered her bun, and her white collar was stiffly starched. She looked at Daniel eagerly as soon as she took the proffered seat, as if expecting a reasonable explanation of the morning's events. Too bad he couldn't offer her one.

"Mrs. Taft, do you have any theories as to what occurred last night?" Daniel asked, rather than going through the usual list of questions. He had no doubt Mrs. Taft would mention anything unusual or unexpected.

The housekeeper shook her head. "I don't, Inspector. Everything was just the same. The master and Miss Grant had dinner at seven, then adjourned to the drawing room, where they remained until they retired. Mr. Hamilton locked up for the night, and we all went to bed. We had no idea anything had occurred until Miss Shaw came to fetch Mr. Hamilton this morning."

"Were there any strangers in the house?" Daniel asked.

"Not in the evening, sir."

"Who was in the house earlier?"

"Judge Grant had visitors around four. I sent up refreshments. Mr. Hamilton saw them out just after five. And there had been deliveries from the butcher and the greengrocer, both before noon. Mr. Hackett and Mr. Grady are well known to us and make a weekly delivery. I saw them leave."

"Mrs. Taft, is there a door to an adjoining room in Miss Grant's bedroom?" Daniel asked.

"No, there isn't."

"What about a secret passage?"

"There are no secret passages that I know of, and I have been housekeeper here these nine years."

"Can you offer an opinion on how the murderer managed to get out of a locked room?" Daniel asked.

Mrs. Taft shook her head, her gaze reflecting her bewilderment. "I cannot."

"Were you close with your mistress?" Jason asked.

"Close, sir?" The woman looked even more baffled, if such a thing were possible.

"Did she ever confide in you?" Jason often confided in his own housekeeper, Mrs. Dodson, and thought other masters did as well, but that wasn't likely in a traditional household. Cool politeness and courtesy were the best a housekeeper could hope for from her mistress.

"No, sir, Miss Grant never confided in me."

"Thank you, Mrs. Taft," Daniel said. "If you happen to think of anything, please send for me."

"Of course, sir."

"Who shall we speak to next?" Jason asked.

Daniel exhaled heavily. "I suppose the next logical choice is Judge Grant's valet. He is one of the few people who would have access to that floor in the evening. All the other servants would have retired after having their supper in the servants' hall."

Jason nodded in agreement. "Yes, at my house, Henley and Katherine's maid are generally the last people upstairs in the evening, so there's a chance the valet might have seen or heard something."

Roy Nevins was a man of indistinct appearance. He was of middling height, middling weight, and middling attractiveness, the sort of person who could easily blend into the crowd and leave no impression on anyone who'd seen him. He did, however, exude an air of confidence and was smartly turned out.

"Mr. Nevins, can you describe your movements last night?" Daniel asked as he studied the man.

"Of course. I came upstairs just after ten to prepare Judge Grant's clothes. He likes to have everything ready when he gets up in the morning, so I laid out the clothes in his dressing room and laid a clean nightshirt on his pillow. He came up shortly after. I helped him undress, hung up his jacket and trousers, deposited the day's linen in the laundry hamper, and wished him a good night before going to my own room."

"What time did you leave him?"

"Around ten-forty," Nevins replied.

"Did you see or hear anything unusual once you stepped out into the corridor?" Daniel asked.

Nevins shook his head. "I didn't go as far as Miss Grant's room, since it's at the other end, but I didn't hear anything unusual. I did see a light under her door," he added. "I believe she liked to read before going to sleep."

"And Judge Grant? How did he seem?" Jason asked.

"He said he was tired. We chatted about the weather and his plans for the next day. He'd intended to dine at his club this evening. I assume he won't be going now that—" The valet didn't finish the sentence. His meaning was obvious. He sat silently, waiting for Daniel to either ask him another question or dismiss him.

"Thank you, Mr. Nevins. You're free to go," Daniel said.

Nearly three hours later, Daniel and Jason finally left knowing no more than they had after examining the body, despite questioning every member of staff, down to the eight-year-old boot boy named Andy. They had searched the house from top to bottom, checking for secret panels in Miss Grant's bedroom and any sign of bloodstained clothes that may have been discarded or burned. The only person left to interview was Phillip, the coachman.

They found him in the carriage house, smoking a pipe while he cleaned the windows of the brougham with little enthusiasm. A tall, burly man, he had a full head of ginger hair with matching muttonchop whiskers and light brown eyes. His cheeks and nose were a mottled red, the spidery capillaries a testament to his love of strong drink.

"I'm Inspector Haze, and this is Lord Redmond," Daniel said as he showed the man his warrant card. "What is your full name?"

"Phillip Astley."

"Mr. Astley, first I will need addresses for Annabel Finch, Dorothea Parker, and Eleanor Gladstone-Smith. Judge Grant said you'd have them for us."

The coachman provided the addresses, which Daniel jotted down in his book. "Thank you," he said. "Now, when was the last time Miss Grant had gone out?"

"Yesterday," the coachman replied. "She went to call on Mrs. Finch."

"How long did she stay?"

"'Bout an hour."

"Did she come straight home afterward?"

"Yes."

"What time was that?" Daniel asked.

"'Round one."

"Did she seem in good spirits?"

Phillip Astley stared at Daniel as if he were daft. "'Ow would I know?" he asked. "Not like we 'ad us a chat."

"Did she seem frightened or upset?"

"No."

"Did she ask you to take her anywhere unusual recently?" Daniel tried again.

"No."

"Did she ever meet any gentlemen on her own?"

"No."

"Mr. Astley, is there anything at all you can think of that might have been out of character for Miss Grant?" Daniel asked, exasperated with the man's monosyllabic answers.

"No."

"Thank you for your help," Daniel said acidly. The man really was a dolt.

"Where to?" Jason asked once they had left Phillip Astley to his task and his pipe.

"Mrs. Finch's. She was the last person who's not of the household to see Miss Grant alive. Perhaps she'll know something."

"I certainly hope so," Jason said. "No one else seems to know anything, which is odd in itself."

"Why do you say that?" Daniel asked as they walked down the street, keeping an eye out for a hansom.

"Someone entered the house, proceeded to Sybil Grant's bedroom, and hacked at her neck after first trying to strangle her. Something must have precipitated this savage act. I highly doubt it was a random killing, which suggests that someone knows more than they are saying, either about a visitor to the house or one of their own."

"Yes, I agree with you there," Daniel said, "but perhaps Sybil Grant had secrets they weren't privy to."

"In a house with a staff, there are no secrets," Jason pointed out. "The servants know and see all."

Daniel and Sarah kept only one maidservant at their rented house, but Daniel was sure she knew every minute detail of their lives. There were ten people looking after Judge Grant and his sister. Someone was sure to know something, especially if they had been with the family for years, as they all claimed.

"If anyone knows anything, it would be Miss Shaw. She was Miss Grant's lady's maid, so she'd not only see her comings and goings but also see to her soiled linen."

"Do you think Miss Grant was conducting an affair?" Jason asked.

"You said she wasn't a virgin. It's possible she had a secret lover."

"Yes, it is, but how did he get in the house?" Jason replied. "Unless her lover was one of the staff."

"A theory worth exploring," Daniel replied as a hansom pulled up to the curb. "Let's speak to her friends and see if we can learn something of Miss Grant's private affairs. Miss Shaw will be more likely to reveal her mistress's secrets if she thinks we're already privy to them."

"Agreed," Jason said.

Printed in Great Britain
by Amazon